The Ratking

– D. A. MATTHEWS –

An environmentally friendly book printed and bound in
England by www.printondemand-worldwide.com

This book is made entirely of chain-of-custody materials

www.fast-print.net/store.php

The Ratking
Copyright © D. A. Matthews 2013

A catalogue record for this book is available from the British Library

ISBN 978-178035-655-6

First published 2013 by
FASTPRINT PUBLISHING
Peterborough, England.

To Liz and Karen

*My severest – and therefore
most welcome – critics*

Chapter 1

Saturday, August 7th, 1962

An Arctic cold exploded in Sara's body.

The red bus from which she had just descended lumbered off. Like an opening stage curtain, it revealed a picturesque village sleeping in the heat of the midsummer sun. Whitewashed stone houses resting in two irregular rows straddled a central street which sloped away towards a castle ruin.

But as she continued to gaze at the chocolate-box scene, Sara's veins remained ice-laden. Brief mental shadows hinted at vague, disturbing recollections.

Almost as soon as the sense of menace emerged, it was gone again. But the perplexing emotions had surfaced long enough. And at once she knew it

S*he had been here before!!*

And there was more.

Despite the apparent peace and calm of the thatched and slate roofs, she sensed that danger had stalked her here. Enigmatic, elusive danger, the wispy recollection of which lurked in deepest memory, inhabiting the dank depths of her subconscious.

Desperately she tried to remember. But the memory she sought refused to surface.

What had happened here? And *When?*

With a strange feeling of trepidation, quite unable to define the cause of her unexpected distress, Sara turned to watch the venerable vehicle. As it trundled away, the shuttered sunlight shafting through the trees cut swathes in the cloud raised in its wake. And as the bus disappeared round a bend in the road, the sound of its engine receding into the distance, a marooned feeling settled on Sara like the drifting dust in the still sunlight.

Suppressing her disquiet, Sara set down the cases outside the small shop and bus depot behind her. 'I'll ask for directions in here, Connie.' she said to her sixteen-year-old companion.

Sara approached the small building with a sign reading VILLAGE SHOP, and underneath, prop. Beth Quincey. Leaning down, she peered through the the glass door, squinting through the gap between an advert for potatoes and a notice for village show.

A plump, ruddy-complexioned woman wearing a flower-patterned dress seemed to be having difficulty reading the label of a parcel just delivered from the parting bus. Another woman of similar age stood watching.

Opening the door, Sara called softly. 'Hello.'

The woman's owl-like eyes creased at the corners as she looked up. 'Hello, there. C'n I help you?' A deep-throated burr in her speech bore witness to her Northumbrian roots.

Moving into the cooler interior, Sara crossed to the counter. 'I'm looking for Mill House. I have to collect the key to Rose Cottage. From Mr. Lumsden.'

'Rose Cottage?...' The woman smiled. 'Oh, yes... You mean *DEATH* cottage. It's about a mile and a half away. Along the clifftops. George'll be driving you there.'

She rounded the counter and together they emerged into the sunshine, the woman shielding her eyes with one hand. Her other arm rose to horizontal, pointing down through the village.

'Go down Village Street. Turn the corner at the castle. Mill House is at the riverside. You'll find George there.' She nodded to the cases. 'These yours?'

'Yes.'

'Leave them here 'til you come back. I'll look after them.'

Thanking the woman and depositing the cases, Sara left, walking with Connie down the broad street, passing the cottages which flanked the road in two irregular rows. The years had altered the symmetry of the whitewashed stones, betraying their age. Imminent collapse of upper storeys seemed inevitable.

As she passed down the hill, Sara's sense of *deja vu* resurged. And as the two girls passed the village inn midway to the castle, the feeling strengthened. White in the sunshine, the inn stood back from the line of houses, its sign - THE KINGS HEAD - swinging gently on top of a black stand of gnarled wood.

As they rounded the right-angle bend past the castle, the downward slope of the road steepened as it started its descent towards the river.

The village had an air of yesteryear, emphasised by a mysterious silence punctuated only by the hum of insects and the occasional call of a bird. It was as if the T-junction at the main road acted as a screen cutting off the village from the present.

'This place looks like a page from a history book!' Connie exclaimed with no little contempt.

Sara smiled. 'It does.'

'Do you think they know *anything* of what's going on in the world? Do you think they'll know that Marylin Monroe died yesterday, for example?'

Sara's grin widenned. Looking at wire "H"s attached to two chimney breasts she nodded. 'There are a couple of television aerials.' she pointed out. 'So they'll have heard, although I know what you mean... But for the aerials and the tarmac road, the clock could have been turned back through centuries.'

'Is it much further, Sara?' whinged Connie. 'My feet hurt.'

'I told you not to wear stilettos, didn't I? Thank goodness I packed a pair of flat shoes for you.'

Connie was silent for a moment. 'I don't know why mother didn't come.' she bleated. 'This holiday was *HER* idea anyway - not mine!'

'She couldn't come, Connie.'

But although trying to pacify the adolescent, Sara was also irritated at Harriet. And although she and Connie got along well enough, there was no escape from the fact that Connie was an immature sixteen-year-old who often acted as if twelve or thirteen.

Sara was not surprised that the adolescent could not understand the selfishness of her only parent. Connie's mother, Sara's Aunt Harriet, a failed actress, ready to clutch at any straw to belatedly get a stage career going, had also been Sara's guardian. Angry memory regurgitated Harriet's words.

'I've been offered a chance to further my career. And I'm taking it. I'm going to California with *'Shivering Timbers'.'*

'Never heard of them!' Sara had been scathing.

'They made a record in the fifties.'

Sara had gazed heavenwards for inspiration. The stardom her guardian aunt permanently dreamed of was an old acquaintance.

'This may seem unkind, but don't you think that at forty-two, you're a bit old to be going to California as unpaid roadie to a has-been pop group?'

'Don't be sarcastic, Sara!' Harriet had almost stamped her foot. 'I'll be Musical Director, not a 'Roadie'! And why don't you come? You'd be a great success on the stage. Black hair, oval face, arresting nut-brown eyes, hourglass figure, long, shapely legs--'

'I don't **want** to be on the stage! I'm a nurse. And what about your promise to take Connie on holiday?'

Harriet had waved an airy hand. 'I can't help it. I must grab this chance. Anyway **you** can take her. And as you're a nurse, you'll be able to look after her if anything happens to her. Better than I could!'

'Which one is Mill House?' Connie's question brought Sara back to the present as they approached a lone pair of bankside cottages near the bottom of the hill.

'The one on the left.' Sara answered, then realised with amazement what she'd said. *'How did I know that?'* she wondered.

The converted water mill had a semi-neglected look. Green moss shrouded thick stone, the odour of mustiness betraying dampness. A rusty knob hung apologetically at the side of the solid door. Sara reached forward, pulled the knob, let it spring back and waited. A Victorian servants' bell clanged distantly in the bowels of the house.

'There's nobody in.' wailed Connie.

But the sound of approaching footsteps shuffling along an inner corridor whispered against Sara's ears.

The latch lifted and the door slowly creaked open to reveal a passageway, dark, even in the sunlight. In it stood a slight woman of indeterminate age with grey hair bundled into a hair net. Her ankle-length black dress showed under her grey jumper, legs covered by lisle stockings. Like the village itself, the woman looked as she belonged to a time already long gone.

'Aye?' she asked bluntly.

'Mrs. Lumsden?'

'Aye.'

'I was told to come here for the key to Rose Cottage.'

'Oh, aye. Mrs. Hopkins?'

'Mrs Hopkins made the booking. She's my guardian. My name is Sara... Sara Goodwin. And this is her daughter, Connie.'

A thin smile spread over the ancient features. 'Aye. Welcome to ye both.' Her accent was a mixture of Northumbrian and Scots. 'Ah'll tell George. He'll bring the car round and take ye tae the cottage. If ye'll jist wait here for a minute...' She turned and shuffled back off into the house.

'George!' Sara heard her shout, 'George!...'

'Aye?' came a distant response from the rear.

An inaudible conversation ensued as both girls waited. A couple of minutes later, from behind Mill House the 'put-put-put' of an engine started. As Sara turned expectantly, round the corner laboured an ancient black car. Square, hard-sprung and of indeterminate vintage. It turned towards them, advanced, and pulled up with a squeal.

Behind the wheel sat a muscular old man with the same grey eyes as the old woman. And, like hers, his eyes twinkled in a kindly weather-beaten face, which looked out from between cap and dungarees.

'Hello.' the man said, climbing out from behind the wheel. 'I'm George Lumsden.' He looked round. 'Where are your cases?'

'At the bus depot. I left them with Miss Quincey.'

His eyes creased kindly as he smiled. 'Beth Quincey.'

'You know her?'

'Very well. Everybody knows Beth Quincey. In fact, there have been Quinceys in Abbots Cross since God-knows-when.'

'Mmm... So it's a pity the line will come to an end now.'

'Why do you say that?'

'Well - if she's "Miss" Quincey...'

George shook his head. 'She has a brother. Harold Quincey. Known as "Hal". He keeps the pub up in the village. He has a couple of young 'uns.'

Sara smiled as George went on. 'Get into the back and I'll drive you up to collect the cases.' He grinned with a wide mouth in which teeth were a rare commodity. 'Then we're off to the cottage.'

Sara pulled open the square rear door to be greeted by a vague odour of oil and leather. Connie bounced in, then Sara followed, turning to close the door before looking out of the vehicle's aged yellow windows.

Leaning his left elbow over the back of the driver's seat, George turned a smiling glance at them. In his hand he held a large key which he passed over to Sara. 'That's the doorkey.' he said, then asked, 'Now before we leave the village, d'ye need anything?'

'I don't if the provisions have arrived'

'They're here.' he said, thumping his hand on a full cardboard box which rested on the seat beside him. 'They'll keep you going for the week.'

Still wearing his infectious grin, George turned weightily forward to bend down and turn the ignition. The engine turned over a few times before spluttering into life with a cloud of smoke. Scraping the gearchange into first, George let out the clutch. The car gradually struggled forward.

Labouring sedately back up through the village, they retraced the way up to the bus depot. Pulling on the handbrake, George alighted, leaving the motor running, and disappeared into the depot. Beth Quincey and he were clearly well acquainted, for George's shouted remarks were interspersed with shrieks of laughter.

Then George emerged, carrying the cases. Beth Quincey grinned from the door as he walked to the rear of the car. Sara heard the boot lid open and close before the crunch of boots on gravel signalled George's return to the driving seat.

'Right! Here we go!' His weight made the car lurch sideways before he slammed shut the door. Then, with a quick wave at Miss Quincey, once more he crunched the gears of the elderly car which then trundled into motion.

For a short way they followed the main road. Speed was steady - no more than twenty miles per hour.

Sara leaned forward and spoke to George. 'George', she asked, 'Has it always been called Rose Cottage? The woman in the depot called it by some other name.'

'The local people refer to it as *Death*Cottage. But we don't advertise it as that. Otherwise nobody would ever want to book it for a holiday!'

'Why do they call it 'Death' Cottage?'

George half-glanced round. 'In the Seventeenth Century, a young girl living here on her own died when the cottage burned down.'

'How awful!'

'Aye, it must have been. Then it was rebuilt as it is now. It also got its name at the same time, and it stuck ever after.'

'Was anything left of the girl?' Connie piped up.

'Only a charred skeleton.'

At a junction they turned off, taking a mud path, more of a farm track than a road. As they continued, the track seemed to be ever-narrowing, with ever-higher bramble hedges. It would have been impossible for two vehicles to pass.

Further along, the track rose. Abbots Cross spread out to their left. Turning to the right again, the track emerged out onto a cliff top. There the view was suddenly open and expansive. The troubled sea on one side contrasted starkly with the steady fields of ripe wheat waving gently in the offshore breeze on the other.

Within minutes they came into sight of a solitary building, far from anywhere else. The thatched house, gleaming white in the last of the afternoon sunshine, had finely restored Tudor lines.

Sara leaned forward to gaze out of the yellowing window. 'Beautiful!' she said in admiration.

'Do people live there?' asked Connie. 'In that beautiful house?'

George smiled back proudly. 'That's Death Cottage!'

Sara could almost feel herself breathing in the historical delight of the Seventeenth Century house with its barns and outhouses backing onto clifftops overlooking the sea. 'So it's the house in which the girl died?'

'Aye. Or rather, that's where it *used* to be before it burned down. '

He stopped and they got out. Connie was first, followed by Sara. George circumvented the car and walked to the garden gate. As it creaked open, he wandered along the short path to the front door, Connie and Sara following.

Turning a key in the lock, George pushed. The door slowly creaked open. Connie turned to look at Sara. 'Spook-e-e--!' she exclaimed with a grin.

The open door led into a large room with a black-leaded fireplace in which hung a now-decorative black pot. Various pieces of heavy furniture stood around the polished wooden floor. Spaces were covered with occasional small carpets. Through an open inner doorway Sara could see a small, well-appointed kitchen.

George led the way up the steep stairs. A small, square landing was flanked by an open door at each side leading into rooms containing ready-made beds.

Sara noticed two or three steps rising in a semicircle to a half-hidden third door. 'What's in there?

George glanced at the third door without interest. 'It's a loft containing junk. The key to that door's back at Mill House.'

They moved between the bedrooms. 'Watch your head up here!' said George, ducking under a crossbeam. 'Some of the ceiling supports are low. You can give yourself a nasty crack if you're not careful!'

The bedrooms with their low beams were small but comfortable. 'Lovely.' Sara said.

* * * *

After watching George disappear back along the track in the old car, Sara and Connie spent quite a time in sorting out. *'It's a lovely cottage.'* Sara thought, *But a week here! In this isolation! Thank goodness I'm off on a proper holiday with the other nurses later in the year...'*

By now, the first shades of dusk had begun to fall.

'What are we going to do now?' Connie asked.

'We'll have some supper... then off to bed.'

She went to the kitchen, leaving Connie in an armchair with a teen mag. As she switched on the tap, the pipes made a humming sound which continued even after she'd switched the water off.

Connie appeared. 'What's that noise?!'

'I think it's the plumbing.' Sara spoke hesitantly.

Connie's face took on an impish look. 'No it's not! It's a ghost! I told you it was spooky here, didn't I?'

Sara nodded at her.

It was not until later, when she was actually in bed that Sara realised how tired she was, how fatigued travelling to new surroundings in the care of a boisterous, rather juvenile sixteen-year old had left her. But soon she, too, dissolved into an exhausted, dreamless sleep.

As she drifted off, she fancied she heard the low moan again.

But nobody was turning the tap this time...

Chapter 2

At first, Sara did not realise what had woken her from the depths of sleep. But as the sounds persisted, and although only slightly alert, she opened her eyes and began to listen. Vague noises, apparently in the house and above her head, persisted. The occasional scrape, the occasional bump, the occasional step, as if something was happening - slight sounds here and minor noises there. There was no doubt about it. Something was moving somewhere in the house.

Was Connie awake?

Yes, that had to be it. There was no other explanation.

'Don't make so much noise, Connie!' she called. 'You've just woken me up!'

Sara expected a response. But none came and for a moment after she had called, silence reigned. The noises no longer persisted. *Perhaps a rodent had taken refuge in the thatch of the roof? Or perhaps her imagination was taking hold in the strangeness of a new and quite different environment?*

Dismissing the sounds as tricks of imagination, she turned over and prepared to go back off to sleep. But then once again the thumping noises restarted, a little louder this time and now enough to waken her to a more major state of vigilance. Eyes wide open, she thought for a moment before sitting up in bed, still listening.

Then another sound from above made the decision for her. Reaching over to her bedside to switch on the light, she heaved the covers back before swinging her legs over onto the floor and standing up. In no very happy frame of mind, she went to her bedroom door, opened it and crossed the passageway to Connie's room. The door to Connie's room was ajar, and Sara pushed her way in.

She was about to berate the adolescent for being noisy when she stopped. Connie's long blonde hair spilled out over the bedcovers which rose and fell gently in deep sleep. Whatever the cause of the sounds, clearly it was not Sara's companion!

Just as she was about to turn to leave, a floorboard creaked under her foot. It was a minor sound, but enough to waken Connie, who started up in bed. Clearly by the light from Sara's bedroom, Connie could see who was in her room.

'What is it, Sara?' she asked in slurred, sleepy tones.

'I just wondered where the noises were coming from.'

'What noises?'

'Connie there are noises going on in this house and I'm trying to find out where they're coming from.'

Connie reached over and switched on the bedside light before looking at the clock. 2.30.a.m. She tuned back, looked at Sara and listened for a moment, holding her breath. But the only sound was the distant roar of the sea.

'Well, Sara, I can't hear any noises.' she said irritably

Sara listened. Silence.

'There were noises a minute ago.' Sara said. 'I thought you must be you moving about.'

'Well, it isn't!'

'No, I can see that now. I think they were coming from the room above here. Behind the door above the three spiral steps. Listen!'

But Connie shook her head. 'I'm too tired to listen.' she said, sleep reclaiming her. She reached over and switched off the light. 'Go back to bed.'

In the gloom Sara could see Connie flop down amongst the blankets again, fatigue consuming her. As she stood looking at Connie for a moment. the sixteen-year-old was already drifting off back to sleep.

Sara watched her for a minute then turned away to return to her room. Climbing back into bed, she switched off the bedside lamp before pulling the covers over her.

She lay straining her ears, but apart from the noise of the waves and the occasional cry of a seagull, now there was not a sound.

Sara stared up at the ceiling. What little extraneous light there was sketched still patterns on its rough surface. Patterns which, like a tapestry, appeared to tell a story of the past.

Or the future...

Eyes wide, she lay awake for a long time. Thinking.

And listening...

The morning dawned cloudy and somewhat breezy, although not windy. But when Sara switched on her bedside transistor radio, the forecast was that clouds would clear, all light rain would go and later in the day the sun would put in a most welcome appearance.

Sara was up and dressed and downstairs for at least an hour before the adolescent Connie put in an appearance. As she came through into the living room she looked at Sara with a half smile and an accusing look.

'Did you sleep well?' Sara asked.

'I did until some idiot woke me up to complain about noises at 2.30 in the morning!'

'I'm sure you dreamed it all.' Sara retorted, stifling a smile.

'Of course I didn't dream it! '

'There *were* noises. I heard them!'

'Then why didn't I hear them?'

'You were asleep.'

'What kind of noises were they?'

'Clumping about noises... like a man in boots...'

Connie looked heavenwards. 'Oh, yea?!'

Sara grimaced. 'All right. Don't believe me.' Then she added, 'Come on, Connie, Let's have breakfast.'

As they sat at the table, Connie asked, 'What plans do we have for today?'

Sara glanced out of the window at the open sea for a moment. The day was overcast, the sun still shrouded in ominous clouds. 'It's beginning to drizzle a bit.' she added. 'We can have a walk into Abbots Cross this morning. The forecast for later in the day is glorious sunshine, so what do you think of going down to the beach?'

'Now you're talking!'

It was late morning when the girls left the cottage to wander down the rear path on their way to Abbots Cross. Near the rear boundary gate, stood a large wooden outhouse, neglected, uncared-for and in a state of some dilapidation. Clearly a former storage place for hay and tools, and stabling for a couple of horses, it now stood disused and empty.

Slowing down to look as they wandered past, Connie poked a curious head through the gap above the half door. She looked for a moment before turning her head to listen intently. Then she turned a look of alarm to Sara.

'Sara!' she called, some distress in her voice.

'What is it?'

'There's something! In the outhouse!'

'What do you mean, "Something"?'

'It sounds like an animal. And it sounds as if it's trapped.' Connie beckoned urgently. 'Come and listen. There's a squeaking noise. From behind a wooden wall at the back.'

'We'd better have a look.'

Putting her fingers under Suffolk latch of the half door, Sara pushed upwards. The door swung outwards.

As they went into the outhouse, the squeaking became more pronounced. In the dim interior, it seemed that the outhouse was now vacant of all save a few pieces of ancient farming debris, reminders of a useful past. In the bottom corner, entry to a small grain store was barred by a stout door.

'The squeaks are coming from behind there!' said Connie.

Sara nodded. 'You're right.' Moving forward, she looked at the door, thinking. *Probably a grain store...* 'Something seems to be trapped behind the door.' Then her stomach tightened as, with growing unease, she spoke. 'Connie...' she warned urgently, 'I don't think we should open that door...'

'Why not?'

'Well... it's just that... I don't think... You see, I don't know... the squeaking might be... '

But Connie was not put off. 'Then let's open the door and find out!'

'Best not to.'

'Sara! There's an animal in there. And it can't get out!'

Sara's stern intent melted. She relaxed, dismissing her fears and conceded. 'All right.' she agreed. 'Let's open it.'

She reached the door and pushed at the catch. But it resisted. Then, grabbing the door firmly, she shook it back and forward. But again, her efforts were to no avail.

'We'll have to lever it open!' Sara said.

She looked round the barn to see what she could use as a lever. Propped up in a corner was a stout stick, an elongated shepherd's crook. Grasping it firmly, she waded back over straw-strewn cobbles to the door, inserted the stick into a small gap between door frame and then pushed in an effort to prise it open.

The door was initially stubborn. And it took several full-force pushes by both girls before progress could be made. Then suddenly it relented, cracked and burst open inwards.

Connie who had been pushing on the door, tumbled forward, her foot catching on a piece of wood. She tripped and fell heavily.

Images flashed before Sara's eyes as she rushed forward to help Connie back onto her feet. Then she saw what Connie had fallen onto.

Sara dropped the stick and started back, feeling herself go faint. She had expected something alive. Possibly horrible. Repulsive even.

But she was unprepared for this!

Reaching for the support of the doorpost, she gazed round-eyed at the grotesque sight as she proffered her left arm to help Connie up and out of the storage room.

'Into the house!' she yelled with stern authority. 'Let's get you washed! At once!!'

Hot soapy water spilled over the rim of the bowl as Sara watched Connie scrub with enormous vigour, making sure that her arms and hands were cleansed with a clinical thoroughness fit for an operating theatre.

'Make sure no germs linger!' Sara commented. 'Pity you ever touched the horrible thing!'

'I fell!' Connie retorted angrily.

'You should have been more careful!'

'It was an accident!'

Sara realised Connie was upset. 'Come on, let's go.' Sara said, feeling that perhaps she had been a little abrupt. 'Once we've had a walk to Abbots Cross, we'll both feel better.' She looked out of the window. 'I think it's going to continue raining a bit longer. We can visit the Parsonage. Harriet said it's worth seeing. Then we'll go down and see George about the things in the barn.'

'Will it stop raining later?'

'Yes. Then we can go down to the beach.'

'O.K. I fancy getting a tan!'

For the second time that morning, Sara and Connie set off to walk to Abbots Cross. The leisurely walk along the clifftops gave them the opportunity to admire the views. Inland lay the gentle folds of rich productive farmland supporting well-tended cattle. Elsewhere, golden corn waved in the sunshine. And on the other side, the sea lay in a semi-dormant, waveless calm.

They continued to walk, and after a few minutes, breasted a hill. Abbots Cross suddenly appeared, spread out below in a view which was beautifully panoramic. Behind the bus-depot at the top of the street stood the medieval church and a very grand Parsonage against a backdrop of trees. It was approached by a drive which left the main road and wound its short, lazy way past the church. And at the other side of the main road, the village street down which they had walked the day before, weaved away in a descending slope towards the river.

Within a few minutes, they passed the first houses. Now it was possible to appreciate better the ancient church, its square tower paternally dominating the village. As they walked past the bus depot, Miss Quincey waved from inside.

'Do you like Death Cottage, then?' she called through the open door.

'It's wonderful!' Sara called back.

'Glad to hear it!'

The church drive was indicated by a metal sign. Imagination fired, Sara wondered what it must have been like in years gone by. A thriving church, a large congregation, carriages arriving to disembark the gentry. 'I wish I could go back through the years,' she said absently. 'Just for a time. Just to see what it was *really* like.'

They walked up the drive, passing a notice advertising a village fete shortly before arriving at the front of the Parsonage. Mounting the short flight of stone steps, they paid admission. Inside, armed with a guide book, they joined the few other tourists and started to tour the house.

In room after room, wax figures colourfully presented a picture of Victorian times, and before. Occasional glimpses of the gardens came into view, and at one point, a magnificent view of the village street spread out before them, leading its downward way past houses and castle.

'Peasants have lived here for hundreds of years.' Sara said.

Connie looked at village street. 'They lived in nice houses!'

'They're nice now. But not then. There's something about it in the guide book.' Quickly thumbing through the pages, Sara found what she sought.

'In former times, the bordars and cotters lived in hovels on both sides of Village Street--'

'What's a hovel? ...and what's a bordar?... and a cotter?'

'There's an index.' said Sara. 'Ah - here we are! -- Bordars were very poor peasants. Cotters were poor peasants with cottages. A hovel's a building infested with rats. Houses had no floors. Damp running constantly down the walls.'

'Oh - *God!!!*'

'They caught all kinds of diseases. That's why people had such big families - because so many of their children died!'

'It's horrible!'

'It couldn't be helped. If you'd lived in those times, you'd have seen why for yourself.'

They moved away from the window and into a corridor hung with oil paintings of all shapes and sizes. Generally the figures were of little interest.

Then Sara's attention was arrested. It was like being struck by a hammer.

She gazed almost open-mouthed at a huge oil painting on canvas. A young man with a firm, square jaw, dressed in Seventeenth Century apparel sat at a desk. Quill in hand, he looked out of the painting and with searing hypnotism, fixed her with his look. And on the instant, an amazing thing happened. For Sara instantly engaged with the figure in the portrait. A bond was forged between the man in the painting and Sara herself. A bond of trust. A bond of understanding.

A bond of... *Love...*

Startled, Sara felt the déjà vu of the previous day avalanche back - as if she'd been through all this before. 'Edward... Edward Makepeace...' she began to say.

Then she stopped.

'How did I know that?' she demanded of herself.

Startled, she glanced down at the entry in her guide book which told the man's name:

EDWARD MAKEPEACE

'How did you know his name, Sara?'

In the midst of inexplicable flummox and fluster, Sara only distantly heard Connie's question. She turned to look at the adolescent.

'What?' she asked, playing for time.

'I asked you how you knew his name?'

'I can't explain.' Sara admitted softly. 'I really can't. I just seemed to know, that's all.'

Sara felt the eyes in the portrait follow her around. Edward Makepeace watched her constantly and intently, no matter how she moved. It was as if the portrait were alive, as if the man were a real, breathing human being, sitting in front of her, ready to speak. She even knew the timbre of his voice - a rich baritone, powerful, commanding - yet gentle. The sensation was more than startling - it was uncanny.

'Why are you breathing like that?'

Once more Sara jolted back to reality. 'Like what?' She spoke defensively, taken by an irrational, unreasonable sensation of guilt.

'Like that!' Connie inhaled and exhaled several times in imitation. 'Heavy - as if you'd been running.'

Sara knew that Connie was right. She *WAS* breathing heavily. 'Oh... I don't know...' she said, 'I suppose I find the young man in the portrait... well, attractive.' With a little shake of the head she added, 'I have a feeling I've met him.'

'*Met* him?'

Sara grinned. 'Yes.' Then, seeing Connie's despairing frown, she went on, 'I know. It's impossible! He must have died hundreds of years ago!'

'Who was he?'

An attendant standing a little way along the corridor, an older, tweed-suited lady, had been listening to the conversation. Now she intervened. 'That was Edward Makepeace' she explained in a quiet Northumbrian accent. 'Parson of Abbots Cross in the early 1660's. Later became Squire of Christ Church. He was advanced for his time, persuading people to be more hygienic. For example, he persuaded the cottagers to drink fresh stream water.'

Sara was curious. 'Where had the water come from before?'

'From the river. They drank the same water in which they poured sewage and washed their clothes. Incredible by today's standards. But common practice then.'

'How did *he* know what to do? Medical knowledge at the time was so basic! When did *he* find out about hygiene?'

'After the Plague.'

'The Black Death?'

'Yes. 1662. There was a much greater outbreak in 1665, of course. That's the one everybody hears about. But plague was an annual scourge in those days.' The attendant turned to look lovingly at the picture. 'In a time when most gentry looked on their tenants simply as economic units - providers of profit, Parson Makepeace regarded them humanely. He helped to stop the plague when it broke out here.'

'How did he stop it?'

'Legend says he had pills with healing properties.'

'Pills?' Sara shrilled in disbelief.

The attendant smiled. 'You're not the first visitor to disbelieve it. I'm not convinced myself. But that's the legend.'

Sara smiled. 'Then I *do* believe it.' She turned to face the portrait again. 'But I didn't know the Black Death had spread this far North? I thought the plague only hit London and the South?'

'That's largely true.' the attendant agreed. 'But there were sporadic outbreaks elsewhere - especially during the great plague of 1665. Eyam in Derbyshire is the most famous.'

'How did the plague get here?'

'Nobody knows. Brought by travellers, possibly. But that's not certain.'

Sara nodded. 'I see...' She smiled. 'The house is beautiful... she commented. Then, looking at the very few pieces of furniture, she added, 'But it seems rather sparsely furnished for a grand house.'

The attendant sighed. 'Furniture was so expensive in those days.' she said. 'In fact, most better class houses would be equally short of furniture.'

Thanking the attendant, Sara and Connie left the gallery and reached a door which opened into the last part of the Parsonage. This was a roofless ruined addition at the end of a long broad passage. Through an outside door, stone steps led down onto a large open area, its surface covered with huge flat cobblestones.

Formerly a medieval banqueting hall, it was dominated by an enormous stone fireplace at the far end and fronted by a Tudor bridge-like mantle.

Perhaps ten feet in height and much more deep, the back wall rose to a broad ledge which seemed to be three or four feet wide, at the back of which another wall rose, leading its way into the now-demolished chimney.

A sudden strange shiver ran down Sara's back as she and Connie wandered over to read the sign on the mantle:

THE HANGING FIRE

AFTER HENRY V111'S SOLDIERS HAD DESTROYED THEIR PLACE OF WORSHIP, TWO MONKS WHO WERE CAUGHT TRYING TO HIDE FROM THE SOLDIERS INSIDE THIS ENORMOUS CAVITY WHICH HAD PREVIOUSLY BEEN USED AS A FIREPLACE WERE HANGED ON ROPES SUSPENDED FROM THE COOKING FULCRUM.

IN AUGUST 1662, A YOUNG WOMAN OF THE VILLAGE WAS FOUND GUILTY OF WITCHCRAFT.

SHE WAS ALSO HANGED IN THIS PLACE.

As Sara read it, a spasm of shock gripped her, speeding up through her body trembling her arms and freezing her neck. An urge to leave, to get away from this dreadful place suddenly surged through her, starting in her feet and instantly reaching all parts. For some reason she could not explain she felt horror so terrible, so fearful, that escape was imperative.

Whirling round to turn her face from the Hanging Fire, she snapped at the younger girl. 'Come on, Connie!'

'Why? Where are we going?'

'Never mind, Connie.! Just come!'

Sara moved swiftly across the cobbles back into the broad passageway, the bewildered, wide-eyed adolescent running after her as she ran through the exit and leapt down the outside stone steps.

It was not until they were well down the drive that Sara's irrational fear began to abate. She allowed her pace to slow down. And only then did she notice that Connie had been yelling at her.

'Sara... Sara... what is it...?' Connie's eyes were wide with terror.

Sara stopped, sorry for her own panic. 'Forgive me, Connie.' she said apologetically. 'I can't explain. But that place gave me the shivers.'

The smooth young forehead furrowed under the still-startled eyes. 'The picture didn't make you shiver. It made you breathe fast.'

Sara relaxed into a smile. As she thought again of the portrait, the terrible vision of the hanging fire abated. And the more she thought of the face in the painting, the more the inexplicable horror receded into an unused corner of her mind.

But Sara was unable to dismiss the memory of the young man in the portrait. Nor did she want to. And as they reached the top of the Village Street, the dominating, searching eyes of Edward Makepeace continued to haunt her...

Chapter 3

G eorge was outside his house, lying underneath his car.

'Hello, girls!' he said, pulling himself out from under the vehicle, his face a toothless grin of pleasure. 'Everything OK?'

'Sara heard noises upstairs in the cottage!' Connie said quietly.

'Noises?' George sat up curiously, laid his spanner aside and scrambled to his feet. 'What noises?'

'It was last night...' Sara began, feeling a little foolish. 'They woke me up.'

'But I didn't hear *ANYTHING!*' Connie said. 'Even though Sara woke me up.'

'Must have been my imagination. First night in a strange house--'

'I think it's *haunted!*' grinned Connie. 'And there are other strange things--'

'What strange things?'

'The strange thing you saw behind the outhouse door, Sara!'

'Yes...' Sara felt a little foolish under George's scrutiny.

'What did you find in the outhouse?' Apprehension masked George's face.

'A rat.'

'A rat?'

'Yes. A *black* rat!' She paused, thinking in digression for a moment. The rat of history, of sailing ships, of lice and typhus. 'But not just a rat.' she went on. 'A *number* of rats. Nearly all of them dead. Dead for some time, judging by the smell.'

George nodded.

'There was one live one.' Connie added.

Sara nodded. 'Yes. Squeaking pitifully as it lay, unable to escape, trapped and helpless. Each rat had been trapped by its tail - intertwined with the tails of the others. Tangled in too complex a knot to be tied by human hand.'

George's weathered face seem to pale. 'The formation of these rats...' he asked, trepidation haunting his voice, ' Were they... er... like the spokes of a wheel...?'

Sara nodded, eyes wide in surprise. George's clear concern came over sharp and clear. 'An enormous, black festering crown.' she went on, almost relishing the horror of the details. 'Each fly-covered carcass was of a rat which had tried to escape in a different direction. A ring of rats.'

George suddenly looked grim. 'Who saw it first?' he asked with quiet meaning.

To Sara, the question seemed strange. 'Why do you ask that?'

As George looked at her, Sara caught a glimpse of his expression. Fear triggered in her stomach. But the look vanished before it registered properly.

'Oh, nothing. But I'd like to see it. As soon as possible. Can I come now?'

'Of course.'

George's face relaxed slightly. 'Were you scared?'

Sara smiled nervously, sensing something more behind his question than was instantly clear. 'I was! But Connie touched them.'

George cast Connie a sharp glance. 'You *touched* them?'

'I didn't *mean* to touch them I fell on them. When the door burst open.'

'You mustn't touch rats, young miss!' George's voice was stern.

'It was an accident.' Connie protested.

'Rats can give you all kinds of diseases!' Then George looked at Sara. 'What happened next?'

'I pulled Connie into the house. Got her washed straight away.'

George shook his head in disbelief. 'Sounds to me like you did the best thing.' He pondered briefly. 'I'll come - at once!'

Then he turned to speak directly to Connie. 'These noises? Where do they come from?'

'From behind the door... the door up the spiral stairs...'

'I wonder if mice have got in there?' George pondered aloud. 'I'll bring the key to that door.'

Disappearing into the house, George re-emerged quickly. Triumphantly he bore a large jailer's key. With a strangely serious expression, he got in behind the wheel. He coaxed the old vehicle into life, and they moved off.

Once there, George followed Sara into the cottage. 'Now,' he said, 'let's have a look at this door.'

They all climbed the steep staircase, George first, followed by Sara, with Connie bringing up the rear. 'Achoo!' Connie sneezed.

'You've caught a cold, young miss.' George observed.

He reached the bottom of the three spiral steps and climbed their few carpetless boards to the door. Producing the key, which looked as if it would have fitted a medieval dungeon, he thrust it into the keyhole. 'OK' he said, 'Let's try!'

The key was stubborn. 'I - don't - think - it's - going - to - move -.' he began. Then just as he spoke, 'CLANK!' The mortise sprang open.

He took hold of the metal knob with both hands and with great efforts, managed to pull it round. With a great creak, the door swung reluctantly open to reveal the interior of the room.

Inside was turmoil. Bits of junk lay everywhere. Old carpets, an ancient washday wringer, an iron bedstead, countless scraps, pieces and bits. All littered the floorboards.

'I'll have to get this junk moved out of here.' said George. 'I keep meaning to do it, then I forget. I suppose this could be used as an extra bedroom if anybody wanted it.'

He switched on the light, but although the bulb lit up, from the bulbholder sounded the fizzing of an electrical fault.

At once, George switched it off again. 'I'd better look at that connection before this light gets used again.'

The three of them made their way into the room. In the semi-gloom, they looked round. But no clue to the noises was evident.

'No sign of mice.' George said. 'Sometimes we get a rodent or two round about, but they never come into the house. I don't think there are any mice here. And I'd have been surprised if there had been!'

Realising there was no point in looking round further, Sara and Connie turned to go. George shut the door, locking it again.

It locked easier than it opened, and to make sure the lock was free, George tried the key two or three times, each time opening the lock easily. The initial resistance was no longer there.

'I've left the key in the lock.' George said as they went downstairs. 'Then you can investigate if you hear anything again.'

As they went downstairs and through the kitchen, George said, 'Now let me see the rats in the outhouse!' He grabbed the handle and pulled the door open, bending his head forward to peer inside. He stood statuesque for a minute, his hand still on the door as he looked down.

Sara poked her head in beside George's. 'They're all dead now.' she said. Then both she and George pulled back from the repulsive sight.

'I thought so!' he nodded. 'That's a RatKing! I've never seen one before, but I've read about them. It's the name given to a strange formation of black rats.'

'These formations... are they common?'

'No, Miss. But they have been documented from time to time. There was a discovery as recently as 1953.' George said. 'In Holland. A farmer found one under a pile of bean sticks in a barn.'

'He could have invented the story.'

George shook his head. 'A photograph exists of the seven adult rats and their intertwined tails.'

'Someone could have tied the knot... the farmer himself, perhaps, after he found separate rats.'

Again George's grey-haired head shook. 'The knot was very complex. It consisted of almost the entire tail of one animal plus the tips of others. The X-ray showed that the knot had existed for some time. In any case - here's a RatKing!' He pointed to the festering formation. 'I didn't tie *this* knot. Did you?'

Sara laughed. 'You're right, George.'

'Which one's the King?' Connie asked.

'None of them.' George answered. 'It's the name given to the formation. Nobody knows how it comes about or what makes the rats do it. Happens with squirrels, too.'

'That'll be a SquirrelKing.' Connie joked.

George smiled. 'I'd better get rid of them at once, or we'll all catch typhus! I've a sack in the car boot. I'll put the rats into it and bury them at once.'

Followed by the two girls, George lumbered out of the outhouse, and round to his car. Quickly he returned, carrying a hessian sack and placed it on the ground. He grabbed an old pitchfork, and carefully forked the limp rat king by the knotted tails.

'What shall I do, George?' Sara asked.

'Just hold the bag, Miss. It won't take long.'

As Sara held the bag open at arms' length, George grinned. 'Don't worry!' he said. 'They won't bite!'

The festering intertwined carcasses were lumped into the sack. Then, throwing down the pitchfork, George grabbed the sack by its neck. He dragged it out of the outhouse, and down the garden.

In the outhouse, beside the pitchfork rested an ancient rusty spade. George now used it to dig a hole at the bottom of the overgrown garden. Within minutes the dead rats were in it, sack and all. Then he refilled the hole, patting the top with the flat spade as if to make sure the rats didn't resurrect themselves.

'That's it!' he said, dropping the spade off in the outhouse. Crossing the courtyard, he stopped at a standpipe to wash his hands.

'I must remember to phone the rodent man when I get back to Abbots Cross.' he repeated. 'Just in case. I doubt very much if there'll be any more, though. They were all dead.'

Sara walked to the gate with George, leaving Connie with a teen mag in the house. Before opening the gate, she hesitated. 'George...?'

'Yes, Miss?'

'You know you asked - back at the village - who saw the RatKing first?'

'Yes?' It was a strange half-whisper.

'I'd like you to tell me why you asked that.'

'Oh, I don't know--'

'George! I really want to know!'

The severity of her tone made his aged eyes look deep into hers. Briefly, he hesitated. 'All right.' he said at length. 'But tell me: Are you superstitious?'

'Superstitious? Not really. No more than anybody else.'

'You don't take notice of old wives' tales?'

Sara shook her head. Then she realised there was something in his tone - something sinister. 'What is it, George? Good or bad, I really want to know.'

He hesitated a moment longer, then went on. 'It's just that there's a legend about a RatKing. Nothing to worry about--'

'Tell me.'

His eyes fell in embarrassment. 'Very well,' he said, then cleared his throat. 'It goes like this:' His eyes turned to the horizon as he began a nervous recitation:

> "Take care that thou avert thine eye,
> If a Ratking nest nearby
> If it ye be the first to see,
> Then evil soon shall follow thee"

He stopped reciting and turned his gaze back to Sara. Sara returned his stare.

'You mean - Connie is threatened with evil?'

'If she were the first to see the Ratking. At least, that's what the poem says.'

For a moment she stared into his earnest face. Then she openly laughed. 'Oh, come on, George. You don't believe that, do you?'

Briefly, he continued to look earnestly at her. Then his expression dissolved. 'No, of course not, Miss. Of course I don't!' he laughed.

But his laugh was unconvincing...

Sara waved at the ancient vehicle as George departed, then turned and went back into the cottage. She was determined that superstitious nonsense would have no effect on her. But despite her determination, George's ancient poem lingered.

'...If it ye be the first to see,
Then evil soon shall follow thee'

Connie had been first to see the RatKing. So, according to the verse, she faced evil. What evil? And had the noises Connie'd heard behind the door during the night anything to do with it?

Sara sat down and surreptitiously looked at Connie without her being aware of it. Connie seemed surprisingly content, sitting in an armchair reading her teen mag.

Sara rose and wandered over to the window. She looked out over the calm sea. And despite her determination to ignore George's warning, questions tumbled through her mind, remaining unanswered.

What evil could possibly follow Connie?
How would Sara be involved?
Could she prevent it?
Or was it inevitable

After lunch a now hot August sun chased the last of the rain clouds, promising a spell of afternoon sunshine.

Distantly, the sea stretched away to the horizon. The end of the cottage garden was bounded by a fence in which hung a gate. 'Connie!' Sara called. 'Would you like to go down to the beach?'

'Yea!'

'C'Mon, then. Let's take advantage of the sunshine!'

Within minutes, both girls had reached the gate. There they stopped to look down. The cottage garden ended at a small rise above a private and very welcoming beach. A short path ran down from the gate, then petered out when it reached the sand.

The girls made their way to the water's edge and spread towels on the sand. Both lay down in the full glare of what remained of the day's sun. Sara glanced over to Connie and took note of her now-fully-formed female figure. Connie really was stunning, with beautiful blue eyes, lengthy trusses of flaxen hair, long legs and a perfectly formed figure.

The dip between the low rise and the beach formed a natural suntrap ideal for the browning of human skin. But unfortunately, other small creatures also found it desirable. Sara did her best to ignore the buzz of insects, but the sting of one on her lower back was fierce enough to anger her into brushing the creature away.

The bite hurt for a few minutes, and by judiciously turning her head, Sara could make out an unsightly weal which was beginning to form just above the top of her bikini briefs.

But there was nothing she could do about it, and she lay down again. In any case, a more insistent problem had begun to bother Sara. The problem had lingered in her mind ever since returning from Abbots Cross.

Connie.

Connie did not seem herself. Normally she would have lain in the sunshine, sunglasses shielding her eyes, the warm rays gently tanning her slim body.

But today she was restless, unable to lie still. She removed her sunglasses as she threshed from side to side, unable to stay still. Her cheeks were now visibly red, her eyes listless.

Sara's concern magnified after a time when Connie sat up to face her.

'What is it, Connie?'

Connie's flushed face pouted. 'I feel hot, Sara, and my back aches.'

Sara leaned across to feel the youthful forehead. *Hot. Extremely hot. Eyelids drooping. Cheeks cherry coloured.*

Glancing skywards, Sara saw that wisps of early evening cloud were starting to filter the weakening sun's rays. 'That's funny!' she said. 'I thought it was getting cool.' Then, hoping not to worry the youngster, she added, 'But it's time to go back anyway!'

As they approached the house, Connie sniffed deeply. 'Don't the flowers smell *LOVELY*?' She closed her moistening eyes rapturously.

'I can't smell them. Where are they?'

'I don't know where they are. But their smell is all over the garden.'

* * * *

Once inside, Connie plumped heavily into an armchair, staying unusually silent as she snuggled against an armrest. Clearly she could not even be bothered to read her teenage magazine. *Not a good sign!*

'Early to bed for you I think, Connie' said Sara uneasily.

'Yes, I think so... aaAAHHCHOOO!'

'You *HAVE* caught a cold!' Sara said. 'I'll put a hot water bottle in bed for you.'

'I don't need a hot water bottle.' Connie retorted. 'I'm *boiling*. Ah... Achoo!'

Sara regarded her young cousin anxiously.

'Achooo...' sneezed Connie again. '...Achooo!' Through her half-open, water-filled eyes, she regarded Sara. 'I don't feel well. I'd better go to bed now.'

Connie pulled herself lethargically from the armchair. Wearily, she began to make her way upstairs, followed by Sara. Once Connie had changed and slipped into bed, Sara returned. She regarded the feverish adolescent nervously.

'I'll go downstairs for a time.' Sara said softly. 'Then I'll be in my bedroom. If you feel worse, give me a shout!'

Seeing that Connie was already drifting off to sleep, Sara closed the bedroom door, went downstairs. There was little she could do for Connie at the moment. Best let her sleep and hope for improvement.

She sat down and picked up the guide book she had bought at Abbots Cross Parsonage. Intrigued by the figure in the portrait, she hoped there would be more information on him in the book.

On first viewing, the Parsonage at Abbots Cross appears very grand for its purpose. And it is. In normal circumstances, the parson would have lived at a level not much above that of the bordars and cotters. But there were reasons for the parson at Abbots Cross living at a much higher standard.

Edward Makepeace was son of the local Squire, who lived in the nearby village of Christ Church. Squire Makepeace's wife, Edward Makepeace's mother, was the only daughter of the family who owned Abbots Cross. When she and Squire Makepeace married, the two estates of Abbots Cross and Christ Church amalgamated, so that the manor at Christ Church became the manor house for both, and the redundant manor house at Abbots Cross became the parsonage.

'I see...' Sara said to herself. 'That explains the grandeur of the house.'

She read on further for a time, but there was little else relating to Parson Makepeace. Eventually, she closed up the guide book and ascended the stairs. Ducking under the low beam, she looked in at the sleeping Connie. The hot, flushed complexion accompanied a troubled sleep.

If you're no better in the morning, Sara thought, *we'll have to see a doctor.*

Chapter 4

The plaintive, piping voice raised in summons interrupted Sara's sleep. Quickly alert, Sara threw back the bedclothes, pulling on her dressing gown and hurried through. But in her haste, she forgot the low ceiling crosspiece. Her forehead collided painfully with the beam.

For a few seconds, she staggered about, cursing her own carelessness. Then, thoughtfully, she felt her brow. No bump. But her head ached.

'What is it, Connie?'

'I feel so *ILL!*'

Sara examined her briefly. The hot figure sweated and trembled.

Sara stood upright, still looking down at Connie. The blonde hair covered the pillow as the lids of Connie's blue eyes half-opened and she looked up. But she wasn't looking at Sara.

'There's a light on!'

Sara frowned. 'Yes. I put it on.'

'No... the light under that door...' Raising a trembling arm, Connie pointed towards the three semi-circular steps.

Timidly, Sara turned her head to look. Sure enough, a ribbon of dim yellow light illuminated a strip of space below the door.

Bewildered, Sara shook her head disbelievingly before turning back. 'I'll try the door.' she said. 'Perhaps George left a light on earlier this afternoon.'

But Sara only said this to allay Connie's fears. Worried about an electrical fault, George had carefully switched off the light.

Gingerly rising from the bedside, Sara went out of the room and over to the stairs. There she stepped up to the door.

Putting her fingers under the latch, she scraped it upwards. Then she stopped, sniffed lightly and let go of the latch again.

A strange odour met her nostrils. It was a foetid smell which could not have been expected in an all-electric house.

The unmistakable dull reek of an oil lamp.

Sara's semi-dormant feeling of alarm burst into life. She moved back. Did somebody live in there?

Momentarily nonplussed, she looked questioningly at the solid carved door. On impulse, she raised her small fist and knocked several times as loudly as she could. She stood back again to wait, listening carefully.

At first it seemed there would be no response. Then a clear sound issued from the other side - the tramp of footsteps on the wooden floor!

Holding her breath, Sara heard the latch being slowly lifted. She watched in amazement as the door swung inwards, slowly and easily opening to reveal an unexpected figure.

The tall outline of an unusually dressed girl of about Sara's age filled the doorframe. In her hand she carried a small oil lamp.

* * * *

Sara stood motionless, unable to breathe, feeling consciousness begin to drain from her as she stared at the apparition in the doorway.

It can't be! she thought. *The loft's empty! Nobody lives here!'*

She blinked her eyes a couple of times, but still the girl remained.

Then Sara pondered. *The beam!* she thought *The bump on my head! I'm hallucinating - I must be!!*

But perhaps not. So, ignoring the fact that this might be a hallucination, Sara quickly assimilated details. The clothes were not bright, but nor were they sober. A russet appearance was conveyed by a weather-beaten complexion. Nut brown eyes were surrounded by deep black curls of long hair which tumbled below shoulder level, framing her oval face.

But while Sara gazed in amazement, the girl's look was one simply of mild surprise - no more. And when she spoke, her Northumbrian voice bore a softness to match her plain simple appearance.

'Aye? What is it?'

For a few moments more the two girls looked at one another before Sara replied. 'Good Evening.' she found herself saying, somewhat inanely, the words coming without thought.

'Good Evening.' replied the girl.

'I... er... thought nobody was here...' Sara stammered, realising she wasn't making much sense.

'Why, Mistress, I live here.'

'You *do*?'

'Aye.'

'Have you lived here long?'

'Since the day I was born. My parents, God rest their souls, tilled this farm before me, as now do I. In fact, I have just come in after assisting a cow to calf. Otherwise I would have been abed a long time ago.'

'You're a farmer?'

'Aye, Mistress, a yeoman.'

'I didn't know.'

There was a brief lull, then the girl spoke again. 'What brings you here?' she enquired. 'Are you in need of aid?'

'Aid?.... Oh - yes... yes, indeed... I need help. Or rather, my young cousin does.'

'Your cousin?'

Coincidentally, at that moment the groggy figure of Connie appeared unsteadily at Sara's side.

'Good Evening, Mistress.' the girl said. 'Are you ailing?'

'My head aches. I feel hot and sick.' Connie spoke in a half-awake murmur.

'My cousin needs medical attention.' Sara told the girl. 'Is there a doctor at Abbots Cross?'

As the girl shook her head, tight ringlets tumbled at each side. 'No. But the Parson is learned in medicine.

He has all kinds of herbs and remedies to aid ills and combat pestilence.'

'Can we get him here?'

'No... but we can take the girl to Abbots Cross. 'Tis not far, and I have a horse and cart.'

Sara pondered for a moment. If she had to walk with Connie - possibly even carrying the adolescent - it would take some time to get to Abbots Cross. If the girl *did* take Connie to the village in a horse and cart, a lot of time and effort would be saved.

'That's very kind of you.' Sara said.

'Please enter.' The girl stood aside to let Connie and Sara pass.

As the two girls went into the room, Sara stopped, her bewilderment deepening. She recalled the room earlier in the day when George had opened the door. But now it was quite different.

The room was the same size. But a fire now blazed. Heating pots which hung down the chimney on chains. Baskets and herbs stood all round. Sara lightly touched the rough plaster of the walls, to find her fingers powdered white.

Taking Connie by the hand, the girl helped her over to a wooden chair. But as the girl turned away, Connie slumped forward. She would have fallen had not the girl caught her.

'I'll lay her on the bed.' she told Sara. Lifting Connie with ease, she laid Connie gently on top of a single four-poster bed, lit from the side by a candle lantern.

Sara sat down on a bench flanking the central wooden table on which stood the oil lamp. She wondered deeply about it all as she regarded the many baskets standing on shelves round the room.

In addition to the changed room, Sara was puzzled by the girl's quaint clothes. She still dressed as in bygone centuries. It was so weird!

But concern over Connie chased all doubts. The girl might be strange - but she was offering a lifeline. One to be grateful for. This was no time to be probing. And perhaps this mode of dress still survived in out-of-the-way places like Abbots Cross.

'My name is Josephine.' the girl said.

'I'm Sara and this is my cousin Constance... Connie for short...'

'Sara... Connie... I shall remember...' Josephine consciously made an effort to commit the names to memory. Then she looked down at the bed. 'The Parson had best examine you, Young Mistress.'

She turned to Sara. 'Perhaps you will make your cousin ready, while I see to the horse?'

Nodding gratefully, Sara got up from the bench, stepping over to the bed. 'I'll get her dressed. And I'll put on my outdoor clothes. We'll be ready in a few minutes.'

Judging by her tear-misted eyes, which only lazily opened, Connie found it difficult to stay awake. 'I really hurt, Sara,' she said, 'I *really* hurt.'

'Don't worry.' said Sara.

Helping her to her room, Sara dressed Connie. Pulling blankets from both beds, she wrapped Connie tightly lest there be a night chill. Then Sara herself dressed fully, pulling on her purple cotton casual blazer and matching trousers lest Connie should have to go to hospital.

A few days earlier, a house doctor had prescribed some antibiotics for Sara when she had developed a slight chest infection. But the infection had cleared up without them. Nonetheless, Sara had made sure the antibiotics the doctor had given her had been packed when she had left. Now she made sure they were in her pocket. If it were decided to give one to Connie and she had to go to hospital, the hospital would want to know what medication the young girl had taken.

Once ready, Sara led Connie back into Josephine's room. Lightly picking up Connie in surprisingly strong arms, Josephine walked over to the door. With one hand she easily lifted the wooden latch to open it.

The exterior flight of steps led down to an earth track. Against a fence, a wooden cart with two solid wheels harnessing an impatient young horse making a 'Brrrr---' sound stood ready. Curiously basket-shaped, the wooden cart was encased by a small lattice fence. Gently, Josephine carried Connie over to the cart, laying her on its rough, unplaned floor.

Sara pulled shut the house door. Then from opposite sides, Josephine and Sara climbed aboard to sit side by side on a single plank which served as a running board.

'Gee - Up!!' Josephine commanded.

The horse's enormous muscles slowly flexed, its powerful legs easily moved, the solid cart lumbered into a lurching motion.

The plodding movement jolted the cart quite savagely. Sara put out a hand to grab hold of the wooden lattice as it swayed wildly from side to side in the deep ruts.

But Josephine appeared accustomed to the violent jerking. She handled the huge carthorse with expertise, guiding it with a leather harness, holding the reins in sinewy hands.

The only sounds, other than the soft swish of the gentle sea, was the clatter of wooden cartwheels and the dull thud of horse hooves. Sara would have spoken to Josephine, but because the effort of driving the sizeable cart was patently strenuous, Sara remained silent.

Periodically, Sara glanced into the rear. But although subject to the violent movements of the cart, Connie remained in an unhealthy, disturbed sleep. Sara's concern mounted.

Looking round at the passing terrain, Sara noticed that in the silver light cast by the full moon, the fields bore a strange, abandoned appearance, irregularly tilled, with few hedges. A curiously longhorned breed of sheep occupied the pasture. Over the unfenced clifftop, the sea was deserted save for a single sailing ship making its way along the horizon, parallel to the coast.

Eventually they reached the hilltop down which they rolled towards the village, dormant in the aluminium lunar glow.

At the fork, Josephine turned onto the main road familiar to Sara from the afternoon's visit to Abbots Cross. At once, differences became evident. In place of the hard, tarmac surface, the main road was mud-caked and deep-rutted. The several cars which had been dotted about that morning were absent.

Josephine now speeded up, coaxing the horse. The powerful limbs responded as it strode out, pulling the cart at a fast pace. The cart crunched along in the deep furrows dug by countless prior wheels, causing Sara to hang on even more tightly.

As they passed the small bus depot, Sara noticed changes. Now it was a miniature cottage, clearly inhabited. In some minor alarm, she thought, 'That was a bus depot' and noticed that the glass door seemed different. Had somebody fitted a wooden door this afternoon? And the notices on the door were no longer there.

Strange?...

The church loomed larger and larger. Although greatly concerned about Connie, Sara looked at it with some affection, recalling the emotions it had so recently aroused in her. Yet although the Parson's house was the same, again there were differences. The signs to the entrance and car park had been removed along with outdoor lamps. A notice board which had borne a notice of a village fete had been replaced by a handwritten sign saying that a special parson was coming to conduct the service on Sunday.

But Sara concentrated on Connie. True, there was now a strangeness in the surroundings. And Josephine spoke strangely and wore outmoded apparel. In addition, the old Parsonage was no longer a museum, but had been restored to its former glory. The entire ambience was one of surreality - as if it were all a disturbed dream, almost a nightmare. *Wake up!* Sara yelled inwardly at herself, *Wake up! You're dreaming!*

But she could not wake up. And the jolting of the cart, the strange unexpected odours and the feel of the wooden bench on which she sat all contributed to Sara's realisation that unbelievable as it seemed, this was *really* happening!

At the head of the village, Josephine circled the cart so that it once more faced the direction of Death Cottage, and as the horse pulled up at a gate, Sara recognised the short drive leading to the Parsonage.

Josephine turned to speak, the perspiration on her brow glittering in the moonlight.

'We'll carry the maiden the last short distance. It would not be seemly to take a farm cart up the carriage drive.'

Too busy to wonder about the word "maiden", Sara nodded agreement. 'She's not heavy. I can carry her.' Then as they stepped down from the cart, she placed a restraining hand on Josephine's forearm. 'Please, Josephine, there's no need to come further.'

By the moonlight, Josephine looked not only tired from the drive, but exhausted from a hard day's work. Sara worried that Connie should be no more of a burden than necessary.

Josephine nodded. 'Very well, Mistress Sara. I must confess to some fatigue - and I will have a heavy day's ploughing tomorrow.' She turned to indicate the Parsonage. 'Knock on the front door. James will answer, and on request, fetch the Parson.'

Thanking Josephine, Sara helped the semi-conscious Connie from the cart. As Connie began to walk trance-like towards the parsonage, Sara turned to thank Josephine. But the cart had already gone away.

Bewildered, Sara went to the gate and looked along the road. The cart was already disappearing round the bend

Now totally confused, Sara turned to Connie. 'Can you stand?' she asked Connie, breaking a silence more complete than Sara ever remembered.

'Yes...' Connie mumbled.

Together they made their way up the drive to the parsonage, Sara supporting Connie as the younger girl stumbled her way along. It took a time, but eventually they were up the steps at the front of the parsonage.

Sara stood Connie against the wall. Then she turned to the huge door and started knocking loudly on its stout oak front before stepping back to wait.

At first, there seemed to be no response. But as Sara was about to knock again, a barely discernible light began to flicker.

Through the windows, Sara could see a candelabrum being carried downstairs. The flame dimly wavered and was followed by footsteps approaching the front door. Bolts were drawn from inside, then the large portal squealed open to reveal an enormous figure. His light hair was swept back behind his head, and held there by a ribbon. His long nightshirt covered by a jacket were discernible by the light of the three-pronged candleabrum he carried.

'Aye? What do you want at this hour?' the giant asked.

'I have a sick young woman here. She needs medical help urgently. Please be kind enough to seek the parson.'

The servant eyed Sara up and down, clearly greatly puzzled not only at her manner, but also by her appearance. He nodded and moved half out of the doorway. Looking at Connie, he studied her for a moment before turning back to Sara. He nodded again elegantly.

'Enter!'

Sara helped Connie from where she had been leaning against the wall, then helped her into the entrance hall.

'Where shall I put her?' Sara asked.

The man nodded sedately towards a curious kind of couch against the wall. 'On the day bed.' He clanked shut the large door, then threw the bolts.

He walked over to where Sara was already laying her younger cousin onto the couch. He looked down.

'Mmm... She looks very sick.' he agreed.   'Please wait here while I seek the Parson.'

He turned to a candle standing on a sideboard, and lit it from the three-pronged candleabrum.   Then, shielding the flames of his candleabrum, he bustled away to seek the Parson, his buckled shoes thumping heavily under his great weight on the wooden, carpetless stairs as he ascended them.

'I wonder why he uses candles instead of switching on the light?' thought Sara, left alone in the dark entrance hall, lit only by the single candle flame...

In a short time, a light reappeared above. Sara looked up to see the servant descending the stairs. Clearly he had dressed quickly, for now he had discarded the nightgown and was wearing a black jacket and britches.

He was followed a few seconds later by a younger man - a man little older than Sara herself.   He was dressed similarly to James, but wore a wig of the Seventeenth Century.

Suddenly, Sara's eyes widened in amazement. Even from the other side of the entrance hall she recognised the hypnotic figure from the portrait of this afternoon, and recalled the entry in the guidebook which she had not needed to consult.

EDWARD MAKEPEACE...

Sara blanched with disbelief as she watched the figure from the portrait descend the staircase. It was as if a figure from a history book had incredibly burst into life. A picture had leapt from a page and taken on a life of its own.

Mouth dry, breathing in huge gasps, Sara spoke as if it were not she but a stranger who'd taken over her voice. 'Is that Edward Makepeace?' she asked the servant.

'Why - do you know him, Mistress?'

'I... er... know of him.' she faltered. Not only was she not in possession of herself, but she also did not know how to answer. 'Is that he?'

'Aye.' the man answered, no little pride evident in his voice. 'That is Edward Makepeace.'

Sara watched silently as, without speaking, the parson crossed the flags of the floor, approached the day bed and bent over the still sleeping form of the teenager.

'Why is he dressed like that?' Sara whispered.

'Why... Mistress... he always dresses like that...' His reply carried no little surprise.

Edward Makepeace then straightened up, turned, and looked directly at Sara. 'Good Evening, Mistress...?'

She recognised it as a question. 'My name is Sara.'

'Mistress Sara.' Edward Makepeace repeated, nodding. He was looking her up and down, a strangely curious expression betraying his fascination at her purple jacket and trousers. Certainly he was dressed very conservatively, so perhaps his taste was for understatement. But was *SHE* dressed so strangely?

The Parson turned to look down at Connie again, then began to examine the adolescent more thoroughly. He placed his palm against her forehead, then opened her mouth to peer in at her tongue. But although he breezed efficiency, there was something about the curious method of his examination which Sara found disquieting.

The servant moved over beside the Parson. He stood watching for a moment before asking, 'What do you think, Parson?'.

'MMM... it's difficult to say...' said the Parson, engrossed in the problem. 'The skin is covered with rossals.'

'Rossals?' asked the disconcerted Sara.

The Parson half-turned, still looking down at Connie. 'Yes, Mistress. The medical term for a rash of fiery red spots anywhere on the body. It is the generic name for spots, be they measles or anything else.'

As he turned back to address the servant, Sara's eyes became circular as she listened to the conversation. Never before had she come across the term 'Rossals'. Now she realised she was hearing other terms she'd only read in history books.

'The maiden may be afflicted by spotted fever... or the flux perhaps... or some other pestilence.' the Parson was saying. 'I hear that there's plague in London, but it's only a small outbreak, and unlikely to have travelled this far North.'

Now Sara listened to the conversation with ears which almost refused to hear. Disbelief filtered through to every part of her body. Not only did she begin to feel the blood drain from her face, but the giddiness she had experienced earlier in the day returned. *No!* she shouted inwardly. *Keep your head!*

She gulped, deliberately breathing deeply as she fought to stave off an urge to faint. She knew her face was draining further as the monumental nature of what she feared might be happening began to dawn on her.

It was incredible.

It only happened in fiction.

It was impossible.

But though it seemed all of these things, she cursed herself for not having realised what was taking place. Now she asked the question she knew she should have asked Josephine before leaving the cottage.

'Pardon me.' she interceded, addressing the two figures bending over Connie.

Edward Makepeace turned. 'Yes, Mistress Sara? What is it?'

'Well...' hesitated Sara, 'this must seem a silly question to you, but... what date is this?'

'Why, Mistress Sara' said the servant, 'surely you know? 'Tis the month of August. You can tell by the ripe grain ready to harvest.' He waved his hand in the general direction of the door.

Sara's trepidation mushroomed as, almost fainting with apprehension, she asked the most important question of her life.

'And what year...?'

Both Edward Makepeace and the other man looked at Sara with an amazement they were unable to conceal. '...Mistress Sara' the Parson said, 'this is...' He stopped.

'Yes?' Sara could now only croak.

'Mistress Sara, why do you ask?'

'Please... tell me...' she begged in soft insistence.

The furrows of the Parson's brows deepened, and he paused before answering... 'This is the Yeare of Our Lord...'

Sara's eyes closed as she waited with dread.

'...1662.'

Chapter 5

The lids of Sara's already-closed eyes tightened in dread disbelief. Her breathing deepened as she moved her head from side to side in motions she neither intended nor could control.

'No!... No!... It can't... It can't be!!!' She reacted with strange resentment, determined to fight this nightmare, desperately willing it to be only a hallucination.

Her first reaction was to treat the answer with scorn. To pour derision on what she'd been told. To laugh at and mock this *STUPID* Parson for his idiocy.

But a deep suspicion stopped her. Now the signals of the past hour came flooding back - Josephine's clothes and her room, the unkempt fields and strange breed of sheep, the lack of tarmac on the roads, the absence of cars and roadsigns, the candles, the dress of the people. All verified what she had just been told! And although inwardly she begged and yearned for a simple explanation, lurking in uncharted regions of her mind lingered the certainty that by some quirk of time, she really *had* arrived back in the Seventeenth Century. All around her verified it.

Faint with dizziness, Sara found a chair and slumped down. Sitting with eyes tightly shut, she desperately tried to assimilate the unwanted information. Leaning forward, she drooped her head to her knees, her hands absently covering both ears. Almost from afar, she heard the Parson's question.

'Are you unwell, Mistress Sara?'

Sara tried to answer. But she found herself tongue-tied. She shook her head, as she searched for a response.

'James, fetch a goblet of water!'

'No... no... no need...' Sara stammered. 'I'll be all right. It's just that... well, I'm worried about my young cousin Connie.' She finally managed to stumble out the words, reopening her eyes and looking up again.

The Parson nodded, then turned back to look again at Connie. He and James bent over her and Sara could hear the two men mumbling to one another. Her brows knitted as she caught snatches of conversation and realised they were discussing Connie's dress.

'These are fine clothes.' said the Parson, looking over to Sara. 'And your own, too. I have never seen the like before.'

The stunned Sara could only manage a wan smile and soundless nod. *IF* this were no dream, and she was actually *IN* the Seventeenth Century, her purple suit must seem very colourful. And strangely styled.

Meanwhile, the Parson turned back to Connie. Without glancing at Sara, he asked, 'From where have you come?'

'From London.'

Her answer was reflex, given without thought. But as soon as she had spoken, she became aware she had said something dramatic.

She looked up. Both men were looking at her with expressions that were not only hostile, but fear-laden. Her brows furrowed and her puzzled glance travelled from one to the other as neither spoke.

Then, with a jerk of near-panic, the Parson whipped round to look down once again at the form on the couch. Quickly, he slipped down the top part of her dress, exposing much of Connie's body. He made a rapid examination of Connie's upper legs. He lifted her arms to examine the armpits.

Steeling herself, Sara rose from her chair. She looked over - and recoiled in horror.

Swellings had formed - dark, angry, reddish brown, hideously disfiguring Connie's body. Thighs and underarms had swollen up to become grotesque mis-shapes. They contributed to a disfiguration Sara had never before seen. Not in a hospital ward or in textbooks anywhere. Whatever Connie's disease, it was new to Sara. And not only new.

Terrifying!

Meanwhile, Parson Makepeace again felt Connie's temperature with his palm. With mounting tremor, Sara watched as in an act of deep despondency, he allowed the senseless girl's limp arm to fall back onto the couch. Slowly and thoughtfully, he rebuttonned the dress in a movement which reminded Sara of a slow burning fuse.

Turning to Sara, he looked across at her. She stared back blankly, fear rising as she observed deep venom in his hooded, accusing look. And when he spoke, his voice was cracked, reedy and thin, quite unlike the baritone resonance of a minute earlier.

"Tis exactly what I suspected.' he pronounced.

Sara's mind raced. She thought of the events of the day. And suddenly she did not need to hear him speak or try to explain his conclusion. The morning's incident took on a new meaning.

'The rat...' she whispered faintly to herself, the room taking on a circular motion, '...the black rat...'

"Tis the most fearful disease known to man.' She only half-heard the Parson go on, his voice rising in accusation.

But Sara was no longer listening. With closed eyes, and reeling head, she moaned quietly. She already knew what he was about to say. 'No... no...' she stammered. Her mind refused to believe the obvious as her brain saturated with despair.

'Your cousin has been struck down by plague.' the Parson croaked. Then his voice rose to a near-shout, heavy with recrimination. 'In God's name, Mistress Sara,' he demanded, 'how could you bring the foul gangrene amongst us?'

Sara turned a pleading gaze to him. Tears which had already welled now spilled freely down her cheeks. 'I didn't know... I didn't know...' she wept. Then she stopped, emotionally overcome, unable to continue, sobbing violently.

But although noting her grief, the Parson's tone did not soften. 'Then you *should* have known!' he said loudly. 'Living in London, you are aware that there is plague there!' He paused, then added in cutting damnation, 'Indeed, I wonder, have you and your cousin fled here to escape the Sicknesse?'

For the first time, Sara felt indignation. Her sobbing halted as, for a moment, the remark displaced her grief. Suddenly she was angry. 'We have *not!'* she almost yelled back at him.

Taken aback by Sara's ferocity, the Parson said no more. Turning back, he looked again at Connie. 'Well, Mistress Sara, I dread what I have to confirm.' he whispered.

Sara gulped, knowing what he was about to say, dreading what she knew he would tell her, yet wanting it confirmed. 'Tell me, Parson,' she pleaded, 'Please - tell me!'

The Parson turned and looked her fully and unflinchingly. 'Very well.' he said in a dread voice of no hope. 'Your cousin is sicker than she has ever been before. Unless God be willing to cure her, she is certain to be dead within two days!

* * * *

A dread-laden silence followed Parson Makepeace's warning, delivered in a deep bass which reverberated the rafters. Then the servant spoke. 'What shall we do, Parson?'

Parson Makepeace shook his head. 'Whatever else, she cannot stay here... in this Parsonage... or in Abbots Cross! The pestilence will spread throughout the village until it reaches every family. Then who will tend the crops? There will be deaths without number, and red crosses on doors in abundance! If we send her away now there is a chance that, with God's mercy, we may escape the foul pestilence.'

'But... Parson Makepeace... look at her, I beg you.' the manservant protested. 'I ask you to think again. She is too ill to be cast out!'

'She *must* leave - else we will all surely *die!'*

Sara sat silently listening to the exchange. Silent anger mounted within her as the discussion continued.

Neither she nor Connie had asked to come to this century! She'd only sought the medical help of her own time. Help she could have relied on. Help which would have been speedy. And expert.

But instead she was here - now - in this forlorn Century. She had to ask for help from people involved in the primitive medicine of the time. And the selfish attitude of this self-opinionated man-of-God was despicable!

'Perhaps if you fear disease, Our Lord's work was not a wise choice of career.' she said. Her mocking sarcasm goaded him fearlessly.

He whipped round. As he glared at her, his look was fierce and unyielding. 'Guard your tongue, Wench!!' he snapped back, eyes like hot coals.

'Why?' Sara's tone was unwaveringly under the onslaught. 'Don't you take kindly to criticism?'

A volcano of anger erupted. 'You should not speak like that--'

'Why not? Are you skilled in medicine as you claim? Or are you only fit to attend old ladies with the vapours?'

As soon as the words left her lips, she knew she had gone too far. But worry about Connie and anger at fate for putting her in this situation made Sara abandon her sense of propriety.

Yet it was a desperate situation. Propriety had no place in it. Goading him might be no bad thing.

And in that, she'd succeeded. Too livid to respond, the Parson did not speak. For a moment, Sara wondered if she and Connie would be bodily thrown out of the house. His breathing came heavily, and his flashing eyes betrayed a barely controlled anger. She waited for the axe to fall.

After an age, he spoke - a chill in his tone, a razor edge to his voice.

'Very well, Mistress Sara!' he spat out angrily. 'I shall attend your cousin to the best of my medical knowledge. With God's will, she will survive.' His chest heaved as he added, 'Although I greatly doubt it.'

Sara closed her eyes and breathed out a sigh of relief. First hurdle crossed! 'Thank you...' she whispered.

But the Parson ignored her as he turned to the manservant. 'James, 'tis vital that no person outside of this room learns the nature of the maiden's sicknesse. No servant other than you must find out. Else there will be panic and fleeing from Abbots Cross such as never before!'

'Aye, My Lord. The secret will be safe with me.'

The Parson turned to Sara. 'And what of you, Mistress Sara? Can *you* keep a secret? Or does your woman's tongue wag like a dog's tail?'

Sara restrained her anger. She'd infuriated him once. It would not be politic to do it again. 'I can keep the secret.' she said quietly.

The Parson nodded, and turned back to James. 'Then an unused bedroom is needed - and at once, James. Prepare the bed. Make haste!'

'Shall it be a naked or brocaded bed, My Lord?'

'Dammit, man, it matters little whether the bed has curtains or not!' Edward Makepeace snapped back loudly. 'Attend to it - at once!!'

James bowed deferentially, ignoring the rebuke. He hurried off at a dignified pace while the Parson turned to look at Sara.

'Now, what about you, Mistress?'

'I shall have to stay with Connie.' she said, adding, 'if you will permit it.' Sara's tone was softer now that she had gained her objective. 'I cannot leave my cousin. I must stay with Connie. In her room.'

Parson Makepeace' already-angry eyes widened further. 'There's great danger of catching the pestilence! Your cousin must be isolated!'

'I can't leave Connie alone.'

'As you wish.' He turned irritably away.

Seeing his reaction, Sara was embarrassed. As a 20th Century nurse, she'd studied medical history. She realised the massive problems the Parson was facing. His knowledge of plague would certainly be primitive. And his ideas of medical treatment based on superstition and without scientific foundation.

But despite her deep reservations, Sara was relieved the Parson had allowed them to stay. She understood his reluctance, even if she disapproved of it, but admired his purposeful handling of the situation once persuaded. From her nursing experience she knew that disease spread rapidly in insanitary conditions like those of Seventeenth Century England. And the ravages could be disastrous.

But to have taken Connie out again into the night air might well have brought about *pneumonic* plague. Without urgent and instant 20th century treatment, that would certainly have proved fatal.

She still resented having had to argue with the parson for treatment for Connie. Yet the more she thought about it, the more she realised that her criticisms had been unfair. Makepeace did not fear the disease for himself. It was the rampant spread of plague amongst the villagers which had worried him.

Sara vowed that she would use her medical ability to contain it if she could. But now she had achieved her objective, it might be tactful to apologise for having spoken impolitely.

'Parson Makepeace' she said softly, 'I am sorry. I was discourteous. Had it not been for worry about my cousin, I would not have spoken to you with incivility.'

Although still angry, as he regarded her pleading look, his wrath subsided a little. "Tis only of minor consequence. Think no more on it.'

He turned back to Connie. Connie lay motionless. But she had begun to mutter in a flushed delirium.

It was a few minutes before the servant reappeared. 'The room is ready, Parson.' he said as he hurried down the stairs, candelabrum in hand.

'Very Well.' Parson Makepeace took the candleabrum before turning to Sara. 'Please follow up to the bedroom.'

The Parson led as James picked Connie from the couch, and began to carry the young girl upstairs. Sara brought up the rear, taking hold of the intricately carved handrail, her feet clumping noisily on the bare wood of the elegant staircase.

At the top, they turned right, moved a short way, then stopped at a door which the Parson opened. James carried Connie into the room, followed by Sara and the Parson.

Inside the large, wooden-floored bedroom was a four-poster bed opposite a casement window under which was a window seat. Beside it stood a small writing desk and a dark sideboard, on which stood a basin and water jug. A door in a corner led away into an ante-room.

Gently, James laid Connie down on the bed. 'Thank you.' said Sara to James and the Parson. 'I can attend her from now on.'

The servant bowed his enormous form gracefully, then turned to walk away.

'Remember, we must isolate your cousin.' the Parson repeated. 'We cannot allow her to have contact with anyone other than you. I beg you to stay in the same room with her, and not come out. If you catch the pestilence, let no-one enter!'

'I agree, Parson Makepeace. I must nurse her. She's my responsibility!'

'Take care not to contract plague yourself.'

Sara recalled what she knew - how, contrary to Seventeenth Century belief, bubonic plague was spread by rat fleas and not from one person to another. She shook her head.

'No fear of that, Parson Makepeace. Bubonic plague is not transmitted by one person to another. It's carried by a flea.'

The Parson looked on in disbelief. 'Tosh!' he said disparagingly. "Tis not carried like that at all! It wells up out of the ground. 'Tis a miasma in the air! We'll have to keep your cousin in this room and keep the windows firmly shut so that no plague can get in or out.'

This was not the time to argue. 'I will nurse my cousin myself...' she repeated quietly, then added, '...if you will agree to that.'

For a moment the Parson stood and looked. 'You are brave, Mistress Sara.' he answered with surprising softness, a hint of admiration in his voice. 'Truly, there are those who sit by bedsides, lance tumours, carry away soiled linen, and care nothing for their personal safety, and yet take no harm at all!' Then he added. 'Yet others going but once to comfort a friend in a moment are stricken!'

A kindly look now displaced his sterner expression. 'I shall leave you now - and may God be with both of you. Good Night.'

Resuming his formality, he turned to walk out. But as he was leaving, Sara glanced round the sparsely furnished bedroom. 'Have you another bed... where I might rest?'

He stopped and turned back, puzzled. 'Why... there's the trundle. Rest there.' Then he turned and left, closing the door behind him.

What's a trundle? thought Sara.

For a moment she pondered, trying to hide her ignorance. Then she suddenly ran to the door. Opening it and putting her head out she called to the figure disappearing along the corridor. 'Parson Makepeace!'

He stopped and turned to face her along the landing. 'Yes, Mistress Sara?'

'Where's the trundle?'

'Why... under the bed... where it always is...'

'Of course.'

Back in the room, as Connie lay quietly, Sara knelt down to discover a cot under the bed. As she pulled, it came out, and she recognised a very low-slung bed, rather large for an adolescent. *So that's the trundle!* she thought.

Standing up, she went over to prepare Connie for bed. Taking off Connie's shoes and socks, she recoiled, nauseated.

For the first time she noticed that the white socks were soiled with a strange yellow tinge. A sharp, unpleasant and sickly odour immediately pervaded the room.

Controlling her revulsion of the pungent smell, she opened the buttons at the back of Connie's brightly patterned summer dress and slid it off, leaving Connie only in bra and knickers.

The discarded clothes gave off the same sickly aroma, and for the first time Sara noticed that Connie was sweating profusely. The youthful body was slippery with a dull jaundiced slime. Connie's complexion was a dusky colour, her eyes subscribed by blue rings. The large swellings had not gone down.

Lifting back the bedclothes, Sara managed to ease Connie into the bed underneath them. Then, satisfied that she had done all she could for the time being, she sat back to keep watch.

Just at that moment, Connie moved with a sudden jerk. Finding her voice, she let out a cry.

'Sara' she said meekly. 'I'm going to be sick!'

Sara looked round and grabbed the bowl. She was just in time, for at once Connie turned over onto her side and began retching. Time and time again she retched until finally she vomited into the bowl. Again she tried to speak, but this time she failed, and, giving up in the attempt, she fell back onto the pillow.

Finding a slop-pail in an ante room, Sara washed out the bowl. Once back in the room, she put the bowl easily within reach. Then she placed herself once more on a stool at the edge of the bed to keep vigil.

Hour after hour went by, time moving like a snail, interrupted only by the occasional moan from the patient.

Then Connie spoke again. 'I need a drink.'

Sara went over to the jug, pouring some water into a wooden goblet and giving it to Connie who greedily gulped it down.

'Oh, Sara,' she said, 'more... please... more water...'

It was at least three more wooden goblets full before Connie had drunk enough. And it was after the third drink that Sara caught sight of something, an added revulsion which magnified her alarm and made horror explode.

Connie's tongue was larger than usual - swollen and misshapen. But it was the protruding section which drove dread into Sara, and brought home the seriousness of Connie's illness.

Sara saw that the end was misshapen, and pointed, its end honed to a pencil-like, bright scarlet tip.

The nocturnal hours stretched endlessly on.

Moving with a constant restlessness, Connie thrashed about in the over-warm bed. At first, Sara tried to make sense of what the girl was saying. But in the end she gave up. Connie was delirious. Her mutterings were gibberish.

But in addition, Connie sweated huge amounts of perspiration. Her body gradually became coated with a sweet- and sharp-smelling yellow slime. This tangy odour filled the room and became more and more nauseous as the long, hot night dragged its soulless way through.

Twice, Sara pulled back the bedclothes to examine Connie. She was reluctant to disturb the sixteen-year-old. But Sara was so worried about her that frequent examinations were necessary.

The first time she looked, Sara was staggered at the amount of sweat. And later, when Sara pulled back the bedclothes a second time, she saw that the lemon coating of pungent discharge had become so extreme that Connie's pants now clung to her.

The room temperature was warm in the balmy evening. Now, mixed with Connie's noxious body odours, the heat increased to stifling. Several times, Sara looked at the firmly closed casement, wondering if she might open it. Finally, almost unable to stand the heat longer, she decided to get some fresh air into the room somehow.

She pulled her stool over to the window. Stepping up, she reached with a foot to the back of the window seat, then jumped over to perch on it. She steadied herself with one hand while stretching up with the other to reach the catch, just within reach of outstretched fingers.

She pushed up. But her efforts were in vain. The casement was fastened firmly. Impossible to open.

Sara didn't give up. Time after time she repeated her efforts. But each time she tried, she failed.

It was impossible. The only result of continued efforts was likely to be a bruised hand.

With heavy reluctance, she stepped back onto the stool and down to the floor. She moved back to the bedside, now stiflingly uncomfortable. Once more she sat back on the hard stool to resume her vigil in the unbearable humidity of the room, now resigned to waiting in dire discomfort for daybreak.

The long night continued...

Eventually, the first streaks of dawn sent notice of the new day. As if in greeting, Connie's retching restarted. She was once more violently sick into the bowl.

Afterwards, Connie flopped back onto the pillow. Immediately she resumed writhing about.

Standing up, Sara looked despairingly down at the adolescent in the bed. Now in the grip of a very high temperature, Connie's movements were greatly exaggerated. She moved first one way, then the other in a vain subconscious attempt to lower her own body heat. But there was no escape.

Leaving the intervening door open, Sara went into the anteroom to empty the bowl. Quickly washing it out, she hurried back to the bedroom.

As she came through the door, she flung down the bowl. 'Connie!' she yelled, dashing forward.

Connie was trying to get out of bed.

Putting her hands on Connie's shoulders, she pushed at the surprisingly strong girl. 'Lie still, Connie!' she urged, 'Lie still!'

Connie resisted, then grudgingly submitted. She lay back on the bed, her knees pointing at the ceiling. For a few moments, she lay still, her groin exposed.

Sara looked with crescendoing dismay. The dark swellings of the angry buboes had enlarged enormously overnight. Now they were twice as big as the evening before.

Time continued at a dismal pace. But eventually, daylight began to strengthen. Sara still sat edgily beside Connie's bed, watching Connie moving restlessly from side to side. The girl muttered constantly, her body now permanently in motion, on her face a hybrid expression of anxiety and agony. Clearly she understood nothing Sara said to her.

Connie again tried to rise. 'Lie down, Connie! Lie still!' said Sara again, pushing at Connie's shoulders.

Chapter 6

A t about seven-thirty, a knock came to the door.

'Yes?'

"Tis I. Parson Makepeace.'

'What is it, Parson?'

'May I speak with you, please?'

Sara rose. Her feet clattered on the oak floor as she crossed to the door. A welcome coolness swept into the bedroom as she lifted the latch and pulled the door open.

Outside on the landing stood the Parson. In his hand he carried a small wooden bowl.

'Good Morning, Miss Sara. I've brought you a mazer of mead.' He reached forward with his left hand to pass the bowl to her.

'Thank you.'

'Perhaps later, you might like to break the night's fast?'

'Break the fast?... Oh - *breakfast!* Thank you - I had not thought of food. I cannot leave Connie.'

He looked at her with a level stare. 'If you believe that the gangrene is spread by a flea, then Mistress Connie's plague is not infectious. Therefore, I can ask a servant to sit with her for half an hour or so.'

'I know it's true. But the servant mustn't find out about the presence of plague. You said so yourself.'

He nodded sagely. 'I did. But Rose knows nothing of Connie's plague. Besides, to keep her out might arouse suspicion amongst the villagers. if you are agreeable, I shall ask Rose to sit with the invalid while you are away.'

'In that case I will be delighted to break the fast with you.'

The Parson called for Rose who turned out to be a plump, homely woman in a heavy brown dress, white apron and dust-cap.

'Good morning.' said Sara.

'Good Morning. My name's Rose.' The servant bobbed a little curtsey.

'Will you suit with my cousin while I break fast?'

'Certainly, Mistress.'

'She has a fever but it's not infectious, so you'll be quite safe. She may try to get out of bed and she may be sick. If she does, please call me straight away.'

'I will, Mistress.'

Once the servant was ensconced at Connie's bedside, Sara and the Parson went downstairs. Shortly, they were in the dining room, sitting at opposite sides of a table which had been covered with a cloth.

'Do you worry about there being a coffin in the tablecloth, Mistress Sara?' Edward asked.

'A coffin?'

'Yes. 'Tis the term for a wrinkled crease in a tablecloth. Personally, I do not hold with the superstition that a coffin means death to one of the diners, but some others do. Do you not, Daisy?'

The servant girl smiled. 'I do, Master. And that is why Rose and I spent the whole day after washing day ironing and folding the tablecloths very carefully into the press so the creases would be perfectly straight when we laid them on the table.'

As she spoke, the servant girl placed a pewter platter in front of Sara, together with a spoon and a knife. Neither knife nor spoon looked particularly clean.

The meal was a curious melange of meat with fruit. The meat was partly chicken - but not chicken like anything Sara had ever eaten before. Butchers' chickens were tender and palatable, but this was an old boiler past egg-laying age. It did not look like the kind of chicken she was used to, nor did it taste like it.

There was also some other meat on her plate, but Sara could not work out what it was, as it appeared to be uncooked. At first she wondered if the cook had made a mistake with hers, then she glanced at Edward. He was tucking into his portion of uncooked meat with great relish.

There was nothing for it - Sara knew she would have to eat it. As she tasted the food for the first time, she had a struggle to hide her revulsion, and as she placed the first spoonful into her mouth, her silent reaction was *'Oh, that's disgusting!'*

'Would you care for some ale?' Edward asked, oblivious to her reaction to the meal. ''Tis small ale.'

'Small ale?'

'Aye - 'tis unbrewed and less expensive than ordinary ale.'

'Thank you.'

Expecting something like beer, Sara watched while from a jug he poured a dirty looking liquid. 'Thank you.' she said with soft apprehension as she raised the mazer to her lips. The small ale tasted as disgusting as it looked.

'*I'd love a cup of tea!*' she thought as she replaced the mazer on the table.

How Sara struggled through breakfast, she would later wonder, but finally they rose from the table together.

Together they mounted the stairs. From a room at the head of the stairs, he produced a bottle. ''Tis mead. Would you care to join me? Small ale is not very palatable, but this is fine.'

'*Can be no worse!*' Sara thought, but simply said, 'I would love some.'

Pouring a bowl of mead, he handed it to her. The mead was welcome, as it was sweet and chased the foul taste of breakfast.

Together they stood on the landing from where they could look into the room where Connie lay.

'You may go, Rose.' The parson said. 'And thank you.'

Rose got up from her seat, bobbed her curtsey and left.

While drinking the sweet, cooling liquid, Sara regarded Connie for a time from a discrete distance. Then she looked at the Parson.

He was smartly dressed in a black, knee-length jacket, frill-edged white shirt, knee-length britches, white stockings and black buckled shoes. His long hair was swept back and fastened behind his head with a bow.

As she looked at him, he shook his head. 'I regret that she seems worse. But thankfully, there is no sign of the plague-tokens. Pray God they never arrive! Do you think we should purge her?'

Sara's brow lined as she looked over the rim of the mazer. 'What with?'

'A drench of yewgh. Much better than an enema - or leeches!'

'What does yewgh contain?'

'The electuary would consist of whatever herbs we can obtain from the herb-gardens, hedgerows or waste lands - together with two grams of trochiske of vipers. It's the time of the full moon, so the drench can be taken now.'

Sara felt her mouth fall agape at his ludicrous medical thinking. But what intrigued Sara was that the confident tone in which he had spoken betrayed his strong belief in the imbecility.

Despite the danger to Connie, Sara almost burst out laughing. But she controlled herself in time. She was determined to be courteous. Despite his primitive medical training, he meant well.

'I think I'd prefer to let the Lord have a free hand in it.' she replied. She knew that such a suggestion would appeal to him.

He looked at her thoughtfully, then nodded. 'Perhaps you are right. But later we might try some feverfew, perhaps. Venus commands this herb, and has commended it to succour her sisters. It is very effectual for all pains in the head, the herb being bruised and applied to the crown of the head.'

This would no cause any problem as I would be an external

application. So Sara was happy to go along with it - and humour him.

Besides, she had read of feverfew, and knew it had certain healing

properties.

'That's a good idea.' she agreed.

He looked past her into the bedroom, catching sight of the

disused trundle. He transferred his puzzled gaze to Sara. 'Have you been

awake all night, Miss Sara?' he asked in disbelief.

'I have.'

'But... Mistress Sara... you must sleep. Else you too will fall ill!'

'Once Connie is past the worst I can rest. 'Til then, I must watch her.'

He looked steadily, his eyes boring deep into hers, just as the portrait had done. 'Then let me help you. I will sit awhile to permit you rest.'

He made to move past her, but she raised one hand to bar the way. 'No, Parson, you mustn't.'

'But, Mistress Sara--'

'We agreed that it would be my responsibility. Besides,' Sara turned to look at Connie, whose movements had stopped for a while, 'she looks more peaceful. Perhaps I can rest awhile now.'

'As you wish, Mistress Sara. But if you decide otherwise--'

'Thank you.' she replied, then added thoughtfully, 'Parson Makepeace, it's very hot in there. I tried to open a window during the night, but it wouldn't open.'

A look of horror crossed the Parson's face. 'But... the night air...'

'What about it?' 'Well... it's very bad... for a sick person...'

'It won't make much difference.'

'But, Miss Sara, the moon is full at this time of the month!'

'What has that to do with it?'

'Well... The moon controls the phlegm!'

'What?'

'Aye... Jupiter and the sun look after the movement of the blood, Saturn the black bile and Mars the yellow bile! 'Tis common medical and astrological knowledge!'

Sara looked at him in amazement. But, not seeing her amazed stare, he transferred his look to Connie. 'I shall return later.' he said. 'Open the window if you wish, although I advise against it.

The rest of the long day was spent in little rest and much threshing about by Connie as she fought the disease. Sara snatched rest where she could, but to little avail. Eventually, night fell, and Sara rested in a high-backed chair, dozing off a little here and there.

The greying streaks of dawn began to wax into full daylight and yet again Sara stood up and looked down on the sleeping Connie. The sixteen-year-old looked more peaceful than she had all night. Sara realised that if she was to get a short rest on the trundle, now was the time. She would not, of course, go fully to sleep. She would just close her eyes and rest...

Without intending to, she immediately fell into a deep sleep.

But her eyes had hardly seemed to close when she became distantly conscious of Connie's voice.

'Sara... Sara...'

Sara blinked open sleeping eyes and looked up.

'Sara... I'm going to be sick!'

Now instantly alert, Sara leapt off the trundle and grabbed the bowl. But too late. Connie was already leaning over the side of the bed and vomiting onto the floor.

As Connie lay back again, Sara cursed herself for dozing off. Now she would have to clean up the mess, spread like an ugly miniature tidal wave over much of the floor.

Wearily, Sara got up from the trundle and made her way into the anteroom. There she found a cloth, picked up the basin and returned. Pulling up her sleeves, she got to her knees, and started the lengthy and distasteful job of wiping up the foul mess.

Cleaning took several minutes of alternately wiping the large area and wringing out the cloth, but tired as she was, Sara eventually managed it. She was just finishing the last of the mess when the sound of approaching footsteps presaged a light tap at the door.

Straightening her back, but still kneeling, she called, 'Come in!'

The door pushed open and Parson Makepeace took a step inside. There he stopped, looking down, startled.

'Why... Mistress Sara! That's a serving maid's work!'

Sara shook her head. 'I disagree.' she said. 'It's my fault. I should have been quicker. Then Connie would not have been sick on the floor. So it would not be fair to expect anyone else to clean it up.' Then she added, 'Especially when you have been so kind to both of us!'

As she laid aside the cloth and rose to her feet, he bestowed on her the most bewitching smile. 'It is not kindness. It is my duty.' He raised a gentle finger. 'That you pointed out when you arrived!'

Sara's cheeks flushed. 'Please don't say that, Parson.' she said, laying aside the cloth and standing up. 'I was rude, and I admit it. Forgive me.'

'Let us forgive one another,' he said with an unexpected kindness before adding, 'And pray to God that Connie survives the sicknesse!'

'I think with good nursing, she will.'

His brow furrowed. 'Have you been able to sleep on the trundle?'

'I... slept... some of the time...' she faltered.

His creased brow expressed deeper concern as he commented, 'You look exhausted, Mistress Sara.'

She gave a slight nod. 'I am deeply fatigued, that's for sure.'

'Because you were awake all night, were you not?'

Sara smiled sheepishly. He knew the truth. 'I was.' she admitted.

He shook his head. 'You cannot continue like that. You will be ill yourself if you do not sleep.'

'How can I sleep? I must stay awake if Connie needs me.'

He shook his head slowly. 'Then I will assist.' he said. 'And I have no doubt that James will be willing to help too.'

'But – Parson Makepeace – I cannot permit you to –'

'I will brook no refusal.' he interrupted. 'Today we will take turns - you and I.'

'But – what about the danger of catching plague?'

'If, as you say, 'tis a flea which carries the plague, then 'twill no longer be here. And we are all safe.'

Sara was pleasantly surprised. *So he had considered her theory?* She smiled, and was about to speak when her smile became a yawn. The mention by the Parson about being awake all night and the still-stuffy atmosphere in the bedroom reminded her of her tiredness.

'I do not fear the plague. So I will sit with Connie for a time. To permit you to take a short walk in the fresh air.'

'Oh - Edward - that is really kind.'

He shook his head. 'A pleasure. I shall sit in the room while you are out. I have letters which can be written at that desk yonder.' While speaking he began crossing the bedroom to the desk.

Sara glanced at Connie again. She slept quietly, breathing quickly, not in delirium. It wasn't a true sleep. But Sara knew she could probably leave Connie safely with the Parson for half an hour.

The Parson had sat down at his desk. He had found quills and parchment, and had already started to write. Sara stepped lightly out of the room, closing the door behind her.

She made her way along the wooden landing and down the stairs. At the bottom, her feet clattered over the stone on her way to the Hall exit. Out in the rear, she wandered round the vegetable garden looking yet not really looking at the vegetables, some known some strange. After a few minutes, she returned inside.

Back in the room, the parson looked at her with disturbed eyes. Then he turned away, pondering for a moment before turning to the open doorway. 'James!'

'Parson?' came from downstairs.

'Come up here, please.'

Following footsteps on the staircase, the manservant arrived and the parson said, 'Have you anything pressing to do this morning?'

'Nothing that cannot be delayed, Parson.'

'Will you sit with the sick girl for a time?'

'Willingly, Parson.'

Edward turned to Sara. 'Please step this way, Mistress Sara.'

Taking Sara along the landing, he opened the door to another room. Although a little smaller than the room Sara and Connie currently shared, it contained a double bed which looked comfortable.

'I suggest you sleep for a time, Mistress Sara.'

Sara nodded grateful thanks. 'And will you call me if anything happens to Connie?'

'I will.' Turning, he left, closing the door behind him.

Taking off shoes and her purple suit, Sara slipped into the bed. Within a minute she had been engulfed by great swathes of fatigue.

Chapter 7

The next two days were largely a repetition of the events of the first two. Sara snatched sleep where she could, and although Connie vomited from time to time, her bouts of heaving became less frequent. And Sara was constantly alert enough not to have a repeat of the accident which had ended up with her having to swab the floor.

At periodic intervals, James or Edward took turns to sit with Connie and during these periods, Sara snatched sleep in the same far bedroom as she had occupied on her second morning here.

By the Monday morning, Connie's multi-coloured nylon dress was wet and smelling pungently. On coming into the room and quickly looking at the patient, Edward said, 'Has she a night dress, Mistress Sara?'

'Has she a night-gown?'

'Not here' Sara quickly regained her posture. 'I didn't think to bring one.'

'I think there will be a night-dress in the chest.' the Parson said. 'I'll have a word with Rose and ask her.'

Turning, he called, *'ROSE!'*

'Yes, Master?' sounded a plaintive reply.

'Come here, please!'

The patter of running feet preceded the arrival of the same plump, homely woman in a heavy brown dress, white apron and dust-cap who had looked after Connie during breakfast.

'Yes, Master?' she asked with a curtsey, her round face creased into a smile.

'Seek out a night-gown for the maiden, please, Rose.'

She curtsied again, and scurried off.

'Now I shall leave you to attend to the wench.' the parson said. 'Farewell for the present.'

As Sara nodded to him, he turned to go back along the landing, and Sara re-entered the bedroom. Connie lay fairly quietly, muttering in unintelligible whispers. Then as Sara looked down at Connie, Rose hurried in with a dark-cream bundle on her arm.

'Here is the night-dress, My Lady' said the still-smiling maidservant.

Sara smiled back. 'Thank you.' she said. 'Please help me to get her into it.'

Together they lifted Connie out of bed, helping her to her feet. Connie was not asleep or unconscious. But neither was she sensible. Weakly she submitted as her hands were lifted and pulled through the arms of the long, ankle-length coarse flannelette nightdress. As she groaned and fell back, Connie protested mildly, still all but asleep. She was supported by Rose who pulled the nightgown over her. Then Connie's head drooped forward onto Sara's chest.

Rose went behind Connie to hurriedly pull back the bedclothes. The white sheets were now stained with the nauseous yellow discharge. But Sara ignored the stains as she lifted Connie and gently laid her back down on the bed.

As Connie lay back, Sara pulled the covers over the recumbent figure.

* * * *

Despite the assistance she received, Sara found that fatigue was mentally stretching her. And this was compounded by the fact that she had not been able to wash for the last three days. So the following morning, when Edward came in and told her to take some time out of the house, she mentioned that she would like to rinse down.

'And I think a walk out would do me good.' she added. 'Somewhere in solitude.'

He pondered. 'Why not take a wander up the glebe, Mistress Sara?'

'The glebe?'

'Yes. 'Tis the name given to the grassy hillocks behind the parsonage. 'Tis part of the parsonage, private land, and is an area rarely frequented by anyone – save a few sheep. If you take the route out through the back door, traverse the vegetable gardens and continue on, you will come to it. Follow the bed of the stream up the hill towards its source and you will come to a large pool. 'Tis surrounded by bushes. People rarely go there and you will be able to wash not only comfortably, but privately too.'

'That's a lovely idea!" she said, and meant it. Then she asked, 'Do you have a towel?'

'A towel? There is some sacking if that will suffice.'

'Yes.'

'You will find it hanging up in the room at the back of the house the servants use.' He smiled at her wanly. 'And might I suggest that when you get back, you snatch at least an hour's sleep? You look exhausted.'

'I feel exhausted.' she said, 'But you have been very kind to me and I do not wish to take up your time.'

'I am free all morning.' He told her. 'This afternoon I have duties to attend to, but I can spare an hour or two before then. In the meantime take advantage of a period when you need not be here.'

Leaving the bedroom, she went along the landing and down the wooden stairs. Making her way through to the rear, she went into the servants' room, found the sacking, then went out of the back door.

Crossing the brick-paved courtyard, she made her way past the outbuildings. Whitewash made their walls glisten in the light of the summer sun. A gardener doffed his cap deferentially as she walked up the rise away from the house and into the vegetable gardens

She took the path winding its way through the vegetable plots. Little had changed over the centuries. The main crops were cabbage, lettuce, carrots and onions. But there were other vegetables growing in neat rows. Irregular gaps indicated that some of the most advanced plants had already been harvested.

The boundary of the garden faced a small wood. This copse consisted almost entirely of oaks, elms, beeches and a few sycamores. Approaching these, she came to a lane which ended in a gate. Sara unlatched the gate which opened onto a primitive footbridge of three boards side by side which crossed a stream. The planks had to be crossed with care, but they were not unsafe.

Holding a horizontal sapling tied at both ends which served as a handrail as she stepped across, she looked down at the water flowing lazily underneath. Insects and small twigs were caught in the osmotic stickiness of the stream's surface.

Once across the stream she followed the path which led on to a small wood. As she entered the wood she took care to avoid a neat row of three thatch-roofed beehives at its edge. Nectar-laden honeybees buzzed industriously. Sara's presence was of no interest to them while she did not trespass too closely.

Once past the hives, she found herself in the glebe, and clearly this area was little frequented, as the path petered out amongst the tumbling green velvet of verdant pasture.

For the first time since her arrival in this time, Sara began to feel a little more relaxed, although it concerned her that she was leaving Connie with a man versed in the rampant superstition that dominated the medical thinking of her newly adopted century. She was deeply conscious of the fact that even with his best intentions, Parson Makepeace had no real idea how to treat bubonic plague.

Nevertheless, she felt that little harm could befall Connie for a short time. All was serene and peaceful and at least she could tell herself that Connie was in the best hands the time had to offer. Reassured, she wandered along, starting the climb the hillocks as she trailed the rising stream bed. And eventually she came to the bushed area to which the parson had referred, where a large natural pool had formed.

She stood on the edge and looked down. The stream flowed into the upper end, then out of the lower, and the water was cool and so clear that she could see to the bottom, the pool bed looking deceptively shallow in the refraction of the water.

Sara would have liked to swim, and the pool certainly looked inviting enough for that. But she had brought no soap, and besides she did not want to trespass on the good offices of her host by taking more time than perhaps he had intended her to. Today she would simply wash herself down with the cold water.

Stripping to her underwear, Sara used copious amounts of water to wash down, making sure she rid herself of all the accumulated sweat and grime of the last three days. Following that, she rubbed herself down vigorously with the sacking, then pulled back on her clothes before setting off to return, climbing back down the knolls and mounds of the glebe to the parsonage.

Although as she wandered back down the gentle descent her head was heavy with exhaustion, she still had time and perception to look round and admire the natural beauty which surrounded her. White sheep sprinkled across the green meadows were interspersed by the occasional cow or horse while in one or two places, the lone figure of a farm worker beavered away at his tasks. All was peace, everything was quiet and there was a ubiquitous air of serenity. No sounds assailed her ears which did not occur naturally.

Although used to 20th Century London, with its hurly-burly, noise and bustle, Sara was surprised at herself to note how attractive she found the serenity she now experienced. Almost mesmerised by the beauty of her surroundings, she slowly descended towards the parsonage while continuing to look all round at the captivating beauty of the rolling hills and fertile farmland of Northumberland.

Finally returning to the environs of the parsonage, she crossed over the plank bridge and made her way back through the vegetable plots and made her way back to the rear entrance to the parsonage.

Replacing the sacking to whence she had borrowed it, she climbed the wooden staircase to the landing, but this time instead of going back to Connie's room, she went straight along to the bedroom which she had used each day. Within minutes, feeling greatly refreshed as a result of her rub-down she had removed her suit, slipped under the covers and was deeply asleep.

Sara calculated that she must have slept for some time, for when she woke, the sun had moved considerably and was about its zenith. Clearly, it was about midday. Swinging her legs over the side of the bed and slipping on her suit and shoes, she left the room to return to Connie.

As Sara tapped on the door and pushed her way into Connie's bedroom, Edward was standing over the bed looking down at Connie. He looked up and smiled.

'How is she?' Sara asked.

He nodded sagely. 'Peaceful.' he said. 'She is sleeping peacefully. Indeed, I think we may have overcome the worst.'

Sara moved forward and looked down at the sleeping form. Indeed, Connie was calm and serene. Her rest was much less disturbed than previously. The worst appeared to be over. 'I think you're right.' she agreed.

'Shall we examine her?' he asked.

'Yes... I think that would be a good idea...'

Pulling back the covers, Sara looked at the sleeping form, simply clad in her long nightdress. Pulling up her dress, she and Edward then examined Connie together, looking at her thighs and under her armpits. The lymph glands had swollen to form ugly buboes. But her nose was not bleeding and there were no other signs of plague, save high temperature.

He nodded again. 'Praise be that the plague-tokens are still absent.'

She knew what he meant. Plague in its advanced stages, burst the ends of the capillaries all over the body and created tiny rose shaped patterns which in the 17th Century were referred to as "plague tokens".

Satisfied, Edward gently laid her arms back and Sara returned her nightdress to position and the bedclothes were pulled over her again. Her beautiful golden ringlets lay on the pillow, framing her perfectly formed features.

'She is quite delightful.' Edward said. 'The most comely wench I have seen in many a year.' He looked up and added, 'Apart from *YOU,* of course, Mistress Sara.'

She looked at him sheepishly, conscious of a slight reddening to her cheeks. *Was he joking or did he mean it?* The smile was totally enigmatic. It was difficult to say.

Not knowing how to respond, Sara went on, 'She is talented too. She really has everything.'

'Talented?' he asked.

'Yes.' She is a beautiful musician.'

'Really? What does she play? Recorder? Or one of the more advanced instruments.'

'Her principal instrument is the piano.'

'Piano?' he asked. 'What is a piano?'

Oh Dear! she thought. *Pianos weren't invented until the 18th Century!*

'I should have said "harpsichord"' she said to him. 'She plays the harpsichord.'

'And the spinet and virginals too?'

'Yes. But she also sketches.'

'Sketches you say? Like Master Holbein, perhaps?'

'Well, perhaps not like that!' Sara grinned. 'But when she recovers a little, perhaps she will sketch something for you.'

'We have paper. I use it for letters. With what does she sketch?'

Sara thought furiously. She was not about to make another mistake. 'I think she uses charcoal. She often does charcoal sketches.'

He nodded. 'We can make charcoal sticks. Quite easily. And I would like to see that.'

'When she recovers, I'll ask her to do a couple of sketches for you.

The rest of that afternoon was fairly peaceful. But later that night things again became somewhat restless. Yet there was no more vomiting, and it seemed that the night would be more peaceful.

Sara decided to risk the trundle, pulling it out from under the bed and resting on it. It was a fitful interrupted sleep but at least she got a little rest.

* * * *

Next morning when Edward came in to tell her that he would take over that afternoon, she said. 'That's good. Although I've had some sleep last night.'

He nodded and smiled. 'Good. I'll come after lunch and allow you to rest this afternoon.'

Within a few minutes there was a knock on the door and Rose arrived.

'May I speak to you Mistress?'

'Certainly, Rose.'

'I would like to ask, What do you want me to do with young Mistress's dress?' She held up Connie's plague-ridden dress.

'Oh!' Sara exclaimed. 'I had forgotten all about that!'

'Shall I drop the dress into the pissbarrel, Mistress?'

'In the *what*?'

'In the pissbarrel, Madam.'

'What's a pissbarrel?'

'Why... Mistress... I thought they were used everywhere...'

'I have never seen one!'

'Oh... well, 'tis used to wash garments and bedclothes. The reeking liquid excellent for removing dirt of all kinds. And the barrel is topped up every morning when the pots are emptied into it by the maid.'

Revolted by the idea, Sara could only stammer, 'But - the clothes will stink!'

Rose chuckled. 'Oh, they are not left like that, Mistress. Once cleansed in the barrel, the clothes are taken down to the river and held under the running water with stones until all foulness has gone. Then they are wrung out, and laid over a bush to dry in the sun. No smell remains once that's been done.'

D. A. Matthews

Sara looked round the bed at the cheap, drip-dry polyester-cotton dress, very easy to replace and costing practically nothing. And because it might contain a flea, Sara was determined not to risk any further contagion.

'I see...'

Sara did not want to tell Rose of the plague. But the clothes had to go! 'I think this dress is beyond cleansing, Rose.' she added softly.

Rose frowned. 'Beyond cleansing?!' she asked.

'Yes.'

Rose looked totally perplexed. 'So... what do you want me to do, Mistress?...'

'I want you to find an old sack.'

'A sack, Mistress?' Rose's dismay was mushrooming by the minute.

'Yes. As quickly as you can.'

With a brief, puzzled curtsey, Rose left. Within two minutes she had returned and in her hand she carried a coarse, Hessian sack.

'Hold it open.'

As Rose held the sack open, Connie picked up the dress by the corner of a shoulder and dropped it into the sack.

'Now tie the sack up.'

Curiosity dancing in her eyes, Rose tied the cord round the neck of the sack. 'Now what, Mistress?'

'I want you to take it out and burn it.'

'*Burn it*, Mistress?!!'

'Yes.'

Rose looked startled. 'Burn her dress, Mistress?'

'Yes. I suppose it could be boiled... but better to burn it!'

Rose gaped. 'Burn it, Madam?' she exclaimed. 'Why... it would be a great shame to destroy it... it is so fine!'

'Yes. But it is very dirty.'

'I would still be happy to wash the dress in the pissbarrel, Mistress.'

'**Burn it**!' insisted Sara. 'And as soon as possible!'

Nodding, reluctant and bewildered, Rose picked up the sack containing the infected dress. She scurried off carrying the sack, leaving Sara alone with the sick Connie in the room.

* * * *

As Rose scurried downstairs carrying the clothes which the strange woman had told her to burn, her mind was racing. The idea of destroying clothes of any kind was repugnant to someone for whom every penny counted and every scrap of clothing had to be worn time and time again until threadbare. The idea of deliberately going outside, lighting a fire and heaping fine clothes onto it was anathema.

She went out of the rear door glancing round to make sure that she was not seen by anyone, then she looked at the bundle in her arms. The clothes were of a very strange raiment, tough yet fine, such as Rose had never seen before. And colourful. With flowers painted on them. It was like that tapestry she had once seen as a girl when she had been taken to a strange church. Yet these were of much, much finer material.

Looking round, she found a sack and put them into it. But although she knew that in not taking them to the open ground to burn on a fire she would be disobeying an order, the prospect of being able to do something with these clothes proved too strong to resist. Consequently, she did what her instinct dictated.

Rose knew she could slip away from the parsonage for perhaps half an hour, and her absence would not be noted. Even if it were, she could claim that she had been getting rid of the clothes as instructed.

Slinking away by a back lane instead of walking down the drive, Rose scurried off, carrying the offending clothes in a hessian sack. Soon she was down to the road just along from the crossroads. Once through a gateway, she crossed the meadow to the path at the rear of her own cottage.

When she came in through the door, Rose's young daughter Lizbeth was there and a neighbour who had come in to give the child some of the pottage which constantly stewed over the fire.

'Why, Rose!' said the woman. 'We did not expect you.'

'I have only a few minutes, Meg. And I have come down because I have something I want to show you.'

Mysteriously she undid the top of the sack, pulled out Connie's dress and held it out. 'What do you think of that?"

'Why... Rose... I have never seen such apparel...'

Marvelling at the fine material, Meg reached forward and gingerly touched the dress with finger and thumb, careful lest she damage it by handling it too roughly. ''Tis enormously colourful. And a very fine weave.'

'Mistress told me to burn it.'

'*Burn it!!*' Meg exploded. 'You cannot! You cannot burn such fine clothes. I have never seen such beautiful yarn. 'Tis the work of a master weaver!'

'That's my belief. But fine though it is, we cannot wear it. What would people say? They would think we were witches or other such evil women!'

Lizbeth was standing in the corner, watching and listening. She moved tentatively forward. 'That is a dress of many colours, Mother. Just like Joseph's. In the bible.'

'"Tis not for the likes of us.' said Rose.

'I would *love* to wear that dress, mother.'

'You cannot, Lizbeth.'

'Why do you say that, Mother? If Joseph could wear a coat of many colours, then why may I not do the same?'

'Because it would not be... Not be...' Rose stopped, unable to summon an argument.

'It would not be what, Mother?'

'Run away, girl.'

Meanwhile Rose set off back to the parsonage. She would have spent longer at home, but she knew she would have to get back to the parsonage before she was missed.

Chapter 8

Sara gave no more thought to the plague-ridden dress and continued to sit with Connie. From time to time during the remainder of the day, either James or Edward arrived and she would go out of the rear of the house and wander amongst the vegetable plots in the summer sunshine in order to take advantage of the fresh air.

When she arrived back that afternoon after a short break, she noticed a change in the atmosphere of the room. The air was fresher, less stifling. Looking across at the window she could see why.

The window had been opened.

Sara looked at Edward. 'Why... Edward... you've opened the window!'

'I have, Mistress Sara. In accordance with your wishes. And whereas it is directly opposed to all medical thinking, I have succumbed so that experimentally we might see if fresh air will help Mistress Connie to recover.'

'Thank you.'

Dusk was falling and Sara prepared to spend another night with Connie. Edward left and Sara lay down on the trundle.

Connie was not sick again, and Sara was able to snatch a fitful period of rest.

Next morning she felt much more refreshed than the morning before.

While James looked after Connie, Edward and Sara had breakfast. She felt much refreshed, and when Edward again suggested that she take a stroll in the fresh air, she gladly accepted.

'I'd like to take a stroll through the village. I have yet to see it by daylight.'

'I think your apparel may raise a few eyebrows, Mistress Sara.'

'How so?'

'The style... and particularly the colour...'

She looked at her purple jacket. 'What's wrong with it?'

'Nothing. 'Tis just that such a colour has never been seen before in Abbots Cross.'

'Purple?'

'Is that what it is called? Is it used in your country?'

'Yes.'

'Who by?'

Sara had to think fast. 'Why... 'it's the colour of kings... It's normally reserved for Royalty.'

'Perhaps they'll think you are a queen, Mistress Sara.

* * * *

Sara went downstairs. Through the double doors, she descended the outside steps, and began to make her way down the drive towards the village.

Beeches and ash trees on either side waved in the gentle breeze. The sun had not yet reached full warmth, for which Sara was grateful. She gulped in huge lungfuls of the fresh, cool air as she walked towards the gate. Crossing the mud road along which Josephine had brought them a few nights before, she started down the street towards the castle. The Church and Parsonage stood at the northern end of the road. From it the houses led away down Village Street like soldiers standing at attention on either side.

Although still early, two women were standing at the junction, gossiping, and both turned to look at Sara as she neared them, surprise evident on their faces. But as Sara was about to voice a greeting, both turned away, clearly suspicious of her. And as Sara passed by, she noticed strong odours from bodies which had clearly not been washed in a very long time. The nauseous stench emanating from the two women made Sara want to retch, and she quickened her stride to avoid smelling them further. She was conscious of their eyes upon her as she walked on.

Coming up village street was a child whose age would doubtless be measured in single figures. In its hand, the child held a short rope at the end of which was a docile pig. It was impossible to tell whether the child was a boy or girl as the figure was clad in a petticoat. Not yet old enough to be breeched!

Sara determined to speak to the child when they met. But she was to be denied. Midway up the street, the figure turned away to lead the pig along a track between two houses where they disappeared from view.

As Sara walked down the road between the houses, deep ruts cut by farm carts made walking difficult, and she had to pick her way with care. Nonetheless, she examined the buildings with great interest, noting much.

The houses had the same deep pitched sloping roofs she had noticed on arrival. Their heather or straw thatch, which had once been bright yellow, had now dulled to a light brown with the passing of time. Moss and lichen added touches of brilliance to the roof colouring, their yellow and emerald irregular patterns contrasting with the deepening hues of the thatch. Dormer windows, each surrounded as though a picture frame with climbing flowers such as morning glories or peripopples peeped out from under the thatch at regular intervals like frogs' eyes in April.

Each cottage was almost completely hidden by huge screens of unkempt bushes. Small wooden gates closed gaps in the hedges. Some had arches of climbing roses, others wandering clematis.

Through the thick screens of foliage could be seen flowers at their summer peak - purple and white, red and yellow, orange and blue - each garden a rainbow of horticultural delight, each vying with its neighbour for scent and splendour.

Sara walked slowly down the street, admiring the delights of the storybook houses. As she walked, her problems with Connie, while not forgotten, at least drifted to the rear of her conscious, allowing a brief respite from the worry which had nagged her for several days.

Then at one house, a door unexpectedly opened. A trim female figure wearing a brown smock and a russet skirt busily emerged.

Determined to speak, Sara called, 'Good Morning!'

The saucer eyes staring out from beneath the white dust cap were followed by a mouth which dropped open in amazement. Then, hurriedly, the woman turned and, picking up her skirts dashed back into the house, slamming the door behind her.

Sara stood in the road, puzzled and a little insulted. *Why had the woman been so impolite?*

She looked down at her own clothes - her bright purple top and trousers, her smart shoes, her string of beads - and realised how outrageous her wear must appear to a Seventeenth Century Northumbrian village woman.

Sara thought for a moment. *Perhaps there were some old clothes up at the parsonage? She might possibly find a dress to fit?*

Making a mental note to ask The Parson, Sara resumed her walk. A couple of stray cats stalked their prey while two infants played. Sara felt dismay at seeing the children making a plaything of the filthy liquid of an open sewer. This channel of putrid liquid ran the full length of the tall unkempt hedges, and gave off a strong smell of rotten garbage.

On the right, past the first hovels, stood the thatched inn. It was fronted by an innyard, and stood back from the building line of the cottages. The whitened stone construction was the alehouse for all the local peasants. Above the courtyard, suspended on a wrought iron arm hung a crudely painted wooden sign. A man with a crown topped the legend, THE KINGS HEAD The sign swung gently in the small movements of air, while the inn door stood closed at too early an hour for peasants who would be labouring in the fields until dusk.

Sara looked carefully at the wooden sign. Something about it was strange. Then she realised. At one time, it had read something different.

Screwing up her eyes, she read in not completely obliterated lettering, 'THE PROTECTOR'S ARMS' Having solved the mystery, Sara smiled wistfully. After the Restoration the innkeeper had changed allegiance! A very wise move in Cromwell's wake!

On arriving at Abbots Cross in the 20th Century, once the bus had gone, Sara had been impressed by the stillness in the village. And she had expected the same lack of noise in the Seventeenth Century. But to her surprise, there was an unexpected level of sound. Even back in the Parsonage, the stillness had been regularly interrupted by bells ringing for servants, or the sound of voices as staff called out to one another.

Next to the innyard stood the blacksmith's cottage. Next to that, his shop. At the other side lived and worked the carpenter. Further down, another tradesman or two. From the open doors of each emanated the sounds of these men plying their trades.

Outside, pigs grunted while they foraged in small enclosures. Chickens proudly proclaimed that an egg had just been laid. People were shouting across the street both to and at one another. Wood was being chopped while a hedge cutter speedily but noisily hacked away surplus growth by means of upward sweeps of a small scythe on alternate sides of the hedge. He was clearly very experienced, for Sara thought the rate at which he worked quite amazing.

At the bottom of the hill strutted the castle. It stood just as it would three centuries later, glowering protectively against the skyline, master of everything it surveyed.

The road turned here and as Sara's feet 'pad-padded' on its earthen surface, she pushed through denser leafage. As nettles brushed against her trousers, she began to hear the running water of the river.

* * * *

'Tis time for me to go.' Rose said to Lizbeth as she prepared for her work at the parsonage. The sun had now been up for some time, and she was well aware that the cleaning and other tasks she had to see to in the big house were numerous. She would not be able to return home until they had all been seen to. 'Now do not forget to go and get the water from the river.'

'I won't forget, Mother. But please may I wear that dress?'

'I don't want you to be seen in it. I was told to destroy it.'

'But nobody will see me.'

'What if the parson or that strange woman came down the village and saw you in it?'

'The parson never comes to the riverside. And even if he did - or that woman - what difference will it make? They told you to destroy it. They did not want it any more. So why may I not wear it?'

Rose fell silent. She knew her arguments were thin. But she could think of no good reason to deny the girl the chance to wear the fine dress.

'Mother, if I only wear it for a short time, what will you say?'

Exasperated, Rose exploded. 'Oh, Heaven take us. Very well. Put on the dress and see what it is like. But you still have to go for some water.'

'Then can I wear the dress to go?'

'Oh - very well...'

With a whoop of delight, Lizbeth grabbed the dress, pulled off her petticoat and pulled it on. It was quite a bit too large, but richly colourful. She would grow into it.

Grabbing a bucket for some water, she flounced out of the cottage.

* * * *

Nearing the river, Sara realised that like the village, the water's edge was a centre of local industry. Two serving wenches came by, chatting away cheerfully to one another while carrying a large heavy garment between them.   They were holding it as far away from themselves as they could, and it was noticeably wet. As they walked past, Sara caught the whiff of stale urine. Clearly it was straight from the pissbarrel Rose had talked about earlier.

As Sara looked on, the two wenches carried the garment to the water's edge.   Then, swinging it in unison, they tossed it into shallow, slow moving current. Picking up one or two stones from the river's edge, they plopped them into the water.   The stones landed on the submerged cloth, anchoring the garment so that the flow of the river would not carry it away.

Four children of indeterminate age played on the near bank with a skipping rope. A fifth child - a pre walking infant - sat on a grassy bank watching.   The infant wailed lustily, but to no avail.   None of the skipping children who had clearly been detailed to look after it had interest in anything other than their skipping game. Curls of various colours bobbed up and down as each child took its turn to jump over the rope.

Then Sara looked at a field just beyond the far river bank where hay was being harvested and at once she realised why the children who were playing were all very young. Anyone from about six or seven years of age onwards was helping to gather in the harvest. Adults - all in a line - used sideways sweeping movements with long handled scythes while children gathered up the newly cut hay and spread it out evenly on the stubble. Sara smirked to herself/. *Making hay while the sun shines...* she murmured.

Further upriver, a woman arrived with three or four pans which she then dropped onto the bank with a noisy clatter. Taking some of the rough sand from the river bank, she proceeded to rub and scrub at the interior of the first pan. Meanwhile, on the far side of the river a younger man arrived carrying a wooden bucket. Reaching the edge, he poured its contents into the water. To Sara's nausea she noted that the bucket's contents had been scraps of meat, much of which had already begun to turn green. And Sara felt momentarily sick as the rancid smell of the festering meat wafted over the water towards her as it began to float away downstream.

Just down from where the butcher had discarded this rotten carnivorous waste, two children of no more than three years of age played happily in the shallow water. One of them picked up a piece of rotten meat as it floated by, but fortunately, discarded it immediately. Even the fish in the river which Sara could see examining the discarded waste chose not to consume any of it.

As Sara stood watching, the running water continued to be a hub of activity of many kinds. George Lumsden's water mill stood at one side, its undershot wheel gently turned by the flow. Nearby, a child was in the act of throwing slops into the water. Several women rubbed away at coarse clothes to beat out the dirt.

As Sara watched, appalled at the unhygienic mixture of activity, a young girl appeared from behind her. She was carrying an empty bucket. As Sara glanced, her mouth fell open.

The girl was wearing Connie's dress.

For a moment, Sara continued to fly-catch with her mouth. The picture of the young girl wearing the dangerous dress which could kill her was unbelievable.

Then realisation exploded. Oblivious to danger, Rose had succumbed to temptation. She'd given the young girl a dress of such finery as she had never seen before.

For a moment, Sara continued to watch the girl's approach. Anger fought with rationality, for her first reaction was to scream at the child.

But she fought to keep control. *It wasn't Rose's fault! She didn't know that Connie had plague! And even if she had, the woman could not have known how the disease was spread.*

Sara planted herself in the girl's way. 'Hello.' she said with as much softness as her still-simmering anger would permit. 'What's your name?'

The immature lips widened to display a mouth in which milk teeth were still predominant. 'Lizbeth.' she said, 'Lizbeth Sprogg.'

'That's an unusual dress' Sara went on. 'Where did you get it, Lizbeth?'

The girl turned pale blue eyes up in surprise. 'Why... Madam... my mother gave it to me...' Sensing something unusual about this stranger in the curious clothes, Lizbeth faltered. Her tone was hesitant, wary, a nervous half-smile playing at her mouth.

'Does your mother work at the Parsonage?'

'Why, Yes, Madam.'

'And is her name Rose?'

A full smile relaxed the small face. 'Yes, Madam, Rose. Rose Sprogg. That's my mother's name.'

Sara nodded. *This WAS Rose's daughter.*

Sara knew the great danger the girl was in. *If the flea still inhabited the dress...*

For her own safety, the girl had to remove it. As soon as possible. But the matter had to be handled delicately.

'What are you doing?' Sara asked conversationally.

Lizbeth looked down at the wooden bucket with the rope handle. 'I've come for drinking water.' she said.

Taking the explanation as a cue, she turned, leaned over the riverbank, and dropped in the bucket. It slowly sank in the near-stagnant water at the river's edge.

Lizbeth allowed it to immerse completely. Then she pulled on the rope. The now-heavy bucket was full of water.

Sara began to feel sick at the water in the bucket. All other kinds of activities had taken place in the river. Scrubbing, washing, discarding of slops...

'You're going to drink *that?*' she asked, her incredulity apparent.

'We always drink it, Mistress.'

Nauseated, Sara spoke more abruptly than she intended. 'I think you should take off that dress.' As soon as she spoke, Sara knew she had phrased her words badly.

'*Take my dress off?*' the little girl shrieked. 'Why... Madam... ' She began to panic.

'Yes. I don't mean *now.*' said Sara impatiently. 'When you get home. That dress does not belong to you. It belongs to my cousin Connie.'

The girl's already pained face wrinkled further. 'Ooohh... Mistress...' she half-cried, unshed tears filling her eyes.

'If you wear that dress, you'll catch a pestilence.'

A sharp intake of breath greeted this statement. Horror displaced timidity. Thoroughly terrified, she began to weep. 'Oh... you're a... you're a...' she wailed, backing away from Sara. She picked up the bucket, cast a horrified look at Sara then set off at speed up the road, the jostled container slopping its dirty water over all sides.

Sara stood at the riverbank watching the girl disappear. Then she turned back to look at the river. The washing women had stopped their work. They regarded her with odd, suspicious, hostile looks. The butcher had gone, as had the child with the slops. The four children continued playing on the near bank with their skipping rope.

Suddenly on the far side of the river appeared a man of average height leading a horse and a cart. Clearly, like the other village men, he worked manually. But his face, hands and clothes were all red - red as plant-pots, a red which covered him completely from hat to toe. The only colour balance came from his face, out of which shone a pair of dark eyes.

The skipping children stopped, looked over the river – and screamed.

'The reddleman! The reddleman!' one shrieked. ''Tis the reddleman.'

The four little girls all turned to look. Then all four began to run away from the river and towards Sara. Catching sight of Sara, they all stopped and two of them screamed again.

111

"Tis a witch!' one of them yelled. Without hesitation they began to run again, giving Sara a wide berth, their eyes resting on Sara as they ran until they were well away from her.

Meanwhile the reddleman led his horse down and started to cross the ford. As Sara watched he made his way over, stumbling from submerged rock to submerged rock, the horse walking alongside him. As they neared, Sara noted that the cart was laden with several pots containing a thick red dye the same colour as the reddleman himself.

They reached the bank where Sara stood. The reddleman led his horse onto the path, looking at Sara as he came by. He looked her up and down, clearly mesmerised by her appearance. Then their eyes met, and Sara spoke.

'Good Morning.'

'Mornin', Mistress.' the reddleman responded in a dull voice. Then he turned his face forward and led his lumbering horse and cart away up the hill.

Chapter 9

Dejected and angry that her order over the dress had been ignored, Sara turned away. She made her despondent way back up the track between the hovels.

Sara was desolate. And angry. Desolate at Rose for her stupidity and angry that she had not burned the plague-ridden clothes.

At least Rose might have boiled the clothes before her daughter wore them! Had she done that, the clothes would have been much safer for anyone to wear.

Sara knew that lack of sleep was shortening her temper. But it was difficult to not be irritated by the servant's ignorance. And Rose's daughter was now in danger.

She strode resolutely back up the road, round Castle corner towards the crossroads, then up the drive to the Parsonage. She reached the steps and burst into the big house, tripping quickly across the stone floor of the entrance hall. Clattering upstairs to Connie's room, she raised her hand and tapped lightly before raising the latch to swing open the door.

Creaking slightly, it yielded. The periwigged figure at the desk turned and threw her a dignified smile of recognition.

Returning the greeting, Sara cast a glance over to the bed. Connie lay in a disturbed, troubled sleep.

'Good Day, again, Mistress Sara.' the Parson said. 'You've arrived in good time for lunch.'

Sara shot him a disturbed glance. 'What about Connie?' she asked. 'We cannot leave her alone.'

He smiled. 'I asked James to sit with her, and he agreed.'

'He did?'

'Yes, Mistress Sara.'

The Parson had risen to his feet, and now went over to the door to call along the corridor. 'James!'. Then he turned to smile at her. But his smile began to die in answer to something in her expression. 'What is it?' he asked.

Sara didn't immediately answer. She wanted to gather her thoughts before she spoke. 'I'll tell you over lunch.' she said.

While James sat at Connie's bedside, Sara and the Parson went downstairs. As they walked, Sara asked, 'Parson Makepeace, what is the reddleman?'

He turned to smile at her. 'The reddleman?' he asked rhetorically. 'The reddleman makes and supplies the dye which is used for marking sheep. '

'I see...'

'You will have noticed his colour?' he asked.

'Yes. That's why I am curious.'

He nodded. 'He gets to be that colour from the process of making the dye. His face, hands, skin and clothes are all that colour. A deep red.'

'Is he always that colour?'

'He is. He cannot remove the colour which sticks to him all the time.'

'Two children were clearly afraid of him.'

'Young children sometimes think he is the Devil. Satan himself!' he laughed.

Together they entered the dining room and soon faced one another across a solid oak table. Sara contemplated the wooden platter of poached eggs in front of her. A spoon and knife were the only implements.

'May I have a fork?' she asked.

Edward frowned. 'A fork?'

Sara nodded. 'Yes. Where I come from we have a three or four pronged implement we use for eating.'

He puzzled briefly. Then he shook his head. 'I've heard of the new Italian fashion of forks at the dining table. But personally, I have no time for such flippancies.'

Smiling, Sara picked up the knife, and cut into her egg yolks. The yellow liquid spread over her platter, and with the wooden spoon, she scooped it up and swallowed it gratefully. Now that she was out of the sickroom, she began to realise how hungry she had become.

'Something seems to be bothering you.' he ventured.

Nodding, she said, 'You remember the dress Connie wore when she came?'

'Yes... Yes, I remember. Rose took it away.'

'That's right. She took it away to burn it. I think you could catch plague from it.'

She could see by the lines of his forehead that he had no idea what she was talking about.

Impatiently, she tried a different explanation. 'I told Rose to burn the dress because otherwise the fleas in the dress carrying the plague could possibly pass it on to others. But Rose didn't burn the dress. Instead she gave it to her daughter to wear." She shook an irritated head. 'If Rose is not careful, her daughter will catch the plague. Indeed, she may have caught it already if there are any fleas still lingering in the material.'

While she spoke, his look changed from disbelief to scorn. 'Fleas!' he exclaimed disdainfully before drinking from his goblet.

'Look!' she said, pointing at him across the table with her knife, her voice rising. 'If my theory is incorrect, then Rose and her family will be safe! But if not, the only way they may well catch plague is from a flea in Connie's dress!'

He looked at her silently for a moment. 'What I can't understand is this: Fleas are everywhere, but normally nobody catches plague from them. So why are the fleas suddenly giving people plague *now?* If plague *does* come from fleas, why does it not happen all the time?'

'Because most fleas are harmless. It's the ones infesting the black rats which carry the plague with them - special fleas.'

His scorning features did not alter as, rising from the table, he walked over to the window. His tall form was silhouetted against the small panes as he looked out. Then he turned to face her.

'If what you say is true, then why is Constance still infected by plague? The fleas you speak of went with the dress.'

'Once she has the infection, it takes time to be cured of it.'

'How do *you* know all this, Mistress Sara? None of the doctors of the land would agree with you.'

Sara fell silent for a minute. Picking up her goblet, she drank slowly and deeply of ale to give herself time to think.

How could she explain it to him? How could she tell him? How could she convince him that she was from a different time? A time of medical advance? A time of ability to cure disease - to effect cures Edward Makepeace and his contemporaries not only did not know about but would never even dream possible.

'Because I am not from here...' She almost whispered as she quietly replaced the goblet on the table.

'What was that, Mistress Sara?'

She pushed her now-empty platter to one side, and leaned on her elbows. 'I was not born here...' she said quietly, looking hard at the straw-covered floor. Then as he began to splutter a protest, she held up her hand. 'I came from a different place. Many miles hence. You might even think of it as a different country...'

'That's ridiculous!'

'It certainly seems so.' she agreed. 'But it isn't...' It's true...'

'How can it be true? How did you get here? You and your cousin? Will you tell *ME* so that I may make the journey?' His voice rose in the scorn for which she could find no blame.

'I can't tell you.' she said. 'Because I don't know. I was staying in a cottage. Connie fell ill. There was a light behind a door. I found myself in Mistress Josephine's house. She brought us here!'

'If I believed in witches, then I would think you were one!' he said. 'For only *WITCHES* would make such a claim!'

'I'm no witch! Witchcraft is the belief of superstitious and ignorant people--' She stopped. *Had she said too much?* 'I... didn't mean that to be offensive...' she added falteringly.

'I'm not offended.' he replied. He came back to the table. He bent forward to lean on both fists on its surface. His face was very close to hers.

'I believe you are right when you say there are no witches!' He stopped as he stood up, and his tone became more sinister. 'But the cotters here do not. Belief in witchcraft is strong in this village.'

For a few moments he was silent. Then he moved round, sat down at the table again, and looked steadfastly at her.

'So - where are you from? Name the place.'

'You wouldn't have heard of it.'

'Is it in the north... or the south...?'

'It's a number of miles from London. I went to London. Then I travelled here.'

'How did you travel? By sea? or by stagecoach?'

Having travelled by long-distance coach, Sara was able to give an honest answer. 'By coach.'

He sat back in his chair. Then he looked at her jacket. 'Were your clothes made where you live?'

She looked at her now-creased, slightly soiled purple jacket and trousers, the fine polyester cotton a product of Twentieth Century technology, a fibre unknown in the Parson's time. 'Yes, they were.'

He leaned forward to examine them closely. 'They are of a most unusual fashion, I grant you. And of a very fine weave.' He leaned forward to look closely at her jacket. 'Let me... let me... touch it...'

She stood up, walked round the table and stood by him. He turned in his seat to face her. Between left thumb and forefinger, he pinched her sleeve, rolling the material back and forward. Then he took away his hand to look up with eyes which displayed the curiosity of a scientific mind.

'Woven from a very fine cloth. The tailors in your country must be very skilful.'

'They are.' Sara responded, returning to her place at the table. As she sat down, she thought about Connie in the bed. *Had she been left too long?*

Looking out of the window, Sara could see that by now the sun was high in the sky. Its beams shone directly onto the table at which she sat.

Sara looked at her watch. It was now after twelve - between twelve and half past.

'What's that?'

'What is what?'

'That! Strapped to your wrist? Be it a bracelet?'

Puzzled at first, it suddenly became clear that he meant her watch. 'Oh...' she laughed. 'This? No, it's no bracelet! It's my wa-- er, my timepiece!'

'Your... timepiece...?'

'It keeps me informed of the time.'

He leaned forward curiously, clearly shaken by her statements. 'May I see?'

Smilingly, she raised her wrist and held forward her hand, pulling back her sleeve to let him see. He gently took hold of her petite hand in his strong, weather-beaten fingers, looking down at the small neat watch with its silver, brushed chrome case and small clear dial.

'It's a miniature timepiece! I've never seen one this small!'

'No. But in the country I come from, these are made.'

'I wonder if science can take us much further?' he ventured.

Sara's response was a grin of relief. 'Having seen the wonders which have already been achieved, it's my belief that there will come a time when carriages travel without horses, and all people - even peasants - have them. '

'Peasants will have carriages?'

'Not only that. I believe that everyone will live in a home without damp. And without rats.'

'You think there may come a time when peasant cots are not damp? And have no rats in them?' His voice rose in incredulity.

'I certainly do. There will be pipes to carry sewage, and Inhabitants of this village-' she waved her hand in the general direction of Village Street - 'will have long leisure hours, and holidays.'

'They already *have* holidays!'

'I don't mean a day her and a day there. I mean for two weeks and more at a time! And they'll travel to countries over the sea! Nor will they sail on ships, but fly in machines which climb higher than seagulls in the air, and travel to America in short hours!'

'Why would peasants want to travel to the colonies? Unless they were transported there?'

For a moment, there was silence. Then he said, 'It sounds like God's Paradise on Earth, this time in the future you predict, Mistress Sara.'

'Not exactly. They'll have problems. But different problems from those we face today.'

For a moment nothing was said by either of them. But Sara was thinking furiously. *Oh, how I wish I could tell you the truth!* she lamented. *But I cannot. It would sound quite ridiculous. It may be that one day I can convince you. But not yet.*

Sara breathed a sigh of relief. *Now she had an ally!* Then again she thought of Connie. 'I'd better go back upstairs.' she said, rising from the table. Then she remembered something.

'I have something to ask of you, Parson Makepeace.'

'Yes, Mistress Sara?'

'The clothes I am wearing are not really suitable for Abbots Cross. They are much too colourful and are of a style and design of my own far-off country.'

'That is true. But they are pleasant to the eye.'

'Nonetheless, I wondered if there are any ladies' clothes in the house? Something suitable to wear whilst I am here? An old servant's dress, perhaps? '

'Mmm...' he thought, standing back and looking at her, 'I think there may be one of my late mother's still here. She was about your size. I shall have a look when we go upstairs.'

He followed her out of the large room in which they had eaten, and back upstairs.

Back in the bedroom, The Parson dismissed James, went over to the bed and looked down at the sleeping Connie. 'Can we cure your cousin?' he asked. 'Have you any potion which might aid her recovery?'

'Alas,' Sara lamented, 'We can only keep her clean, and comfortable, and hope that she gets no worse.' She sat down at the bedside.

The Parson said, 'I shall return directly.' and went out. A few minutes of worried solitude for Sara passed, then the Parson returned. Over his arm he carried a russet brown-green dress.

'Try this, Mistress Sara.'

She held it up in front of her. It was woven from thick, heavy wool, but it looked close to her size.

'I think it will fit you very well.' he said.

'I'll try it on right away.'

He turned and left the room, closing the door behind him. Quickly she slipped off her jacket and trousers and pulled the heavy dress over her shoulders, It came down to mid calf, slightly full, but a good fit.

Turning to her Twentieth Century wear, she picked up the trousers and folded them over. *It might be possible to wash them before wearing them again.*

She picked up the jacket and was about to hang it up when something small fell out of the pocket and rattled onto the bare floorboards. Curiously, she looked down. There lay something small which had just fallen out of her pocket, and which she did not recognise at first. Then as she looked at it inquisitively, her face suddenly lit up with delight as she recognised what it was!

Sara dashed over to the door, opened it and went to the landing. The Parson and James were engaged in conversation, so she called out, 'Edward... Edward...'

The Parson turned to look up at her. 'Yes, Mistress Sara?'

'May I interrupt you for a moment?'

'Certainly, Mistress Sara.'

James left and the Parson went over to the staircase, ascending it quickly and lightly. As he reached the landing, he looked her up and down approvingly.

'Well, Mistress Sara, that is an almost perfect fit.' he said. 'A little adjustment here and there--'

'How on earth do you walk about in this?' she asked.

'What is the problem, Mistress Sara?'

'It's such a weight! But I like it. So thank you, Edward. But that is not why I asked you to come.'

'It is not?'

'No.'

'What is it, then?'

'Do you recall - just a few minutes ago - that you asked whether we might be able to help young Connie survive the plague? And that you asked me if I had any potion?'

'I do. And I shall pray for it--'

'Yes. But I think I may be able to assist your prayers.'

'How?'

'With these!' She raised her arm. In her hand were the capsules the doctor had given her for sore throats a week earlier. *Now they could be thrown into the attack against a much more lethal disease!*

'*Streptomycin!*' she had thought with delight, reading the bottle label with unconcealed glee. 'Edward! Now we **can** help her!'

'How?'

'With these!'

'What are they?' Lines on his forehead betrayed his complete bewilderment.

'Pills to combat plague! I was given them before I came here.'

'May I see?'

She handed him the bottle. He took it gingerly.

'I must take care not to damage it.' he said, carrying it over to the window and holding it up to the sunlight. 'Such fine coloured glass must be very fragile!'

'This glass is unbreakable!' she laughed, taking the plastic bottle from him and tossing it onto the table with deliberate carelessness. 'Now - let's get some water for Connie.'

'Certainly.'

Picking up a wooden goblet, he turned to the water jug. He would have immersed the goblet, but Sara stopped him.

'No!' she said, laying a hand on his forearm. 'Please, wait a minute.' She remembered how Rose's daughter had filled the bucket with the foul water the villagers were content to drink. 'I'll get some water from the glebe.'

'Mistress Sara - a servant may go in your place.'

But she shook her head. 'This is something I must do for myself. I'll return as quickly as I can.'

Quickly, Sara went into the anteroom. Picking up a wooden bucket, she made sure it was relatively clean. Then she returned to the room.

'Back later!' she called as she left.

Leaving The Parson to look after Connie in the room, she walked hurriedly downstairs, making her way along a corridor and went out of a rear door.

It was still early enough for the air to be yet fresh. Sara breathed deeply, exhilarated that at last she could do something to help Connie.

Happily swinging the bucket by its handle, Sara shut the door behind her - and smiled briefly at the horseshoe nailed to the lintel for protection against witches.

'Witches!' she thought disdainfully as she turned away. 'Ridiculous!'

She walked the same direction as she had done when going to wash. Crossing the brick-paved courtyard, she made her way past the whitewashed outbuildings, through the vegetable plots, past the small wood. Unlatching the gate, she crossed the footbridge and past the three thatch-roofed beehives at its edge.

As she made her way to the glebe, she noticed that her dress was heavy - far heavier than it appeared. And in addition, its rough weave rubbed against her skin, so that she found herself beginning to scratch because of the coarseness of the material.

But she had more major concerns than her own comfort. And as she strode along a short, bracken-strewn path she came to the far end of the wood which opened into hilly pasture through which flowed the creek she had just crossed. But its downward movement was much more purposeful here. It ran and raced, gurgling and gushing over boulders and through plant roots.

Following the stream, she climbed alongside for a short way until she came to the natural pond where she had washed, into which she could dip the bucket. The stream was just as she remembered it, for it flowed with pure, clean water.

Why did the villagers chose to drink river water when this was available?

Leaning over the running pond, she dropped the bucket into the crystal water four or five times. She paused after each immersion for the stream to carry off the dirt now suspended in its flow. Only when she was satisfied of the bucket's cleanliness did she finally fill it with water she thought fit to drink.

As she turned to make her return journey, she looked across the tops of the trees where the roof of the Parsonage could be glimpsed like a whale at sea. The full leaf of the trees made occasional movements in the soft breeze while the constant chatter of chaffinches sounded dissonantly against the droning ground bass of marauding insects.

Sara's feet bounced in the springy turf as she made her way back down the hill. The serene delight of her surroundings lightened her step. On such a day as this, she cared not a jot if she never again returned to the Twentieth Century. And suddenly she realised that if necessary, she could happily spend the rest of her life in her adopted time. The Century she had left certainly held no attractions for her.

But what about the Parson? Would he be happy to have her stay? Would he be willing to continue as host to a couple of girls from an alien Century?

As she considered him, her thoughts softened. *What a remarkable man he was!* Not only had he been willing to shelter the girls in the face of the most dread disease known at that time, but he had treated both of them - Sara in particular - with extreme kindness. And his acceptance of a woman almost as an equal had shown remarkable foresight for the age in which he lived.

When she arrived back at the Parsonage, Sara soon noted with pleasure that the Parson was now clearly convinced of Sara's integrity, for he became a willing helper. Together, they aroused young Connie from a sleep from which she did not wish to awaken. As he cupped the young blonde head, Sara administered the first pill with as little water as possible. If Connie drank freely, she might vomit the pill back up!

Connie's temperature was now alarmingly high - the highest it had been all day. The buboes disfiguring her thighs and armpits were now huge. But the rings of roses Sara had been dreading had not appeared. Nor had her nose begun to bleed - a sign that her blood vessels were breaking up.

Having attended to Connie, Sara turned to the Parson. There was something she wanted to say.

'Parson Makepeace...' she began.

'Yes, Mistress Sara?'

She found his smile disconcerting, but determined to continue. 'I regret that I was forward in being familiar with you earlier today.'

'How 'familiar', Mistress Sara?'

'I addressed you by your Christian name. And I wish to apologise.' She cast her eyes to the floor in embarrassment.

'Why... Mistress Sara...' he said kindly. 'It was a compliment! There is no need for an apology!'

'You aren't annoyed?'

'On the contrary. I am delighted that you felt so relaxed in my presence.'

'Then - shall I address you as 'Edward' in future?'

'Please do, Mistress Sara.'

'Then 'Edward' it shall be.'

Sara felt a sneaking gratification that Edward appeared reluctant to go about his Parish duties. He seemed happy to stay, to assist with tasks Sara could have managed on her own.

But at length he took leave of her. 'I shall be back later, Mistress Sara.' he promised. 'And then perhaps you will be gracious enough to tell me more of the advances made in your home country?'

'It will be a great pleasure.'

After he had left, Sara took the chance to rest awhile until a low moan from the bed roused her from her thoughts. Almost at once, Connie began to retch again. Sara held the bowl, praying that Connie would not vomit, lest she spew up the antibiotic. But thankfully, the retching ceased and the troubled figure returned to lie back on the pillows.

During the rest of the long, long afternoon, Sara sat with Connie, administering another pill as twilight started to pursue the remainder of the sunlight. Although Sara dozed off on occasion, it was never very long before Connie needed further attention.

Then Edward returned. He came into the bedroom, and looked at Sara with concern.

'You should sleep, Mistress Sara. Go along to the bedroom.'

'I can't leave Connie.' Sara replied, her head now dead from fatigue, and knowing that Edward was right.

'I am willing to stay.'

'She's my responsibility.'

'Then rest on the trundle while I remain here.'

It was an offer from Heaven - one not to be refused. 'Yes... yes, I suppose I could do that.'

Before pulling out the trundle, Sara told him the timing of the pills, then she lay down and was asleep within a minute, exhausted beyond endurance.

The shades of twilight were beginning to metamorphose into dusk, and when Sara woke again, it was dark. Although to judge by the last of the light, she could not have been asleep long, she felt refreshed. She rose, and walked over to the window - then realised why she felt so much better. The sun had been down, and risen again.

She'd slept all night.

Looking round, she saw Edward, his clothing slightly dishevelled, asleep in his seat, and she went over to him.

'Edward!' she said in a semi-whisper, shaking him awake. 'Have you been here all night?'

He stumbled into wakefulness. 'Why... yes, Mistress Sara.' he said, shuffling round in the seat. 'I must have fallen asleep.'

But he had not just fallen asleep, as Sara knew, but had deliberately stayed in that uncomfortable seat so that she might have a night's rest.

'I am most grateful to you, Edward.'

He nodded, but did not say anything as he got up and went out.

Sara turned to look at Connie. Her temperature was still extremely high. But the tell tale roses, the capillary end bursts which frequently sounded the death knell of the plague's host, were still absent.

But the pungent stench of the yellow body discharge once again assailed Sara's nostrils. 'Great Heavens!' she thought. 'She's *GOT* to have a bath!'

Sara walked over to the door, opened it and shouted, 'Rose!'

Leaving the door open she returned to Connie, gazing down at her as she waited.

A tapping came to the door, but instead of Rose, in came the huge form of James, Edward's manservant.

'I am sorry, Mistress.' he said. 'But Rose has not arrived this morning.'

'Oh dear!' said Sara. 'I hope she's not sick! What ails her, James?'

'Why, Mistress Sara, have you not heard?'

'No...' Sara suddenly felt apprehension rising by the minute. 'No, I haven't heard. Please - tell me.'

'Then I regret to have to tell you that Rose's daughter has contracted the same vile sicknesse as your cousin, and 'tis feared she may die.'

Then suddenly Sara stopped short. *'My God!'* she thought. *'The dress! Connie's dress! Now plague has hit the village - and it's my fault!!!*

* * * *

Crushed by the news as she looked at the sombre face of the giant figure, Sara asked, 'What makes people fear that she will die?'

'Well... Mistress Sara... many people die of sicknesse...'

'Yes, but I hope that Rose's daughter will recover.'

'I hope so too, Mistress Sara. But, it's different with Lizbeth Sprogg.'

'Different?'

'Yes. When Luke Sprogg spoke to me this morning, he told me that young Lizbeth is greatly sick.' Then he asked, 'Will that be all, Mistress Sara?'

'Yes, James, that will be all. Thank you'

The black cloak of the enormous man whirled about him as he turned towards the door. She watched, filled with apprehension as without another word, he went out.

Sara wondered if James was right - that Lizbeth WAS likely to die, for although Sara suspected she had plague, it was a disease from which sometimes the patient recovered. When plague was fatal, it killed some victims swiftly, yet others with agonising slowness. There was no telling.

But Sara had problems of her own, and for the moment she put Lizbeth Sprogg to the back of her mind. As she looked down at the troubled form on the bed, she again noticed the pungent, searching odour with which she had lived all night. She looked up at the casement. The window to the room was still firmly shut.

A tap came to the door. 'Come in!' she called, and Edward entered, carrying a goblet of ale.

'I understand Rose is not here this morning.' She nervously took the goblet from his hand.

'No. It is as you said it would be. Her daughter has plague. I have examined her this morning - and she is very sick. I have taken care not to let it be known that Lizbeth has plague. It would cause terror amongst the villagers.'

'What did you tell them?'

'I said I thought Lizbeth has flux. It will be the same outcome whether or not they know it to be plague.' He looked at the floor. 'I wish we could chase the vile distemper from the sufferers!"

He was clearly upset. Sara was sorry for him as she watched him walk across to Connie's bed. 'God's tokens be still absent!'

'Yes. Thankfully! - But her temperature runs high.'

'We must await God's judgement upon her. We seek to aid the recovery of the afflicted - but the knowledge escapes us.'

Sara turned to look again at her cousin. As she regarded the dark pallor and abundant sweat, she asked. 'I wonder if she might have a bath when she feels a little better?'

'A bath? But... Mistress Sara... bathtime is past for this year. 'Twas in the Spring!'

'You're right. Perhaps we can wipe her down with clean water later?'

'If you wish, Mistress Sara.'

The mention of a bath reminded Sara that she herself was clammy and sticky. 'It might be an idea if I were to go and wash my face and hands.'

'Shall I fetch a bowl of water for you?'

'I'm more sticky than that. Some running water would be better.'

'There's a pump in the yard. Or perhaps you will wish to wander up the glebe as you did for the drinking water?'

'Yes...' In her mind, the deep, broad pool lingered invitingly. 'May I borrow a cloth with which to dry my face?'

'Certainly, Mistress Sara. I shall tell James to provide one - and soap too. We have a new barrel of Castile just arrived from Bristol. It will be kinder to your fair skin than the soap the servants make.'

'I shall wash Connie down later.' she said, adding, 'If you will be so kind.'

'Of course! 'Twill be no trouble.'

James produced a pale green bar of coarse soap labelled 'BRISTOL', together with a piece of sacking. Sara noted its large size with satisfaction.

She made her way up the glebe and arrived at the pond formation where she had obtained Connie's drinking water yesterday. The hillside pool made a natural suntrap, screened as it was by an outcrop of boulders on one side and large bramble bushes in full leaf on the other. In the absence of humans, insects felt free to hum merrily about in the August sunshine, while a pleasant odour wafted gently over from the hayfield being hand-scythed by half a dozen men further to the South.

Sara looked round. The spot was completely deserted. Reassured, she took off the borrowed dress and removed her underwear, piling them in a neat bundle beneath a bush. Then, completely nude, she turned to face the clear natural pool.

Gently testing the temperature, she dipped first her feet then the rest of her body into the running creek where it started to form the deep pool. The water was invitingly cool and beautifully clear. Leaning down, she immersed her naked body, pushing forward with a gasp as the coldness of the water made her shiver momentarily. Gently floating on the surface, she gasped again in the cool water. But within minutes she had adjusted to its welcome temperature.

The only sound to be heard was of water falling in at one side and splashing out at the other. The constant feeding and draining gave the water an ever-replenished freshness which Sara found exhilarating.

Ducking her head under the surface, she revelled in the cleansing, a complete contrast with the unbearable clamminess of Connie's room. Becoming more adventurous, she swam down, reaching the deep bottom before turning up again.

Bursting to the surface, she breathed deeply before moving over to the shallow side to reach for the soap. Standing in the shallows, she rubbed herself with refreshing vigour, rejoicing in her first bath for several days, making sure that all parts of her body were cleansed. Replacing the soap, she pushed out again, once more swimming to the bottom to clear all suds.

Surfacing again, she lay back in the water to enjoy the cool rinsing, temporarily free of worry. She rolled her head back and forward under the water, her eyes lazily drifting over the bushes at the side of the pool.

Then something caught her glance...

She started up in the water. Reaching for the shelf with her feet, she stood still while searching the foliage.

At first nothing moved. Then a slight movement in the bushes caught her attention.

Was she being watched?

'Who's there?' she called. The movement stopped as more forcibly she repeated, 'Who's there?'

Up to her neck in water, Sara scanned the shrubs again. Only stillness greeted her gaze. Not a twig moved.

Beginning to feel she must have imagined it, Sara swam over to the side of the pool. She emerged from the water, taking care to watch all round. Grabbing the sacking, she rubbed herself down, drying body and hair with brisk, vigorous rubs.

But just as she drew the sacking away from her hair, a loud rustling in the bushes behind demanded her attention. She whipped round, pulling the sacking over her naked body, tying it with a fold just above the thrust of her breasts.

As she watched, a huge young man with an enormous jowl and wide-set eyes which stared wildly from under bushy, unkempt hair, suddenly parted the tall shrubs. He lumbered towards her with enormous strides. Taking a huge gasp, she screamed.

'No!... *No!!* Go *away!!!* Don't *touch* me!!"

But the young giant ignored her pleas, moving relentlessly towards her. 'Ugh... Ugh... Ugh...' he panted in senseless grunts.

'No!... *No!!*' she screamed again, backing away. 'Get *away!!!*'

But as he flung his arms round her, instantly overwhelmed by a putrid body odour, she squirmed to be free. Her face pressed unwillingly against the brown sackcloth smock which hung loosely on the unwashed giant.

He moved, and she pulled free her arms. Her small fists drummed upon his powerful shoulders as his huge misshapen face came into contact with hers. A huge hand arrived to cover her mouth.

'Don't cry...' he said quietly, 'Don't cry... Lancelot not hurt...' His speech was slurred, as if drunken. But Sara sensed that a mental defect was the cause.

Sara was not in a mood to accept Lancelot's assurances. 'Help me!' she called, 'Somebody help me!'

With little effort he lifted her from her feet. He carried her upright for a couple of yards towards a rock. There he sat her down and stood back to look at her in admiration.

'Pretty...' he said, spacing each word deliberately, as if speech were difficult. 'You... are... pretty... Pretty wench...'

'Go *away!!!*' she screamed again. 'Don't *touch* me!!

Despite being clad only in the sacking which she'd brought as a towel, Sara took her opportunity. She leapt up and started to run down the slope. She could hear the figure behind her thrashing through the longer grass in pursuit.

Was nobody around?

Glancing up as she ran, Sara espied a figure, not too far away, walking along the road to Abbots Cross. Without waiting, she yelled out.

'Help!!!...Help me!!!...'

The figure stopped, turned and looked. Clearly he saw on the instant what was happening. Turning off the road, he began to make his way up towards her. As he hurried, he shouted.

'Lancelot!... Lancelot!!... Do as she says!!...'

The voice from behind was Heaven sent – but only for a brief moment. And, looking back, she saw that the pursuing figure had stopped, clearly wary of the shouting man.

But when Sara turned back to look down the hill again, her spirits plummeted. The owner of the voice was a heavy-set man whose appearance did not inspire Sara one bit.

Nevertheless, it was best to be civil. 'Thank you... thank you... Mr...?'

'John Sprogg' he said. 'My wife is Rose.' Then he called again to the youth.

'Go on, Lancelot! Go home! To your mother!!'

'Er... Lancelot...' Sara began, but too late. Lancelot had already begun his retreat.

She turned to face John Sprogg.

'Lucky I was passing by.' he said in a sweet-sour voice.

'Yes...Thank you again. Now, I shall return to the pool and [ut my clothes on. Goodbye.'

But John Sprogg was already looking at her figure. It was a mental undressing, a removal of the sacking which was acting as Sara's towel, and Sara knew it.

'Now... now..., Mistress...' John Sprogg said. 'No need to be hasty.' He advanced towards her. ''Twould be a great pity were the charms of one so lovely as yourself left untouched.'

'What do you mean?' asked Sara, knowing exactly what he meant, but playing for time.

He took a step towards her. 'Why, I think you should get to know me better.'

'I don't think that's a good idea.'

'Yes it is.' He took another step.

'No... Don't touch me...'

But he was not about to stop. He stepped up close, and took her round the waist with both hands, pulling her towards him.

She struggled to be free. But she was too weak. His powerful arms reached out and encompassed her in a bear-grip of such firmness that breathing became difficult.

She knew she would have to act - or be raped. The stink of his body mingled with the cheap ale on his breath. And the nauseous combination spurred Sara into a reflex response.

Reaching up with both hands, she drew her nails deeply down both cheeks of Sprogg's face. He shrieked with pain, releasing her and covering his face with fingers through which ran rivers of blood.

'Bitch!!' he screamed in pain. 'Bloody bitch!!'

He advanced towards her again, but she was quick to realise his intentions. Ducking under his outstretched arms, and still wearing nothing but her sacking, she set off down the hill at the fastest pace at which she could make her legs work.

'Bitch...' she heard John Sprogg call again. She glanced back. Suddenly he was gone, out of sight. Then she saw him, continuing to walk away from the glebe and back towards the road from Abbots Cross to Christ Church.

Further over, she could see Lancelot following down the hill. He continued to look across and looked as if he would try again.

Whimpering with apprehension, she turned back to run down the glebe. And ran straight into a pair of strong arms.

'Lancelot... Lancelot!!... What are you doing?'

Lancelot stopped at once. As he turned to look, a childish expression crushed his features. Sara expelled an enormous gasp at the sound of Edward's voice and the youth's reaction to it.

Shouting over to the giant, his arms remaining in position, Edward reprimanded the tall man again. 'What are you doing, Lancelot?' he asked a second time.

'Oh... Parson... I, er... the pretty wench--'

'You- are- a- bad- boy!' Edward interrupted as if speaking to a five-year-old. He dropped his arms, stepped forward menacingly and barked out successive commands. 'Now- be- off- with- you! At once! Go home. Now. Your mother needs you!' The words were spoken with deliberate spacing as if to allow them time to penetrate the young giant's brain.

'Er... yes... I'll go home...' The giant nodded subserviently. 'I must see mother.'

'I'll come later. I'll ask your mother if you're home.'

The young giant's voice rose. 'I'll go, Parson.' Clearly, the mention of Lancelot's mother germinated feelings of subservience . He turned and began to step and stumble his way down the glebe.

When he was out of sight behind a green rise, Edward turned back to her. A gentle smile brightened his expression. 'I hope he did not frighten you, Mistress Sara.'

'He did for a few moments. But I'll get over it. Who is he?'

'Widow Parkinson's son - the village simpleton. Harmless. I cannot understand why he attacked you.'

'He was not the only person to attack me.'

'No? Was there someone else?'

'John Sprogg.'

Edward looked round. 'I cannot see him. Did he harm you?'

'No. But I harmed him.'

'*You* harmed *him?!* How?'

'I scratched his face. On both cheeks. He'll have scars for a few days!'

'Then he will be correctly served!' Edward chuckled. 'But where is he?'

'He went back down to the road. I saw him walking off in the direction of Christ Church.'

'It is not usual for either of these men to approach other women. At least, not so obviously!' He paused to smile. 'Perhaps it was the sight of your shapely body.'

She coloured at the compliment as he took her arm and subconsciously drew the sacking tighter about her. 'I must get my dress and put it back on.' she said.

Together they wandered back up to the bank of the pool. At the pool, they sat down side by side on a grassy knoll.

Sara's gaze wandered round at the outcrops of rock which gave the land a sense of tumbling undulation. For a few moments, both remained silent. But she was conscious of the occasional movement of his eyes towards her. Again she drew the sacking more tightly round her body in subconscious defence.

She was flattered by his interest. And when he spoke, he both overwhelmed and delighted her.

'Mistress Sara, I have something to tell you.'

Breathing in slight, shallow intakes, she turned to face him. 'Oh?' she croaked.

He nodded, averting his eyes. 'Yes. I want you to know that... I take a delight in your appearance... and indeed, in your entire presence... I have only known you for a few days, but I feel as if you have been here forever...'

She sensed what such an admission must have cost him. Yet his words created such excitement in her stomach that she felt suddenly weak. 'You are most gracious.' she croaked in a faltering semi-whisper.

His chest was visibly heaving. But not through the effort of running up the hill. He was much too fit and athletic for that.

She suspected that he had never before experienced the sensation of attraction to a young woman. Interest in the opposite sex was a new emotion to him. Something he had heard of but never experienced.

Absently she tugged the sacking tighter around her for a third time. Yet although it preserved her modesty, it covered only the area of her body from bust cleavage to mid-thigh. Her legs and shoulders remained exposed, reflecting the bright sunshine with softness and whiteness.

Normally, she would have felt very shy at being dressed this scantily in male company. But for a reason she could not explain, in the presence of Edward, such feelings were absent.

Nor did he seem embarrassed. A tranquil ease permeated his being and his relaxed smile reassured.

She was pleased at his lack of embarrassment. And all seemed perfectly natural. Ever since her forced entry to his house she had felt a growing warmth and regard for him. The more he talked, the greater grew her attraction to him.

'You know I have not yet taken a wife.'

She nodded.

''Tis not for want of offer.' he went on. 'I hope you will not think me unchivalrous. But there are several ladies of the district who from time to time have set their caps at me. Yet I have spurned them all. None have raised in me the fires of desire such as I believe must exist between man and wife. Until now. Now that I have met you, I realise that I have never met such a well-educated woman in my entire life. Your ideas are amazing, your accomplishments astonishing.' Suddenly his eyes widened. 'I trust I do not disconcert you, Mistress Sara?'

'I'm not disconcerted. On the contrary, I am very privileged to hear your intimate remarks, Edward.'

'I also find you a constant source of intrigue. I long to learn more of your country. More of the advances made there to which we may all look forward eventually. Indeed, when Mistress Connie is recovered, I wish to learn all you have to tell me. I thirst for knowledge of betterment for the people which we may all expect in future times.'

Her lips melted into a wisp of a smile. Raising her hands to cup them behind her head, she lay back beside him. She stretched out on the grassy mound while he continued to speak. Here was a man who aroused interest in her such as no Twentieth Century male had ever done!

She looked up at him, not surprised at the tears of desire which misted his eyes. *'Come on...'* she thought,

'Kiss me, for God's sake! Can't you see how much I want you!

In a reflex act of provocation she slowly raised one knee. The sacking slipped back a little until it only barely covered the most intimate areas of her body. She knew she was acting with out-of-character provocation. But she could not help herself, for by the telltale stirring in her upper thighs and the rock-hardness of her nipples she realised what was happening:

Despite the brevity of their acquaintance, she was falling in love with him.

But as she continued to endeavour to evoke a response, she sensed the reservation both of the age and his calling. She knew that if she wanted to make progress, she would have to prod him, to entice him, to snatch the fleeting chance fate had offered her.

She breathed in deeply as he looked down at her, her bust rising provocatively under the sacking. 'How attractive do you find me?' Her voice was a low, semi-whisper. She knew the question was brazen. Yet she was determined to grab her opportunity.

A lack of understanding flitted over his face. 'How can it be measured?'

'By actions.' She kept her voice low and sultry.

His breathing quickened yet further as he leaned over her. The deep brown of his eyes fixed hers in place. 'I' faith,' he whispered, 'I long to kiss you, Mistress Sara.'

She understood his dilemma and the rigidity of the moral code by which he lived. His eyes betrayed the inner conflict he was feeling. But despite this, she knew she must not let this moment slip away. Held by unbelievable excitement, she croaked a reply which seemed to be spoken by somebody else.

'Then kiss me.'

Slowly she raised her chin and unclasped her hands from behind her head. His face came close to hers. Her mouth opened slightly to receive his as softly their lips met.

But it was not the hard, passionate embrace she had expected. A gentle, tender touch caressed her. The subtlest of movements stirred sensations in extremes of her body before driving them on sublime highways along her limbs. The various passions collided at a massive complex in the centre of her body. They exploded into flames of the purest ecstasy.

Tremors sent waves of shock reverberating through her. She was gripped by such extremes of trembling that he mistook her shaking for shivering.

Pulling back, he asked, 'Are you cold, Mistress Sara?'

'Cold?' she croaked, completely dominated and in his power. 'No... not at all...'

This time, he did not ask. Once again his lips caused an avalanche. This restarted her trembling, exalting her to unscaled mountain peaks of bliss.

As he lifted back his head a second time, she spoke, yet again possessed by a superior being, words being spoken *for* rather than *by* her. 'Edward...' she whispered, seeking the intention behind his eyes, 'I've done the impossible... In two days, I've fallen in love with you...'

An expression of supreme joy remoulded his features. 'You do me a great honour, Mistress Sara! One which I delight in, for I believe I love you too.'

'I hope you mean it.'

'I never lie, Mistress Sara. I am true to my vocation. As from now on, I shall be true to you.'

For a moment longer, they lingered. Then she sat up. There was an urgent problem.

'You know I must take Connie home once she has recovered?'

He turned away from her to sit, hands clasped, elbows encircling hunched knees, gazing away towards the village. 'Yes. And when that happens, it will be a grievous day. Will you return to me after you deliver the maiden?'

Her face relaxed into a warm smile. 'Of course.' she almost whispered. 'As soon as Connie is safely in the care of an adult, I shall return.' Then she added, 'If I can.'

She sat up beside him, reaching forward with her hand to place it on his left forearm. Feeling the heat of his black jacket, she digressed. 'You must feel very warm?'

'I am. I envy your coolness.'

'I'm only cool because I went swimming in there.' She nodded to the pool.

'Would that I could join you.'

'Why don't you?'

'Mistress Sara! It would not be seemly for me to cast eyes on your nakedness. Or you on mine. Without us being wed!'

'Nobody will ever know.'

'God will know.'

'God will *understand*. And there is no *mortal* being to see us.'

Despite her arguments, he still hesitated. And on the ocean bed of her soul she knew that a little extra would be needed to persuade him.

Before even speaking, she had decided what she would do next. Now, feeling his eyes following her, she got to her feet and turned to face him. 'Whether or not you join me, I plan to re-enter the water.'

Through eyes which were unashamedly hot and desirous he watched. Without taking her eyes from his, she reached up with one hand to slacken the supporting fold of the sacking. Slowly, in a deliberate act of provocation, she peeled it away. It slipped from her shoulders, exposing the upper part of her perfect body. She held it at her waist for a brief moment before allowing it to fall, where it lay slumped in a crumpled heap round her ankles.

Now completely nude, she stood in front of him for a moment. Her hands were limp by her sides, one knee still slightly curved, her eyes continuing to peer deeply into his.

For a few moments, he sat wide-eyed and almost motionless. He seemed unable to breathe, his cheeks flushing hotly.

Meanwhile, she kept her face expressionless, her eyes remaining on his as they wandered over the perfect cones of her breasts, down to her thighs and up to her face. Apart from his eyes, his only movement was a quiet gulp as he drank in the overpowering attraction of the perfectly-proportioned Venus standing unashamedly in front of him.

At one point, he tried to snatch away his eyes. But clearly he found her attraction too strong. Without moving, she continued to allow him the luxury of gazing at the beauty of her nude body. Defeated, his eyes took on a life of their own as, with a face of deepening red, he continued to caress her with his vision. Timelessly, they stood, silent, not breathing, the atmosphere between them Heaven-sent.

Then, deliberately, she broke the spell. She allowed her eyes to broaden into a wide smile. With her arm she indicated the pool, still looking at him. 'Come and join me, Edward.'

'I' faith, Mistress Sara, you are the most beautiful creature on God's earth. I must confess that you are the first maiden on whose nakedness I have ever gazed in my life. But I cannot imagine any other surpassing your beauty. And now I know it. God *WILL* understand. Indeed, I do not believe that Our Lord would have sent you merely to play havoc with the deepest of my emotions!'

He began slipping out of his jacket, then undid his tunic buttons. Quickly he finished unbuttoning his white frill cuffs, and the front of. Slipping off his shirt and untied his long, dark hair which fell to his shoulders at both sides of his face. Finally, he slipped off his shoes before removing his long black trousers.

For a moment, they stood face to face, naked and unashamed, screened by tall bushes from the outside world as they gazed lovingly at one another. It gave Sara a wry satisfaction to see that he was unable to hide his interest from her.

'Come on!' she said. 'I'll race you to the bottom.'

Turning away, she dived into the pool. Looking up from underwater, she observed the surface disturbance as he followed her. He swam down towards her with long, easy strokes, seal-like in his agility.

They touched the gravel of the bottom almost at the same time. She reached forward to hug him quickly before, catching one another, they rose to the surface. Breaking through into the air, they trod water, tangled together, looking deeply into each other's eyes. Then she broke free, turned onto her back and paddled with her feet. He followed her across the pool about a yard behind.

With a deep breath, she turned onto her front and sped down to the bottom again. The second time he arrived close behind her. Now she wound her legs round his waist which even underwater she found solid and muscular, yet trim and without surplus flesh.

Locked in this liquid embrace, they allowed themselves to tumble over and over, thrust upwards by the force of water. And as they again broke surface, their lips remained glued together.

For ten minutes longer, they relaxed gleefully in the pool, all cares and worries subordinate to happiness. When finally they quit the water, splashing out of the shallows hand in hand, they walked the two or three yards over to where their discarded clothes lay in two neat piles. Sitting down side by side, they said nothing for a time as both looked over from the suntrap of the bush screen towards the Parsonage.

Then Edward spoke. 'In God's name, Mistress Sara.' he said, continuing to gaze away, 'we must wed. I cannot bear the thought of you leaving me.'

Despondently she shook her head. 'I must return Connie to her own country. Once I've done that, I shall come back.'

'Perhaps I should come with you? Your home sounds marvellous.'

She concealed her horror from him. She was unable to imagine Edward amongst the brash discourtesies of her own time. 'It would be better for me to come to you.'

'Will you be able to return?'

'I hope so...' she half-whispered. 'As I live and breathe, I hope so... Otherwise the rest of my life will be wasted...'

'Do you think you could tolerate the privations of Abbots Cross?'

She shot him a wistful glance. Then she looked out over the great expanse of luscious grass. A few shorthorn sheep stood lazily munching grass. Further over, cows contentedly chewed cud. She turned her look to the Parsonage in the wood. Wisps of smoke rose from the village cottages while the castle provided the final backdrop. Then she made a quick comparison with the plastic-chromed efficiency of the Twentieth Century, with its monochrome values and petty problems.

'In all honesty, My Darling Edward, I would rather spend a short lifetime here with you here than a thousand years back home.'

Once more their eyes interlocked. Her look of complete sincerity evoked an expression of longing on his face. Then she lay back in invitation and he leaned forward once more to meet her lips with his.

As he reached out to put his arm round her back, he inadvertently brushed against the hard nipple of her naked breast. At once he pulled back in dismay. 'Oh - Mistress Sara - I am sorry!' he stammered in horror.

Her mouth widened into a reassuring smile. 'Don't be!' she said.

He leaned forward to lay his right hand on her left breast, touching her with such delicacy that rivers of fire burned their way tinglingly and quickly to her feet and back again, burning and scorching on the way. He pressed forward with his mouth, finding the nape of her neck, his lips scorching a passage across and under her chin as she relaxed completely in his power, arching her back and raising her head to look up at the cloudless blue of the summer sky.

Slowly shaking her head back and forward, she waited while his hand moved between her breasts, playing with the pebble nipples - first one, then the other. She found herself sinking, drowning in a sea of ecstasy as his hand slowly moved down from her cleavage, sliding with unbelievable delicacy over her firm, flat stomach, coming gently to rest on the milky white lower abdomen and finally moving to caress her pubic mound with an incredible lightness of touch.

She waited, breath held, preparing to receive him in the final act of love. But to her intense disappointment, he made no move towards consummation. 'Go on... Go on...' she pleaded, whimpering beneath closed eyelids as with unbearable disappointment she began to realise that he was stopping - that he would go no further. Reopening disappointed eyes, she turned her face to look at him in surprise as he raised his head to look at her, taking his hand from her body.

'What is it?'

He turned to sit up, facing away across the luscious grass. 'Mistress Sara, I cannot go on unless we wed. It would be no more than an act of lust. I do not condone concupiscence in others and cannot permit myself what I deny them.'

'But Edward, things between us are different! We're a special case! In the sight of God--'

'In the sight of God we would be as guilty of lasciviousness as anyone else! For me to have carnal knowledge of you before marriage would be a great sin.'

'Edward--'

'Please, Mistress Sara, forgive me. I love you more than I thought it possible to love any woman. But I am forbidden by God and the nature of my profession to consummate our love. That *must* wait until we wed. Meanwhile, I shall retain the memory of your beautiful body. And if you be unable to return to me, the knowledge of your love shall sustain me through the long dark years that may lie ahead without you, even though it will be as if you had died.'

Sara realised the pointlessness of prolonging the argument. 'Then once Connie has been taken back, I must return if it be in any way possible. Then we shall wed.'

'You are the first woman I ever loved, Mistress Sara. The first, and the last. If I wed not you, I shall not wed at all.'

For a moment their eyes met, then he turned away and looked up towards the sky. 'The sun is well up. I think it as well if we go back.'

She smiled, scrambling to her feet, quite unashamed of her nakedness. She picked up Edward's mother's dress and slipped it over her head and shoulders. He pulled his own clothes over his now-cool body which had completely dried in the hot sun.

Slipping feet into shoes, Sara picked up soap, sacking and other clothes. Then, together, they started to make their way down the soft springiness of the virgin turf.

'Take my hand, Mistress Sara. Lest you fall.'

She held out her hand and he took it in his. But she knew the handclasp was not for protection. It was an expression of his love. And as they wandered towards the wood, she knew that whatever the future brought, this love would be forever.

They retraced their way back down the hill, feet lightly springing on the soft turf. Once through the wood, across the creek and through the vegetable plots, they arrived back at the Parsonage.

Now she was convinced. Were it not for her concern about Connie and Rose's daughter, she could happily spend the rest of her life in this place and in this Century. She belonged here! She could feel it! The freedom from crowds, the absence of extraneous noise on the roads and in the air, the unpolluted clarity of the atmosphere - all led to a sense of peace which Sara found soothingly delightful.

Happily, she and Edward re-entered the Parsonage. But once inside, Sara realised that something was amiss. The glowering expression which greeted both Edward and herself confirmed it.

'What is it, James?' Edward asked. 'What's happened?'

'Rose's daughter, Parson.' he answered in a low voice. 'She began to sink shortly after you left.'

Sara grimaced sadly. 'I should have gone to her!' she exclaimed. 'I shall go immediately and give her a pill.' Then, noting his askance look, she asked, 'How sick is she?'

James averted his eyes. 'She be dead,' he said sorrowfully, 'And to make things worse, Rose now also has the foul pestilence upon her.'

Sara looked away, stricken with remorse. 'Why didn't I go at once?!' she demanded of herself. 'I might have saved her. At least I could have tried!'

'Is Rose likely to recover?' she heard Edward ask, and turned to look at James with a heart which feared the answer.

James shook his head sagely. 'I doubt it, Parson, I doubt it very much.' Then, as Sara hung her head in dejection, he commented, 'John Sprogg, Rose's husband, is nearly demented.'

'Was Lizbeth their only child?'

Edward shook his head. 'No. He has one other - older than Lizbeth, - a grown son, but Lizbeth was his favourite.'

'Will there be a funeral?'

Edward cast a heavy gaze at her. 'There will, Mistress Sara.' he said. 'There will be a funeral on the morrow. Indeed, now I must go to the Sproggs, for they will be in sore need of comfort. After that, I shall prepare for the Funeral Service at which Missy Lizbeth will be despatched to the Lord...'

James added, 'And I think Rose will not be long in following!'

Overwhelmed by a deep sympathy for the Sprogg family, particularly Rose, Sara knew what she had to do.

'I'll go to her.' she said. 'Perhaps I can help.'

James' face contorted in consternation. 'It would be unwise, Mistress Sara.' he said hastily.

'Unwise? Why?'

'John Sprogg believes you responsible for his daughter's death.' He hung his head as if feeling he had spoken out of turn. 'Nonetheless,' he continued. 'T'would be unwise to go while Rose lies sick.'

'But - perhaps I can help.'

'I fear for you, Mistress Sara.'

'Very well. Thank you, James.' Then she asked, 'How is Connie?'

'Much the same, Mistress Sara.' said the tall servant. 'I have left Daisy to sit with her.'

'Daisy?'

James smiled with some reverence. 'Yes, Mistress. Daisy is the daughter of one of the local farmers. She works at the parsonage from time to time.'

'Is she not afraid of catching plague?'

James shook his head. 'I have given her my assurance that the time of danger is past.'

Sara was curious. 'And she was ready to accept that?'

'She was, Mistress. '

'Daisy must have a great amount of trust in you, James.' As she spoke, Sara noticed the slightest hint of a reddening in James' complexion.

'Well... to be truthful, Mistress... I think she... she...'

Edward helped him out. 'I think she casts a favourable eye on James.' Edward said with a wry smile.

Sara smiled widely. 'Is that so, James?'

Now the reddening was definitely there. 'I... er... believe so, Mistress...' he stammered.

Sara turned to Edward. 'I'll go up to Connie.'

'I shall come with you before I visit Sprogg's cot.'

As he followed in a dread silence contrasting dramatically with the recent mood at the poolside, she led the way to Connie's bedroom. On opening the door, Sara saw a girl of about sixteen sitting beside the bed. She wore an ankle-length, full-skirted black dress and a white dustcap.

'Thank you, Daisy.' said Edward.   'You may go now.'

As she rose, Sara noticed her hourglass figure, fashionable at the time. Full bosomed and cow-eyed, her large bust and wide hips were emphasised by the narrowing of her waist with a band.

With a slight bob of a curtsey, Daisy scurried past and away while Sara went over to look at her cousin. The stench of the yellow discharge was still nauseating.

'I'll clean her down.' she said.

Occasionally, a moan escaped from Connie's lips, and clearly, her eyeballs were busy under closed lids. The flushed face, the deep red of her cheeks, the bloated tongue with which she kept licking her lips, were all symptoms of the desperate illness which continued to grip her.

Yet there were still no capillary bursts.   Sara's hopes that she may yet conquer the ravages of the plague continued to flicker.

'I hope she may pull through - with luck...' said Sara

'With God's help!' Edward added.

'And the assistance of some medicine!'

'The medical care in your country must be greatly advanced. A potion to cure the plague! Who would have thought it?'

Sara smiled. 'There are other scourges in my time of which you cannot dream! Be thankful you are spared them!' Then a sobering thought plunged her into an agony of self-recrimination. 'Would to God I had attended Rose's daughter! My pills might have saved her from the plague.'

'Your pills might yet save Rose Sprogg!'

Sara's eyes lit up. 'That's right!' she agreed, then sprang into action. 'Forget Connie's bedbath.' she told him. 'If you will sit with Connie for a short while, I shall go to Rose straight away.'

'But, Mistress Sara! John Sprogg--'

She ignored Edward's warning - and that of James. 'I have no time either to argue with you, Edward. Nor to worry about John Sprogg.'

Sara hurried over to the window. Holding up the large brown bottle to the light streaming through the window, she examined the contents. 'I think there will be enough pills in the bottle.' she calculated.

She was already moving towards the door when Edward stopped her. 'Mistress Sara...' he tried again. 'I... I doubt if that is wise. Perhaps I should attend Rose?'

Sara glanced at him obliquely. 'Because of John Sprogg?' she asked. 'I'd rather risk his wrath to save Rose's life than let her die!'

She held up the pill bottle again. 'Plenty of pills in here! I'll give Rose one straight away.'

'Will it act instantly?'

'Speedily.' She turned towards the door. 'Which house is Sprogg's?'

''Tis the cot below the Inn.'

'I'll go now. With luck, we'll yet save Rose's life.'

* * * *

Hurriedly, Sara left the Parsonage and, clutching the bottle, she half-ran down the drive towards the village. Breathing heavily, she crossed the main cartroad, and half tripping, half running, made her way amongst the dry ruts of the dusty mud-track to the cottage next to the red-bricked inn.

Arriving breathlessly at the door, she raised her fist. Banging on the stout door, she stood back to wait impatiently. The sound of footsteps approaching sounded from the inside the cot.

'Who is it?'

The words were called in the deep bass of a male voice from the other side of the closed door.

'Open the door!' Sara mustered as commanding a tone as she could. Her haste was feverish. Time was a precious commodity.

'A pestilent gangrene is in the house. Its foul talons have already taken my daughter. Now it grips my wife!'

'Open the door!' repeated Sara. 'I have a remedy that will *CURE* your wife!'

A short silence. 'A remedy?'

'Yes.'

After a few more seconds, the door began to creak as the bolts were worked aside. The door was swung slowly inwards.

Sara hesitated. The figure confronting her was that of the short, stocky thug who had confronted her at the glebe. He glared at Sara from a weather-tanned, ugly-jowled face.

'What do you want here?'

Sara gulped, a little disconcerted, strangely threatened by the man whose wife she had come to treat.

'I have a pill which may cure your wife.' she repeated, speaking with unintentional timidity.

157

'Are *you* the visitor to the Parsonage?'

'Yes. I am Sara. Let me see Rose at once.'

Sprogg hesitated. His wide eyes were clouded with understandable suspicion. As she waited, he decided, nodded, and wordlessly stood aside.

Entering quickly, Sara hastily glanced round the candle-lit damp-smelling gloom of a two-roomed hovel in search for a bed. The first impression to hit Sara was the smell of wringing damp. The walls, once white, now stained and lined with soot and black from dark, dirty rivulets. The straw which lined the floor had not been changed for some time. At one end a baretoothed mongrel dog growled at Sara as she went past.

Beside a pallet in a corner stood a young man of perhaps sixteen. He looked down at the figure for whom she searched. The wood-ash, dank smell of the dark hovel mingled with the same pungent odour of Connie's bedroom. But intermingled with the mustiness was a rancidity which wafted through from an entry in the side wall. Glancing across at this opening, Sara realised that the adjoining room was not a bedroom. It was a cow-byre.

Although appalled at the unhygienic arrangement, Sara took care that the men in the room should not detect her revulsion. Instead, she directed her full attention at the bundle on the bed.

She began to examine Rose. Thankfully, like Connie, Rose's face did not bear roses, so that Sara's visit was not yet futile.

Sara turned and spoke to the silent figure of John Sprogg. He stood behind her, gazing down in wonder. 'I'm sorry for your daughter, Goodman Sprogg,' she said, 'but I hope I am not too late to save Rose.'

'How can *you* save her?' He spoke the words with exaggerated scorn.

'With *these!*' She produced the dark brown pill-bottle and held it up to the disdainful eyes.

Sprogg took the bottle with reverential care, pinching it between two gnarled fingers. Holding it up, he examined it in the semi-darkness with cynical disbelief. He passed it to the young man.

'Pills!' he scorned. 'I've heard of empirics, quacks and astrologers with their 'infallible' preventative pills against plague and corruption of the air! I may as well buy hellish philtres and charms and other trumpery as have Rose take these!' He half-turned away, displaying his disgust.

Sara shook her head. 'Without these pills, Rose will certainly die. I am not asking for money. I only wish to cure your wife!'

Sprogg paused to think before turning to the young man. 'What do *you* think, Luke?'

Luke pursed his lips. 'I doubt if they will work, Father.' Grief lent the young voice an unsavoury rasp.

Sprogg handed the bottle back to Sara.

'If these pills will save my wife,' he asked, 'then why did you not save my precious Lizbeth with them?'

Sara shook her head. 'I was too late.'

'Too late?!'

Sara nodded. 'Had I realised the urgency, I would have come here to administer to her.' She paused. Her voice was thick with regret. Then she added brightly, 'But I hope I can save Rose.' She looked directly at him. His grief was a crushing burden. 'You've nothing to lose.' she added.

He looked at her with searching distrust. Then he turned to Luke. The lad nodded slightly.

Sprogg looked back at Sara. 'Very well.' he whispered.

Rose's troubled delirium was similar to Connie's. Sara put her arm round Rose's neck and raised the head on her arm. She fingered the pill onto Rose's swollen tongue. With an earthen cup, she administered the smallest possible amount of water to wash down the pill.

Gently lowering Rose back, Sara turned to the others. She had one more thing to do before returning to the Parsonage.

'Where is Lizbeth's body?'

Sprogg raised tear-filled eyes and spoke in a croak. 'Out in the barn!'

'Did *you* carry her there?'

'Aye! Alone.'

'How is she dressed?'

'In swaddling, ready to go to her last rest.'

'Not in a coffin?'

'A coffin, Mistress? Do you think I be a yeoman? A coffin be eight pence to buy!'

'Aye,' joined in Luke. 'Swaddling be only *SIX* pence.'

Sara ignored the economics of the impending burial. 'Where are Connie's clothes?'

'In a corner of the barn where Lizbeth presently lies.'

'Then leave them there if you value your lives!' she warned forcibly. 'Later they can be burned - or boiled.

They must not be touched before then.' Her voice lowered. 'I must go. Pray to God I am not too late to save Rose!'

'I wish to God you had never come to this village in the first place!' Sprogg's tone festered with deep-felt anger. 'I wish to God you had stayed away - and kept the pestilence with you!'

Sara had no answer. She turned to the door. As she quit the cottage, Sara had the suspicion that both John and Luke Sprogg were watching her. She sensed their deep, fiery resentment. And as, in full depression, she made her way back up the empty street, she was conscious of being followed by other, unseen eyes.

Chapter 10

Sara entered the Parsonage. A worried Edward stood in the entrance, pacing up and down on the rock stone floor.

His face lit up with recognition at her entry.

'Thank Goodness you're back, Mistress Sara' he said. 'I fear that Constance has taken a turn for the worse---'

Deafened by her own frantic apprehension, Sara heard no more. Leaving him standing in the entrance hall, she took the stairs two at a time. She sprinted along to Connie's room. The door was open. As she raced in, she was shocked by the sight.

The bed was empty.

Sara turned. She shot out of the bedroom into the ante-room to search frantically. But the ante-room was also empty.

Wasting no time, she turned in near-panic and sped back through the bedroom. As she ran out onto the landing, she hurtled with full momentum into the robust figure of Edward. It was like colliding with a brick wall.

'Where is she?' Sara screamed.

'I left her in bed...' Eyes wide with concern, Edward poked his head into the bedroom. He gaped at the empty bed. 'Why... Mistress Sara...' he stammered, '...she was here only a minute ago... I only left her when I heard you coming back... She was very ill of the pestilence--'

He was interrupted. From the far end of the landing, came a shout. A scream of pain reverberated along the corridor.

Sara recognised the voice. 'Connie!!!' she yelled frantically, setting off in the direction of the scream.

Sara and Edward banged open each of the oaken doors to the landing rooms in turn as they carried out a frantic search. Both moved with a frenetic speed which underscored the urgency of finding Connie before the comatic girl injured - or killed - herself.

At the end of the landing, Sara came upon a closet. As she burst open the door, she allowed a huge sigh of relief to escape. Connie half-lay, half-leaned on a bench alongside the wall. She moaned irrationally, out of her senses. Sickly sweet-smelling vomit lay in a spreading pool on the floor beside her. 'Mum... mum...!!' she was shouting over and over in soulless sobs.

'Connie!' Sara moved quickly forward. She put an arm round the small waist and tugged. But as she was about to lift the girl, Edward stopped her.

'Allow me, Mistress Sara.'

The strong arms of Edward Makepeace reached past her to pick Connie up. Sweeping her easily into his arms, he turned to make his way back to Connie's bedroom.

Connie's moaning grew louder. As she tried to fight against Edward, her arms and legs thrashed in a fever of high intensity. Her busy eyes opened and closed constantly.

Because of her struggles, the Parson had some difficulty with her. Even after he had laid her onto her bed, Connie continued to flail in wild agitation. Arms and legs continued like a windmill. Her head moved hurriedly from side to side on the pillow. The process reminded Sara more of an epileptic fit than anything else.

Sara leaned forward to place a palm on Connie's brow. Connie was not only hot - she was at a temperature beyond anything Sara had previously experienced.

'My God!!' she exclaimed. 'We *HAVE* to cool her down!'

She turned to look at Edward whose eyes looked appealingly out of worried features.

'We'll wash her.' said Sara as James came into the room. She was unable to think of anything else. 'Bring as cold a water as you can find, James.'

James bowed sedately and hurried away. He was back in a minute, the wooden bucket full to the brim. He deposited the bucket, then left.

Sara found two cloths in the ante-room. She dipped each of them into the cool liquid. Placing one across Connie's brow, she lifted Connie's head and placed the other in a knot behind the neck.

The odour had returned. But it was not so nauseous as before. And although the young body was once more slippery with abundant sweat, the yellowness was much less evident. The roses were still absent.

'I will attend to her, Edward.' Sara said. 'I want to get her temperature down. If we can keep her cool, she'll have a chance. Meanwhile, I'll give her another pill.'

It was now two hours since the previous capsule. And although to administer another would be to stretch the dose beyond adult maximum, Sara preferred to risk an overdose than try to fight the disease without medicinal help. Once done, she turned to Edward.

'There is no need to stay, Edward. I know you have many things to do.'

He nodded. 'I have. Now I shall prepare for the funeral.'

He approached her as she stood facing him. 'Mistress Sara, I want you not to blame yourself for spread of the sicknesse.' he told her solemnly. ''Tis no fault of yours.'

Feeling her lower lip tremble, she moved slowly towards him. Softly, he placed a kiss on her forehead, then clasped her arms round his neck. She reached up to embrace him on the cheek. She continued to hold him for a moment, then relaxed her arms, and stood back.

'I shall return later.' Edward told her. Then without another word, he left.

Sara sat down to keep vigil. She continued to sponge and wipe Connie's forehead. The disease racking the sixteen-year-old figure was a distressing sight. But Sara tried to be as objective as possible in her fight. Periodically she administered another pill, knowing she continued to risk exceeding the limit of the adult dose, but deciding it was a risk worth taking.

Come dusk, the fever seemed to start to wane. Connie's sleep drifted towards more rest and less disturbance. The constant thrashing gradually died. The temperature seemed to have peaked.

Late in the evening, a tap came to the door. Sara's body involuntarily relaxed in pleasure. Edward had returned.

'I think Connie is a bit better.' Sara told him, looking at her watch. 'And now it is hours since I saw the Sprogg family. I must visit Rose again.'

'Very well. I shall stay here until you return.'

Leaving Connie in Edward's care, Sara started on her way down the drive to the village, making sure she had the bottle of pills with her. Picking her way carefully down Village Street in the deepening twilight, she reached the Sprogg house, and raised her fist to bang on the door.

'Who is it?' called the voice of John Sprogg from inside.

'It's me - Sara Goodwin.'

'Go away - witch! And take your foul pills with you!'

The response was unexpected. 'What is it?' she called back in surprise.

'So much for pills and potions!' she heard him shout. 'A second death will occur at any time. Then Rose will join our daughter in Paradise!' As his words came, the door was flung open to reveal a grief-demented figure.

But Sara took little notice of him. Brushing past, she hurried into the dark interior. She looked down at

Rose as she lay on the straw pallet. There was little light. It was impossible to see the invalid properly.

Looking round, Sara saw one dim candle standing on a table. Picking it up, she brought it over so that she could see Rose more clearly by its light.

Sara caught her breath sharply. By the flickering yellow glow, rings seemed to have arrived on Rose's cheeks.

The interior of the hovel swirled in Sara's dismay. 'Oh...' moaned Sara. 'Oh... My God!!...'

'Do not besmirch the Lord's name with your foul tongue, Wench!' Sprogg reacted venomously. 'Had it not been for *YOU*, this sicknesse would not now be in our midst!'

Sara had no answer. What Sprogg said was true. She should never have brought Connie here in the first place. If only the clock could be turned back! Or was it forward?

Bewildered, Sara was unable to say anything of comfort. As John Sprogg continued to rave, she bent down, raising Rose's head from the pillow to place another pill on the swollen tongue before administering a minimum of water in a last despairing effort to save her.

Once done, Sara replaced the semi-sleeping head gently before turning away to make her way from the cottage. Behind her was a man who, two days earlier, had enjoyed both wife and children. His happiness was now destroyed. His beloved daughter lay dead. His wife was about to join her.

No wonder Sprogg resented and hated Sara. No wonder he looked at her with eyes of fury. Search as she might, she could find no excuse.

But Sara sensed there was an additional dimension to Sprogg's anger. In a time of complete male domination, for a woman to have not only spurned his advances, but to have fought back and left scars was a dent to his manhood which he probably found unbearable. He was going to be an enemy from now on!

Burdened with self-recrimination, Sara made her fatigued way up Village Street to the crossroads, and thence to the parsonage. Wearily climbing the staircase, Sara cursed herself - bitterly. Why hadn't she burned Connie's plague-infested clothes *herself*?! It would have been only a few minutes' task to take them outside and set fire to them. Then the plague would certainly have been stopped.

But she'd asked Rose to do it. Now Lizbeth was dead and Rose struck down. And apart from her forlorn attempt to cure Rose, she could do nothing to atone.

Edward shot a querulous glance across Connie's bed as she dolefully entered the room. 'What is it, Mistress Sara?' he asked, getting to his feet.

'Rose is near death.' The words came out in a croak of despair.

Edward came round the bed and placed a comforting arm on her shoulders. 'Blame not yourself.' he said softly.

Sara smiled up in recognition of his attempt to console her. But she continued to feel the weight of responsibility deeply. She moved away, and sat down on the stool at the side of the bed. Then, suddenly, she slumped forward to bury her head in her arms. 'Oh... Edward...' she moaned through desperate tears, 'It's my fault. I did it. I brought the plague. I am responsible.'

'You could not have known.' he said, bending down to touch her gently once more. 'Think no more about it.'

His cleanliness as he stood near her contrasted greatly with the sweat-laden body odours of John Sprogg, Lancelot Parkinson and the other villagers. She covered his hand on her shoulder with hers, and gently kissed his fingers with affection. Her love for him blossomed with each meeting.

'Your forgiveness is most chivalrous.' she said, turning to look up at him.

'The Lord will forgive.' he said, moving to sit beside her on the edge of the bed. 'So why should I not?'

Sara nodded.   She would never fail to have reservations about the complete faith of the Seventeenth Century in a true and just God.

Then, looking down at Connie, she instantly thought of Lizbeth Sprogg. 'I shall attend Lizbeth's funeral tomorrow.' she said, almost to herself.

Edward's mouth opened, and he gasped. 'I doubt the wisdom of *that!*' he said.

She nodded. 'Whether it's wise or not,' she answered stubbornly, 'I must be ready to face the hostility of the people I have wronged.'

'But - Mistress Sara - You may find yourself in danger.'

'Danger?' She looked back up at him, now standing beside her. 'What danger??'

'The fear of the people that they might be next to succumb to sicknesse.   That has made them resent you. Unjustly, in my opinion.'

'I'm aware of their hostility. Yet whatever they think of me, I shall go. John Sprogg may take comfort from that act of penitence.'

'Very well...' Edward spoke dubiously. 'I shall ask James to sit here while we are at Lizbeth Sprogg's funeral.'

Sara looked up sharply. 'There is no need---' she began, then stopped. She had been going to complete the sentence with '---for you to attend just because I am going.' but she stopped herself. Of course he would be going! As Parson of Abbots Cross, he would conduct the funeral service.

As he rose to leave, he said, 'Now I shall go to the Sprogg house to offer what consolation I can.'

* * * *

Two hours passed.

To stay awake all during another night was going to be impossible for her. This would be yet another night without complete sleep. She was beginning to pay the penalty for several nights' lack of rest.

For an hour, Sara sat guard over Connie. Her sleep was now much more restful, much less of a delirium. For the first time, Sara began to feel hope.

But she also felt an overwhelming tiredness.

She looked at her watch. She had been in Connie's bedroom now for just over two hours. But the time had been elongated and stretched by fatigue. She wondered if Edward would relieve her again for a time tonight as he had done previously.

Sitting on her stool, Sara cast hopeful glances towards the door from time to time. She hoped to hear his solid knock, see his tall form come in.

But she dismissed the thought. He had much on his mind tonight. And despite his professed love for her, she knew that his concept of honour meant that duty would come first no matter how great his affection for her, or how great her need for him.

Yet when the tap finally came to the door, Sara woke up with a start. 'Without intending to, she had drifted off into a doze.

Sitting up, she coughed nervously. 'Come in, Edward!'

But it was not Edward's figure, nor the tall form of James which appeared in the opened doorway. Daisy was carrying a candle and bobbed a curtsey as she came in. 'Good Evening, Mistress. James and I will be taking turn about to oversee the sick maiden tonight.'

'Why, Daisy, that is most welcome. Did the Parson send you?'

'No, Mistress, 'twas James' idea.' Daisy closed the room door behind her. 'He wants me to stay until the middle of the night. Then he will come and remain for the rest of tonight. He is asleep now and will remain thus until he comes to take over from me.'

'You will be fatigued tomorrow.'

'James says I may sleep until I am fully rested. I shall probably not rise until mid morning.'

'What about Parson Makepeace?'

'Parson Makepeace has not yet returned from the Sprogg house. He plans to keep vigil over Rose Sprogg for a time. He may not come back at all tonight.'

'I see...' Sara turned to look down at Connie's peaceful form. 'Connie is improving, I think. Her temperature has gone down a lot. She should give you no trouble. She has stopped being sick now, and may awaken tomorrow. You'll probably be able to sleep a little in the chair.'

'Certainly, Mistress Sara. James told me to say that your room is on the other side of the landing. The bed is prepared for you.'

'Which room?'

'Oh - I do not rightly know, Mistress. 'Tis the second or third along.'

Sara got to her feet. 'I'll find it.' she said, adding, 'You are most kind, Daisy.'

Daisy curtseyed again and came forward to take her place beside Connie on a chair. She handed Sara the candle in passing. 'You will need to see your way to your new room.' she added.

'Is there a night-dress?' Sara asked.

'Why, Mistress, I am sorry. I do not know.'

'Oh, well, it's a warm night. I need not wear anything--'

'Oh - Mistress!'

Sara shot Daisy a sharp glance, to see the shocked look on the servant's face. 'What is it, Daisy?'

'Why... Mistress... not to wear *anything*...'

Sara smiled. 'Don't worry, Daisy, I won't freeze to death unclothed in bed tonight!' she joked.

But Daisy's expression made her disapproval plain. Yet she made no comment. 'No, Mistress...' she murmured.

Sara turned and made her way out of the bedroom. Her candle flickered against the polished wood of the panelled walls along the landing.

She ignored the first door, then tried the second. She entered the room, but inside, the bed was not prepared for use.

Closing the door, she entered the next room. There all was ready for habitation. Maids had prepared the bed. This must be it.

Sara closed the door, and laid the candle on a writing bureau which occupied one corner of the room.

The room was not unlike Connie's bedroom, but if anything, it was a little bigger, and had the appearance of rather more use. In addition to the desk, a wardrobe filled another corner. A stand for clothes stood beside a small table behind the door. The casement curtains stood open.

Sara quickly pulled Edward's mother's dress over her head and hung it onto the tall hanging stand behind the door.

Completely exhausted, she noted the position of the bed, snuffed out the candle and in complete darkness, lifted the covers, getting into bed at once. The bed was neither too warm nor too cold. Sara's nudity was unimportant. Happily, she laid her head on the pillow.

To Sara's surprise, the linen on bedclothes was not pleasant to her skin, but coarse and uncomfortable. And as she laid her head on the feather pillow, she became aware that it was untreated, and smelt of wild duck. Furthermore, the feather stalks began scratching as soon as she was into the bed, and in addition, the feather mattress was very uncomfortable.

She recalled as a child staying with a great aunt whose beds had feather pillows. She recalled that although soft, they were purgatory. Little feathers worked their way through and scratched the sleeper's face all the time. This bed was like that, and she thought, *this bed is foul!*

Then, realizing what she had said, she chortled merrily. Foul? Or Fowl? she thought ticklishly. And despite the shortcomings of the bed, within a minute, she had fallen into a deep, refreshing sleep.

Chapter 11

Closing his book which he had been reading by the light of a single candle, Edward looked down at Rose Sprogg. The sick servant lay unmoving except for the gentle rise and fall of her bosom as she breathed. She had not moved so far this night. Thankfully, her plague had not worsened.

Getting up from his stool, Edward moved over to the corner. John Sprogg snored heavily there, his body supported by straw which had not been changed for several days. Edward had persuaded him that the son who still lived with them should not stay the night in the house lest he catch the pestilence.

Reaching down, Edward shook the shoulder. By the soft yellow of the rush lamp's glow, the scratches Sara had inflicted on Sprogg were clearly visible. 'Wake up, John, wake up!'

'Ger off, Rose... Geraway, woman!!'

"Tis not your wife, John, 'tis Parson Makepeace!' Edward held the candle near the sleep-laden, deeply scratched face, wondering if he dared leave Rose in his drunken keeping tonight. But Edward reminded himself that Sara also needed to be relieved of *her* vigil. He should return to the Parsonage before too long so that Sara could get some sleep.

He shook Sprogg's again-sleeping figure. 'Come on, John, wake up! This be Parson Makepeace speaking!!'

'Ugh... ugh...' One bloodshot eyelid raised and Sprogg's eyes began to roll into wakefulness. 'Oh... 'tis you, Parson Makepeace...'

'Aye, John, 'tis me. Now wake up. I must be off home. There are others sick this night.'

Sprogg sat up and snorted disapproval. 'They deserve to die. They brought the plague here. Little Lizbeth would still be alive had they not come.'

'Rose should have burned the dress, John.'

''Twas too fine a dress to commit to flame, Parson Makepeace. She had it in a sack ready to burn it, but I told her not to. I wanted it for Lizbeth.'

'Then 'tis you who are guilty, none other. Lizbeth caught plague from the dress.'

'Tosh, Parson! She caught it from speaking to the wench with the black hair and the fair skin.'

'You are mistaken, John, but I cannot stay and argue further. I have other things to do. Rose sleeps well. I think you will not be disturbed this night.'

Leaving John Sprogg sitting on the straw, rubbing his eyes awake, Edward moved over to the door, yellow in the flame of the rush lamp, and moved out into the night.

Thankfully, the moon was just past the full. The way back to the Parsonage along the deep-rutted track was well enough moonlit for him to walk without stumbling. He knew that in honour he should try to relieve Sara from her task. But he also suspected that a desire to meet with and talk to her again played a large part in his hurry to leave John Sprogg's cottage and return to the Parsonage.

Silver moonlight picked out the ribbon of the drive as Edward walked towards the large house. Its dark shroud of trees contrasted with the stonework, unreal in the lunar glow. Climbing the steps, Edward pushed open the unlocked front door. Inside, a single candle burned a welcome glow on a corner table in the entrance hall. Closing the door quietly behind him so as not to awaken the household, Edward made his way across the flagstones of the hall. Taking care to make as little noise as possible, he climbed the stairs. The single candle in one hand flickered a soft yellow onto the ornate carvings of the balustrade.

He reached the top and with anticipated pleasure, moved softly towards the room in which Connie still lay sick. Tapping lightly with the back of his knuckles on the door, he leaned down on the handle to push it open.

Inside, another lighted candle doubled the glow from his own. By it he could see Sara sitting on the stool, her head leaning forward to rest on folded arms lying on the bed. Edward wondered why she had decided to put on a dustcap as he moved forward to touch her lightly on the shoulder.

'Mistress Sara... Mistress Sara...' he whispered softly.

The figure stirred, and the head looked up. 'Oh - Parson Makepeace!'

He started back in surprise as Daisy sat back on the stool, gathering her sleep-laden senses. She rose to her feet with a quick curtsey.

'Please - don't get up, Daisy.' he said. 'But what are you doing here?'

'James thought that you might want to stay at John Sprogg's house all night, Parson. He thought that Mistress Sara might not be able to stay awake on her own, she being greatly fatigued after the last two nights. James suggested that I stay the night here and take turn about looking after Missy Connie.'

Edward nodded. 'I understand. Have you told your mother that you will not be home tonight?'

'Aye, Parson.'

'Is she happy about that?'

'Aye, Parson. She is happier for me to be here than in the village - there being plague an' all...'

Edward silently cursed John Sprogg. His drunken tongue had wagged in the Kings Arms! 'Then would you like to go off to bed now?'

'Parson, I may get into trouble from James should I leave you in my place.'

'I see.'

'Besides, James has said to me that you yourself will be tired and that you should get as much rest as possible, there being the funeral tomorrow an' all.'

Edward smiled to himself. 'Very well, Daisy. That is kind. I shall see you in the morning.'

'Thank you, Sir.' The young girl sat down again on the stool.

As Edward turned to leave he hesitated at the door. 'Oh - Daisy - what about Mistress Sara? Where is she?'

'She be in a room at the end of the landing.' She raised a bare arm to point.

'Goodnight, Daisy.'

'Goodnight, Sir.'

Edward tiptoed along to his room door. Gently pushing down on the catch he went in. The door closed silently behind him. Conscious of the creaking floorboards and the noise they made when walked on, he was as quiet as possible so as not to wake the sleeping beauty in the end room.

Softly, he slipped off his jacket. He moved over to the wardrobe, where he opened the door and hung it inside. Slipping out of the rest of his clothes and shoes, he deposited them in their correct places.

Completely nude, he extinguished the candle and made over to his bed. Pulling back the wide covers, he reached under his pillow for his night-shirt, then stopped. In the balm of the summer heat, he was already too warm! The night-shirt would be no more than an encumbrance!

Changing his mind, he slipped into bed unclad. But as he pulled the covers over his naked body, a movement in the bed beside him startled him into sudden vigilance.

'What?... Who?...' stammered a sleeping voice.

Exhaling deeply, he allowed his face to relax into a broad smile in the darkness as he recognised the voice.

'Mistress Sara...' he whispered.

As Sara turned over to snuggle against his body, her arm laid across his broad chest while her breasts cushioned against his ribcage.

'Mistress Sara...' he began in a whisper, 'Mistress Sara... You cannot stay here!' Unwilling to move because of her nearness, and because of his reluctance to wake her, he turned only his head and looked longingly and lingeringly at her by the faint glow of moonlight streaming through the diamond panes of the casement.

She was in the depths of a sound, refreshing sleep. He knew she desperately needed this rest after the irregular pattern of sleep during the previous two nights.

'Mistress Sara!   You cannot stay here!' he whispered again, raising the sound hoarsely. But she was much too deeply asleep to take notice. 'Mmm... Edward...' she mumbled, '...I love you...'

He realised she was dreaming and felt a thrill of ecstasy that her dreams were about him. And as he gazed at the soft silkiness of her abundant dark hair spreading over her head now lying on his chest, he fleetingly wondered if he should extricate himself and move to the room next door.

But their bodies were much too closely intertwined for him to easily untangle himself from her. He tried a couple of times, but each time, she merely snuggled to him yet closer, and escape was that much more difficult.

As he turned over to face her, she cuddled him closer, gripping him tightly.   Resigned to remaining with her for a time, he lightly moved his arm across her body, clutching her to him.

Her delicate skin was gossamer to his touch.   The bouquet which arose from her thick, well-groomed tresses sent a flood of desire through his body on an orgy of awakening passion. Lightly, he nuzzled her hair in a gesture of affection, caressing her with his nose before laying his cheek against her head.

But retribution shouted questions at him. *What if they were caught by the servants in the morning? What would the position be for both of them if this became common report amongst the villagers?*

He considered the position, weighing each side of the argument. And he quickly reached conclusions.

He was certainly willing to risk it for himself. To be accused of lechery was a thing he could cope with. He could explain that, for within sight of God, he felt justified. He knew that the villagers' criticisms were nothing compared with the delights of the beautiful creature who lay with him and whom he loved more than any woman he had ever known.

But what of this girl beside him? She was a more serious problem. If discovered and exposed, she would be the main target for verbal attack. And it was supremely important that her name remain untarnished. If caught, she would be branded a lecher, thought of as a harlot, spurned as a fallen woman for whom morals counted little.

He *must* leave. There was nothing else for it. Otherwise criticisms of her conduct would make life unbearable should she be able to return after depositing Connie in her home country - wherever that was!

But if she departed and remained in that far-off place, all he would have would be the fondest of memories and nothing else. Marriage is normally the natural progression from falling in love - and consummation of that marriage the proper step thereafter. But marriage might be impossible - forever!

Then he thought again about servants. Only Daisy, Rose and James either slept or worked in the house. Of these three, Daisy would sleep late in the morning because of her vigil long into the night with Connie. Rose was sick at her cottage, and James was a man of complete integrity on whom Edward knew he could rely.

For a moment more, his thoughts lingered. Then he decided. Pulling the bedclothes over her to cover her slim body lest she catch a chill, he settled down and closed his eyes.

Presently, he slept.

* * * *

Sleep was saturated with beautiful dreams of Edward. In a Heaven-sent trance, she hugged him, pulling his muscular body to her as she lay beside him.

But the bed was unfamiliar, and at one point of the night, she woke up. For a moment she could not recall where she was or why.

Then she remembered talking to Daisy, and the instructions she had received. Now she recalled moving into this, a spare bedroom.

But - somebody was in the bed with her! Who?

It couldn't be?...

She sat up with a start, and as she moved, Edward stirred. 'Edward...' she whispered quietly, 'what are you doing here?'

He moved, sitting up beside her, the bedclothes tumbling from him, his face plainly visible in the moonlight. 'This is my bed.' he told her. 'When I arrived back during the night, you were asleep in it. In sleep, you put your arm over my chest before I could get out again. I didn't want to move for fear of waking you.'

She smiled, a thrill germinating inside her in the semi-darkness. 'Was that the *only* reason?'

She watched intently as his lips spread into a wide smile of admission. 'No, Mistress Sara.' he said in slow admission, 'I am ashamed to confess that it was not...'

She lay back, lying invitingly in the subtle, seductive shadows. As she looked up at him, her mouth opened slightly in an involuntary movement. 'Then kiss me.' she said in a soft, sultry whisper.

He moved his head down slowly, coming to her gently, just as she expected. But unlike their previous kiss, this was a much more passionate embrace than the gentle, tender touch with which he had caressed her up the glebe. This time the movements were not so subtle, much more direct, much more urgent and desirous. Her fingers, her toes, her head hair all tingled as her body began an involuntary shivering which she fought, but failed, to control. She had not expected to surpass the flames of ecstasy she had experienced during their previous kiss, but the explosion of desire which flooded all areas of her body was atomic in size and golden in intensity. The shock waves became tidal and she knew that this time - *this time* - he must not stop.

'Edward...' she whispered as he moved slightly away to look down at her, 'Edward...'

'Mistress Sara! Will you permit me to cast eyes on your nakedness again? And you on mine? Without us being wed?'

'Of course.' she whispered in gratitude, 'In any case, nobody will ever know.'

'As I told you last time, God will know.'

"And as I told you last time, God will *understand*. And there is no *mortal* being to see us.'

He nodded acceptance of her argument, and looked at her for a moment longer. His smile was one of total commitment and as he bent to kiss again, he brought his hand to rest on her thigh. As the kiss intensified, his fingers moved to gently begin a caress of her most intimate, sensitive parts. She suspected that he had never before made love, but he quickly displayed a natural expertise - an ability to arouse her with gentle movements which were mere throbs of his fingertips. And as the excitement grew to become climatic, he timed his entry to perfection so that she accepted him when approaching her peak of desire. Then as he took her, she experienced a gradual crescendo of burgeoning emotions which mushroomed in intensity until it culminated in the most outrageously wild, total ecstasy she had ever experienced.

The event was timeless, the sensation electric, the place Heaven. And as he gently pulled from her to lie back in the bed beside her, she was conscious of a gossamer, all-pervasive shivering which possessed her, carrying her on wings so that she soared to undreamed-of peaks of pleasure and hovered airborne for an ecstatic eternity.

Finally, she gently found herself descending again, and as the involuntary body-shivering drifted to a halt, she became possessed of a gentle soothing warmth which flooded into every remote region of her being.

She lost count of the length of time she basked in the afterglow, but presently she was conscious of a stirring of the body next to her. Turning her head, she looked up at him again, parting her lips in preparation. As she accepted his gentle kiss, he started again, the welcome, immensely satisfying process repeating until again she was taken once more to the very doors of Heaven.

During the night he made love to her several times. She lost count after the second, but submitted willingly and eagerly each time until finally utter exhaustion sent her off to a welcome, deeply satisfying sleep.

Chapter 12

As dawn began to filter into the room, she was vaguely aware of Edward leaving. She knew that in his eyes, he had committed a fundamental sin. Several times. And that she had been instrumental in leading him into several sinful acts.

But as Sara had reminded him, the Lord who saw everything, would see and understand that their love was genuine and everlasting. God knew that people made excuses for indulging in lechery, which was a sin. But these had been no mere acts of fornication - their love making had been beautiful, the expression of two souls deeply and irrevocably in love, one with the other. And Sara knew that God would understand that Edward was making no excuse for himself and for Sara, for he and Sara had done no more than express physically their undying and everlasting love for one another. Shortly, if the all-seeing God willed it, they would wed.

If not - they had the memory of one night of unbelievable ecstasy to treasure forever...

Some time after Edward had gone, Sara rose and pulled on the dress. Leaving the room, she walked along to Connie's bedroom.

James sat on the stool, and rose when he saw her.

'How is Connie this morning, James?'

'She has had a much more comfortable night, Mistress Sara. I believe her fever has departed somewhat.'

Sara nodded, and went over to the bed. She placed a palm on Connie's brow. Connie's temperature was lower. Now it was clear that she would survive the 'sicknesse'.

Sara stayed with Connie after James left. Later, Edward paid a morning call. He said little, but there was a strange distance between them. It was as if he part-regretted the night just gone.

Daisy came in shortly after, and Edward said, 'Let us break fast, Mistress Sara. I have asked Daisy to remain here while we eat.'

* * * *

At the dining table, for a time they both ate in silence. But clearly he was mustering courage to speak once alone with her.

'I am deeply ashamed of my fornication with you last night.' he said, clearly regretting his actions.

She shook her head instantly. 'There is nothing to be ashamed of.' she said. ''Twas not fornication, but two people expressing their love for one another.'

''Tis forbidden outside of marriage.'

She smiled. 'I think I may have a solution to that.'

Edward's brow knitted. 'You have?'

'Yes.'

'What is your solution?'

Sara eyed him for a moment. 'You know we have agreed to marry?'

Edward's face relaxed. 'Yes.' he said softly.

'Then let us wed. But soon. Within a short time. As soon as I have taken Connie back home and returned to you.'

He leaned back in his chair, nodding slowly. Clearly he was much happier. 'Yes...' he said with a slow drawl. ''Tis later in the year than is normal for marriage... but that matters not... Once my immediate duties have been executed, we can arrange our nuptials!' He grinned widely.

'Why is marriage normally earlier in the year?'

For a moment, Edward looked puzzled. 'Why - Mistress Sara - a marriage is normally held as soon after the annual bath as possible. Normally May or June. The bride and groom will still smell quite sweet then. And the evenings are long and light, so that festivities can continue until late darkness. Unlike the winter when the nights are short and the bride will smell of grime and sweat.'

'Won't she smell a little anyway?'

'She will carry flowers to disguise any unpleasant odours about her person.' He made to rise from the table. Then he said, 'I must go.'

She smiled at the revelation as to why brides - even in the 20th Century - carry flowers, and wondered what 20th Century brides would have thought had they known the origins of why they were carrying a bouquet!

Sara felt much more at ease now that his self-recrimination had eased. But her concern rose a little when on parting, he said ominously, 'Many are the things which must occupy my time this day. The funeral in particular.'

Still gravely ill, Rose clearly would not be able to attend the service. Sara visited Rose twice in the morning to administer pills - against John Sprogg's wishes. But on Luke's advice, Sprogg had relented, since, as he said, 'Later this day, she will join my daughter in Paradise'.

For the funeral, Sara again wore Edward's mother's dress. Although dark, in fashion and suitable, it failed to stop Sara feeling uncomfortable. She suspected that the villagers would regard her with deep, relentless suspicion. Nor could she blame them. Even in her own eyes, she had unwittingly been the cause of Lizbeth's death.

Leaving the Parsonage that afternoon, Sara walked down the short way to the graveyard. A number of parishioners had already gathered. They stood about in huddled groups in drab clothes, waiting for the service to begin.

This was the first time Sara had seen most of the village people. Although apprehensive about their attitude towards her, she hoped it might be possible to talk to a few of them. She wanted to hear their views and understand them better, particularly if she might help them. Besides, if she were able to get back to Seventeenth Century Abbots Cross after returning Connie to Harriet, she would marry Parson Makepeace. That would make her a prominent figure in village life.

But Sara's hopes were quickly crushed. She realised that the whispered discussions all around were about *HER*. And although she made the occasional friendly gesture, only hostile looks and responses came in return.

Sara soon realised what they were saying. They wanted no contact with her.

Because of her part in Lizbeth's death, she understood her rejection. She resigned herself to standing dismally at the newly dug grave in silent isolation.

The sound of feet softly padding up the gravel drive caught her attention. She turned to see Edward enter the gate at the crossroads leading the procession. John Sprogg, dressed in a dark woollen smock, was at its head. He was followed by a large flat cart with no sides and two huge wheels.

Sara was surprised that although the adult mourners were dressed in a sad colour, there was a small group of five or six young girls in charge of the conveyance, dressed differently from the adults. Although dressed in dark garments, around their hoods they wore white headbands.

As the procession slowly approached, Sara caught a glimpse of the body of Lizbeth Sprogg. Lying on the hamper, it was shrouded in a white winding sheet. The

body was completely covered, secured round the middle with a white swaddling band which also swaddled the arms and knees. But the sheet was left loose at the hands and at the feet.

The procession rumbled slowly on until it arrived at the graveside. Sara looked sideways at Edward. He was reading from his prayer book, and paid no attention to her as he stopped and turned.

'Let our dear Lizbeth be moved from the parish hamper,' he said in a voice from the sepulchre, 'and laid in her last resting place.' Then, while he continued with prayers, the young girls turned to the parish hamper. Using the white bands round the corpse, they lifted it off and carried it over to the grave where they lowered it into the hole. The bands were then pulled free and, still without saying a word, the girls returned to the cart. Meanwhile, Edward moved to the head of the grave.

All heads bowed. Sara was no longer able to see faces. The hoods covered the sides of the bowed heads like horses' blinkers. Only the apex of each hood was visible, each like a rat's tail. Sara could not help reflecting on the irony of the sight, considering the reason for Lizbeth Sprogg's untimely death.

Shutting her eyes at the graveside as the service progressed, Sara's imagination flared. Suppose it had been Connie who had succumbed to plague instead of the Sprogg child? Suppose it had been Connie being buried today instead of Lizbeth? Suppose...?

A tear softly slipped from the corner of her eye. As a stone of grief materialised in her throat, Sara's heart went out to the Sproggs. And the fact that Rose had herself infected Lizbeth by not burning the clothes brought little comfort.

Sara opened her eyes and looked about her. As she glanced at the others, she knew herself to be an outcast, a stranger in their midst. Nevertheless, she still felt she had a moral duty to attend the funeral. Later she would try to offer some comfort if she could to the grieving John Sprogg.

Thankfully, Rose was not yet dead, albeit there appeared little change in her condition. Edward had said that Sprogg's son, Luke, would be left to look after Rose during the time of the funeral service. He would have instructions to send a message to the graveside should Rose's condition deteriorate.

During Edward's sermon, Sara continued to steal looks at the mourners. By now, she was beginning to feel uneasy. Venomous glances were still being cast in her direction. Privately, she started to wonder. The idea began to form that perhaps Edward had been right in advising her not to come. The longer the service went on, the more uneasy she became.

Eventually the Parson finished. Closing his prayer book, he stood silently for a few moments. Then he spoke again, softly this time, in a voice full of feeling and genuine grief.

'She was a child of ten thousand... full of wisdom, of womanlike gravity and knowledge, sweet expressions of God and apt in her learning...'

As Edward spoke, Sprogg's tear-drenched face looked Heavenwards, the grief at his loss engraved in the lines on his face.

Then, stepping to the graveside and looking down at the swaddled body of John Sprogg's dead daughter, Edward continued to speak in words which Sara found so poignant and heartbreaking that tears began to form.

. 'Lord! we rejoice we had such a present for thee!' His voice rose almost to a shout, as if to yell away his grief. 'It lived... and died lamented... Thy memory is and will be sweet unto all of us...'

Silence settled on the mourners like dust. Edward paused for a few moments of silent prayer, then he snapped shut his book, turned and walked away from the open grave down the path and out of the gate.

But none of the others moved. Like them, Sara remained, wondering what was coming next.

Meanwhile, Sprogg remained at the graveside, silent at first. Then he lapsed into such a shouting, moaning wailing that Sara was moved to console him. She stepped forward, lightly touching him on the shoulder in an expression of support.

But she was unprepared for his reaction. Instantly he sprang back. Now his expression was no longer one of grief, but of violent hatred, a hatred which filled Sara with instant fright.

'Don't touch me, Witch! ' he yelled in a deep-throated rage. Then, turning to the mourners, as if a thought had just come to him, he repeated the accusation. 'Aye, that's what she is!' he said in strong voice. 'A Witch! A Daughter of Satan!'

Sara snorted in disbelief. Forgetting for the moment the strong belief in witches, she did not recognise her considerable danger. But, mistaking her snort for a laugh, John Sprogg at once embroidered it.

'See that!?' he shouted, looking round at all the villagers. 'She laughs! She brings flux down on my wife and child, then she laughs!!'

The crowd began to mumble and grumble to one another, nodding assent, their voices signifying agreement. For the first time, Sara realised her danger.

By this time, John Sprogg had turned to face her. 'Where have you come from?' he demanded to know. 'Nobody knows you... nobody has seen you before. You suddenly appear out of the night, spreading sicknesse... You're a witch!!!' He screamed the repeated accusation at the terrified Sara.

But her fear was tempered with anger - rage that because of forces outside of her control, she should be facing superstitious accusations. She fought to retain control of her resentment.

'I'm NOT a witch, you fool!!' she shouted, finding her voice at last. 'I've been trying to help you!'

One of the women behind her spoke for the first time. 'Why aren't you married? You're well past the age.'

Sara turned to face her accuser. 'Well past the age?' she demanded incredulously. 'I'm only nineteen!!'

A shriek of laughter caused Sara to turn and look behind. A mature woman's face was contorted into a humourless grin of disbelief. 'Nineteen?' the woman demanded. 'You're nineteen! Why, I'm nineteen!!!' Then, as Sara's eyes widened in impotent alarm at the remark, she continued, 'I was married at fourteen. My sister was sixteen. And she left it very late! If you're nineteen, comely as you are, why aren't you wed?' Then before Sara could say anything, she concluded, 'It's because you're one of Satan's daughters, Witch!'

Angry agreement swelled. Realising she would not convince the nineteen year old woman, Sara turned in panic. She looked wildly at the silent fat, aged woman at her other side. 'I'm a student.' she told her in a thin, frightened voice.

Most of the crowd laughed scornfully. 'A student!' barked John Sprogg. 'Women aren't students! Only *men* become students! And only *rich* men, too!'

Again, Sara's scant knowledge of history had betrayed her. It was no use, she knew, telling them she was from the 20th Century.

'I'm here from… somewhere else…' she protested.

Then another man spoke. His voice carried a sinister quality. 'From where have you come?'

Sara responded at once - and made the same mistake of a few days earlier. 'From London.' She answered without thinking.

The effect was electric. They drew back from her in communal distrust as the man expressed their feelings. 'London!' exclaimed the man. 'London!!' He paused for breath, raising a bent finger and hovered it accusingly within an inch of Sara's face. 'You came from London to flee the plague!'

Although their anger was boiling over, the wary crowd stayed back from her, listening as she responded. She realised that they had guessed it - that there was no point in hiding any longer the fact that Connie had plague.

'I'm not suffering from plague!' she screamed. 'My cousin is - but she's getting better!'

'I came from London in 1625.' an ancient hag at the back said. 'I remember how many fled from London to get away from death. Some riding, some on foot, some without boots, some in slippers, by water, by land. In shoals swam they westward! So great was their need that hackneys, watermen and wagons were not so much employed in many a year!'

'So did *YOU* flee!' continued the first man, still shouting his disbelief at Sara. 'And now the foul distemper is amongst us! As well as being a witch, you've carried plague here!' His voice rose in a bass of doom! 'Now we're all going to die!'

The moment's complete silence which followed was broken by a shriek from behind Sara. 'In every house there will be grief striking up an Alarum!' she heard the nineteen-year-old yell. 'Wives will cry for husbands and parents for children!'

Things were getting angry - very, very angry. 'Look,' said Sara, trying to plead her case, 'I came from Death Cottage so that my sick cousin could be treated by Parson Makepeace.'

'Death Cottage? Where's that?' demanded the man next to Sprogg.

'About a mile and a half... along the coast...' Sara answered, realising too late that in this time, the cottage would be known as 'Rose' cottage. 'I'm sorry...' she faltered, 'you know it as Rose Cottage...'

It was a simple mistake. Yet it was fuel for distrust.

'Yes... *you* brought her... *you* brought the plague!' came Sprogg's voice.

'That's right - I brought her with the plague.' Sara protested. 'But I did not know that at the time - and she's recovering now! In a room in the Parsonage!'

'Very cunning, Mistress!' scoffed the nineteen-year-old. 'To put your familiar in the Parsonage! Nobody would think of a leveret hiding under the roof of Parson Makepeace!'

'Aye!' shouted a man. 'Your cousin recovers - but what about Rose Sprogg? There's no recovery for her, is there?'

'No!' agreed a tall hag with thin, greying hair poking out from her cap, 'It was a Satan's trick. You brought her to pass on plague, after which she will recover. You'll escape, and the pestilence shall kill us all!'

'The plague only spread because...' Sara stopped. She was going to say 'Because Rose didn't burn the clothes' but she realised how that might be mis-interpreted. Yet it was the only explanation she could give.

Her voice dropped. 'I told Rose to burn the clothes, but she didn't.' she said. 'Instead of burning them, she dressed her daughter in them, and Lizbeth contracted plague.'

'Burn the clothes!' exclaimed the hag. 'You give Rose Sprogg the brightest, finest clothes ever seen in this or any other village - then tell her to burn them? Why was your cousin not dressed in ordinary clothes like the rest of us?'

'Why was she wearing such finery?

'Connie's clothes aren't 'finery" protested Sara. 'They are simply the clothes any young girl would wear!'

The angry mumbling which interjected each of Sara's protests crescendoed again. The crowd did not believe it.

'Are YOU afflicted?' Sprogg asked.

'Afflicted?'

'With the distemper?'

'No. If I'd had plague, I'd have been ill before now - possibly dead.'

Sprogg nodded, then turned to the others. 'She has condemned herself!' he said. 'Others have the pestilence. But on her there's no sign. Take her away and hang her for the witch she is!

The seething of the crowd's anger was now mirrored in their treatment of her.

Roughly seized by both arms, Sara yelped with the sudden pain of the metal claw-like fingers as they gripped her arms Unable to resist because of the overpowering force used against her, Sara was quickly half-pushed, half-carried off by a number of strong hands towards the unkempt side of the small graveyard. Here the grass was not only waist height and above, it was liberally sprinkled with thistles and nettles leading up to a large untended hawthorn hedge whose vicious barbs stood ready to harm any being brave enough to attempt a way through.

But this meant nothing to the heavily-clothed villagers as Sara was half-dragged, half-thrust through the unrelenting hawthorn and the mature and vicious stinging nettles on the other side. Once through the nettles, she was hauled, half-stumbling, half-crawling across an open sewer on a narrow plank leading onto a track to the village. Now she knew what was about to happen! She knew she was about to pay an awesome price for attending the funeral!

As she continued to be forced down the path, untended bramble bushes continued to scratch her bare arms and legs. Now she stung and was scratched in various parts of her body. The thorn-inflicted wealds opened on her skin which rapidly criss-crossed with unsightly, painful wounds, caused by conflict with other hostile plants which in many parts crossed the path along which she was being dragged so uncomfortably.

By now she was sobbing. Quietly at first them a little louder, unable to control the pain. But none of the villagers was ready to show any compassion. Mercy was a non-existent commodity.

Then suddenly the plants and bushes intermittently barring the path ended and Sara found herself being dragged across the green fronting the castle. Standing alone on the centre of this green was a solitary oak tree, its crooked, irregular branches jutting out in all directions above her. Here she was brought to a halt.

The venom in the air was tangible and overt, and was voiced by John Sprogg who pushed his way to the front of the crowd to stand within inches of her face as he spoke, his words addressed to her but meant for the crowd behind. Ominously over his shoulder Sara could see a rope hanging down from a branch, a rope on which Sara had seen the village children playing. But with terror she realised that this was going to be put to a more sinister use - and very shortly.

'You are a damnable witch!' John Sprogg shouted at her, 'A Daughter of Satan! A Harlot of the Devil! And you will pay the penalty with *this!*' He leaned back and grabbed the rope with his right hand. Bringing the noose forward, he shook it in her face. This will surround your neck then you will be punished by *death*!! - Death which you richly deserve. Death which will atone for your infliction of plague upon my lovely daughter!!'

He paused, his chest heaving with the effort of speech and the adrenaline of the emotional moment. 'Bring her forward!' he shouted to the men who still gripped Sara tightly by the arms.

Sara felt herself being propelled towards the rope.

Meanwhile Sprogg leaned towards the tree and pulled himself up to stand upon the lowest branch. Throwing the noose up, he hurled it over another branch so that when the noose dropped towards the ground again, the rope was much shorter. At once, and with terror now gripping her in every corner of her body, Sara realised that she was about to be lynched.

'Up here!' Sprogg shouted, and at once the arms gripping her biceps changed position, taking hold of her body and thrusting her - not forward this time - but upwards to the low branch beside Sprogg. Sprogg grabbed her round the waist and pulled her towards him. The foul stench of his proximity mingled with the metallic taste of terror in her mouth as he took the noose and placed it round her neck.

This is it! Sara thought. *This is the day I die!*

'Now witch,' shouted Sprogg, clearly savouring the moment,' take your last breath, for your death is going to--

'*HOLD*!!!'

Her lynching and the excited babbling of the mob were prematurely arrested by a shout from the back of the crowd. A spark of hope ignited as Sara recognised the voice.

Edward.

John Sprogg, still holding her round the waist, was first to speak.

'What is it, Parson?'

'Where are you going with that young woman?'

'We're going to hang her. She be a witch!'

'You cannot! And take that noose from her neck, John Sprogg!'

Silence followed. Uncertain, still, breathless. Then Sprogg moved. Releasing Sara, he removed the noose from her neck. Just in time, The moment it was off, she lost balance and fell to the ground.

Nobody moved to help her, but luckily she was not badly injured and quickly got to her feet. Meanwhile the rough Sprogg and the cultured Edward faced one another. Edward's bland superiority contrasted with Sprogg's obvious limitations.

Sprogg spoke first. 'Why not, Parson Makepeace? She's a witch!' He half-turned, raised an arm, and indicated the crowd. 'We all know that!

Reassurance at Edward's presence flooded Sara's body. He would protect her from this mob, baying like wild dogs, howling for blood!

But to Sara's dismay, Edward did not defend her. Eyes suddenly wide with fear and disappointment, she watched him nod agreement.

'She may be...' Edward began thoughtfully. Then she listened with incredulity as he added, '...but we cannot hang her. Not immediately.'

'Why not?'

In the awkward silence, the slight breeze caressed the treetops, and the rustle of leaves was the only sound. 'Why not, Parson?' Sprogg repeated.

'Because she must be tried first!'

Sprogg hesitated. But when he spoke, it was clear that he intended having his own way.

'Why?' he demanded fiercely. 'Why waste time with a trial? She's already condemned herself!'

Edward nodded. 'That may be!' he agreed with a calm which infuriated Sara, 'But she must be tried properly.'

'Aye!' shouted another man, 'we'll prick her 'til she confesses!'

The hullabaloo greeting this remark was cut short when Edward's voice again rang out. 'We've no need to prick her!' he shouted. 'A trial before the magistrate will suffice!'

Again Sprogg spoke. 'The magistrate will not be in this district for another four months! We cannot wait that long!'

'We cannot hang her without trial. And I am against the pricking. Hanging without trial is murder. And you will all go to purgatory for it!!' Edward's arm shot up and an accusing finger slowly moved round them all.

The petrified crowd fell silent. The grip on Sara's arms loosened a little. Then Sprogg spoke again.

'We cannot wait until December!' he repeated. 'The witch will kill us all in that time! Better to hang her now than have us all die in our beds!'

During the exchange, Sara's eyes had wandered little from Edward. She had believed him to be something remarkable in his time.

But this incident made her now realise the truth.

He was no less ignorant than the rest of the superstitious serfs! She had thought him open-minded and receptive. But here he was, not arguing that witchcraft was no more than a medieval superstition, but actually agreeing that she might be a witch! And the discussion centred, not around whether or not witchcraft existed, but whether she would be executed *before* a trial or *after!*

'What do you think, Parson?' Sprogg asked.

'I suggest that I speak to my father. As you all remember, he is a Justice of the Peace. Meanwhile, let us search for a third nipple. If it be found, I shall ask my father to try the wench!'

A mumble of discussion broke silence amongst the villagers. They were clearly unsettled by the proposal. But they were unwilling to cross the Parson.

'Very well.' Sprogg agreed. 'Should Squire Makepeace be willing, tomorrow she will be tried - and found guilty! And if he is not willing, we shall prick her and swim her!!'

The sound of 'Aye!' and 'Let her be swum!' grumbled from various sections of the mob.

Sara was grabbed more tightly. Her panic grew as she looked round at the faces of the blood-crazed mob.

Now she would have to face a kangaroo court without support from anywhere. She was alone!

Edward had failed her. Edward, with whom she had thought herself in love, was unworthy. Edward, whom she had thought cultured and strong was at best superstitious and weak.

Yet in the midst of her huge disappointment, there came one minute spark of humanity from Edward. The Parson held up his hand. 'Please...' he asked soothingly, 'please, be silent...' Then, turning to face Sara amidst the renewed calm, he spoke directly to her for the first time since arriving in the graveyard.

'Now, mistress, you are to be searched by the village goodwives for a third pap. After that, you may be tried by the Squire for witchcraft. If you resist, the alternative is to be pricked or swum!'

Sara knew that pricking was a hideous process where needles were thrust into the flesh of the body to find non-responsive parts. But that was not so bad as 'swimming'!

Sara would rather die than be 'swum' - the ignominious process in which, stripped naked, her thumbs would be tied to opposite toes, and she would be thrown into water, there to drown, and thus prove innocent, or not, in which case she would be guilty and hang for it.

She did not want to be searched for the mark of Satan. This would confirm her as one of Satan's daughters. But such marks could be found on ANY living person with enough searching - and enough imagination. The gross humiliation of being stripped bare while strange women sought the 'third nipple', 'proof' of witchcraft, was abhorrent.

Yet although this was degrading, the alternative was immeasurably worse. Almost imperceptibly she nodded agreement.

'Take her!' Edward ordered. He stood up, continuing to display a lack of any sympathy.

'Where to?' asked Sprogg.

Edward thought for a moment. 'Has Quincey a cellar?'

An approving chorus arose. 'Aye, we'll keep her there!' Sprogg proclaimed above the noise of the crowd.

Rough hands again propelled Sara forward. She was frog-marched away from the churchyard, stumbling along mud paths beside small gardens and beech hedgerows then over the main street. Through frightened tears, she looked up at the thatched cottages she had so admired on her first day. With what affection she had looked and wished she could have visited the Seventeenth Century! Now she realised what living in a remote village in Seventeenth Century England meant!

The iron grip of Sprogg's arms on one side and of an equally muscular man on the other whom Sprogg addressed as 'Berb', together with the excited, hysterical crowd behind gave Sara no chance of escape. She darted fearful glances in all directions, desperate to get away, frantic to return to her own Century. But there was no chance of breaking free.

This was not the first time she'd come into close contact with the village people. In addition to their appalling ignorance, she once more found herself nauseated by their earthen smell, the unpleasantly moist odour which all gave off, and which none seemed to notice. No wonder disease spreads so readily amongst these people!

Yet instantly, she rebuked herself. They were not to blame! They simply didn't know. Nor could they be blamed for locking her up and trying her as a witch. In the Seventeenth Century, Satan lived. He was a very real being. His daughters existed as certainly as the sun, moon and stars.

Now they were across the village main street and within another minute came to a stop in the inn courtyard. As Sprogg lifted a mighty fist and pounded on the door, Sara looked up at the repainted wooden sign which in the windless day hung motionless on its wrought-iron support.

The inn door's wooden latch lifted from the inside, and the door swung open. A black jacketed man dressed in knee-length britches and white stockings similar to those worn by James stood there. At his side was a woman whose face seemed familiar to Sara. *Where had she seen this woman before?*

'Why, John Sprogg!' said the man. 'What brings you here at this hour?'

'I laid my daughter Lizbeth to final rest today.' Sprogg replied in high emotion. 'My young daughter. She was killed.'

'Aye' regretted the man, ''Tis a fearful thing, sicknesse!'

'It wasn't sicknesse that killed her!' said Sprogg. 'It was *witchcraft!*'

The innkeeper's eyes became saucers of alarm. Softly, he whistled through his few teeth. 'Witchcraft, ye say? Well, now, who would have thought that?'

'Aye, who? Well, 'tis here, I tell you. Here, in Abbots Cross.' Sprogg's tone quietened. 'But we have the witch. There will be a trial on the morrow.'

The woman standing beside the innkeeper looked past Sprogg at Sara. 'Be this the witch?' she asked, and as soon as she spoke, Sara found her voice familiar. Where had she heard it before?

'Aye, Mistress Quincey.' said Sprogg.

Quincey! At once the woman's identity was confirmed.

The woman in the bus depot. Her name had been Quincey - Miss Quincey. *Descendant of the woman now facing Sara!*

'A pretty wench!'

'True!' agreed Sprogg. 'Satan often dresses his daughters in comely fashion. Not all are old hags on broomsticks.'

'What will you do with her in the meantime?' Hal Quincey asked.

'We'll have to lock her up in your cellar until the morrow.'

'But, John.' protested the innkeeper. ''Tis full. I doubt if you'd get a mouse into it.' He paused for thought. 'There's a stout outhouse.' he suggested. 'Will that do?'

'Aye, anywhere! Only let us get her locked up.'

The innkeeper nodded and moved back, opening the way for them. 'Bring her through.'

Sprogg turned and grabbed Sara roughly by her arm. He pulled her down the step onto the irregular stone floor of the low-ceilinged inn. Under its beams stood rough hewn tables with long benches. A large fire at one side was piled with logs. Although summer, the firewood crackled fiercely, occasionally spluttering with driblets of fat from the roasting pig above it. Sara recoiled with disapproval as she saw the spit being turned by a dog in a cage shaped like a wheel which rotated, revolving the spit when the dog ran inside the cage. A boy sitting in attendance occasionally applied hot coals to the feet of the animal to torture it into running inside its wheel.

Marching to the rear of the room, and still gripping Sara painfully, Sprogg pushed open another heavy door. The central feature of a large white kitchen was a solid table littered with pewter jugs, plates and tankards. As Sara was rudely pulled past, she felt the heat of another fire. Down its chimney hung a chain and cauldron in which lethargically bubbled a thick brown liquid.

Sara was pulled out of the door of the hot kitchen, and bundled into a brick-paved sumpyard. Standing in the hot sunshine, as the villagers spilled into the yard beside her, Sara could see a barn at the far side. A large, solid wooden construction. So that was to be her prison!

Sprinting past the group, the innkeeper reached the barn. He grabbed the latch, unhooked it and moved quickly in a semicircle, pulling the door open.

'In there, fiendish wench!' yelled Sprogg. Pointing into the dim interior, he grabbed Sara by the elbow and hurtled her into the barn. She tripped over a stone block and fell heavily.

Letting out a short cry of pain, she leaned up. She rubbed the elbow which had banged on the floor.

The arrogant figure of Sprogg stood framed in the doorway. The others crowded in to stand behind him, listening with awe as he spoke with assumed authority.

'Today you shall be tested, and tomorrow will be your trial, Witch!' He breathed in dramatically. 'And tomorrow shall be your end! A trial for Witchcraft is what you shall have. And at the end of it, a hangman's rope!' His lips curled in a sneer. 'You're a witch and you shall be sent back to Satan for your villainies.'

'I'm no witch!' protested Sara. 'I'm from the--'

She stopped. Again, she had been about to say, 'from the 20th Century.' but she stopped. Such a protest would only make her seem more witchlike.

'You're from Satan! Daughter of Hell!'

A metallic taste pervaded Sara's mouth as she looked round the faces. They had clear conviction of her guilt!

'How shall we test her John?' asked 'Berb'.

A lone voice intervened from behind the crowd, the timbre of which raised in Sara a curious juxtaposition of emotions. 'If she be witch, she will bear the third pap!' she heard Edward say callously. 'Let her be stripped and searched. If it be there, there be no need for swimming.'

Despite her disappointment at his change of attitude towards her, Sara saw that this suggestion brought calm to a volatile situation. Nodding heads with choruses of 'Aye!' brought to an end the prospect of having to endure the horror of being 'swum'.

'Who shall do the searching?' demanded a crone.

'I shall!' called Sprogg.

Sara gazed up saucer-eyed from her prostrate position. As he moved towards her, she surveyed him like a vixen defending cubs. A new fear now joined the others as she sensed the lechery in his words.

But for once, Sprogg's leadership came under question. 'You shall not, John!' A toothless, shrew-like hag laid her wrinkled hand on his shoulder, arresting his movement by sheer tone of voice. ''Tis women's' work!'

'Aye! 'Tis women's' work!' agreed another.

'Aye, 'tis women's' work!' echoed isolated comments as a consensus came from sections of the gathering.

Sprogg's lechery waxed into disappointment, then resignation. 'Very well.' he agreed. His lust died as he turned away from Sara. 'Let women do it. But do it quickly! Do it now! Then we shall have enough evidence to execute her on the morrow!'

Without another glance at Sara, Sprogg left. Following his leadership, several other men turned to leave. Only Edward and the women remained to discuss the coming search.

Edward was the first to speak. Surely, thought Sara, now he will help her escape from this nightmare!

But again she was thrust into an abyss of disappointment.

'The searching will be done by four goodwives.' said Edward. 'Kate, Meg, Beth and... Agnes. Go into the barn. The remainder of you shall stay in the yard. I must now leave to attend Old Tom Tomkins at Christ Church. I shall also consult my father about the trial tomorrow. I shall be back later.'

He turned to address the four searchers. 'Search thoroughly!' he warned, 'But remember. We agreed. No pricking!'

'No pricking... No pricking... No pricking...' the three searchers assured him.

Edward turned and without so much as a glance at the still-prostrate Sara, he led the others from Sara's prison, banging shut the barn door in their wake.

'No pricking... No pricking... No pricking...' the four searchers had assured Edward. But as they towered over Sara like harpies in the semi-darkness of the closed barn, she sensed that they were unlikely to be true to their promises...

Chapter 13

Sara was left alone in the barn with the women. One was her adversary from the graveside. Another was Beth Quincey.

Warily, not quite sure what the 'searching' would entail, she eyed the leering faces with mounting trepidation. But she knew it was pointless to resist.

For a moment, she watched defensively. Their faces were contorted into expressions of glee. Then, as if on cue, with one lunge three of them grabbed her simultaneously. Beth Quincey was the only one to show consideration by not handling Sara at all.

But the other three showed no compassion as they rolled her face down on the filthy straw. They pulled at her woollen dress, removed it and flung it aside. Then six beady eyes creased into expressions of leering delight at her embarrassed nakedness.

With nothing to cover her, Sara cowed away, attempting vainly to hide her nakedness with bare arms. But, catlike, the women pounced on her, pulling at her arms and forcing her to her feet until she was forced to stand, flushing and unclothed, in the middle of the floor.

But she had no time to be shy. A rough-hewn table stood in one corner. The searchers dragged it out, then pushed Sara onto it.

'Gently... gently...' wailed Beth Quincey, 'Don't be rough with her...'

But her intervention was to no avail. Splinters attacked Sara's fair skin as she lay face up on the unplaned wood. But the crones not only ignored her discomfort, they revelled in it as they began to examine her closely, nipping and probing her body in a search for 'the mark of Satan'.

Sara submitted. The indignities and humiliations heaped on her were worse than the pain of the splinters. But one thought comforted her. There could be no 'Mark of Satan', for she was no witch!

Several times she cried out in pain as the handling of her became more brusque. Repeatedly Beth Quincey attempted to intervene, to persuade the handlers to be more gentle. But her attempts were fruitless. Obviously the peasant women were unable to find what they sought. 'Not so rough...' pleaded Beth yet again, but the others continued to ignore her. Examining Sara in an ever-roughening cycle of pulling and prodding of her soft flesh, they examined in minute details all areas of her body. But they appeared to fail.

Eventually, all three stood back and looked at one another. 'Dammit!' shouted one, and kicked at a pile of straw at the side.

It was an involuntary action - but one with consequences. As the straw flew aside, it laid bare what was underneath.

Sara was the first to see what had been exposed. And her innards appeared to collapse within her.

A RatKing! The rat formation which was the root of all her troubles!

She looked across at the old women. They were all eyeing her with curiosity - and were clearly unaware of what she had seen. And at once, George's poem flooded back into memory.

'What is it, Mistress?' Beth Quincey asked softly.

'It's a ratking.' Sara told her. 'A formation of rats. Not very common. But they forewarn of evil.'

'How do *you* know?' Agnes Brown demanded.

'I know because my cousin saw one quite recently. And she caught the plague! It's all in a poem. Listen:

> *"Take care that thou avert thine eye,*
> *If a Ratking nest nearby*
> *If it ye be the first to see,*
> *Then evil soon shall follow thee"*

As she finished reciting, Sara became conscious of four pairs of eyes on her. She looked at the trio of old hags. 'What?' she demanded.

'You *are* a witch!' said Agnes.

'No, I'm not!' Sara protested, suddenly realising how foolish it had been to recite George's poem.

'Yes you are. And I plan to prove it!!'

As she looked, from the corner of her eye Sara saw something which made her revulsion rise. Looking slyly round, Agnes drew a bodkin out of her bodice.

'Agnes!' Beth Quincey whispered hoarsely at her. 'She's not to be pricked! The Parson forbade it!'

Holding the bodkin, Agnes looked scathingly back. 'I see no Parson in here!'

'I'll have no truck with this!' Beth responded. 'Search for the nipple, but there it to be no pricking!'

'Do you plan to stop me?'

'This is an act of evil!'

'Oh - shut your stupid mouth, Beth Quincey!' the other woman spat out.

Turning quickly, the landlord's wife strode off, out of the barn and away across the inn yard. Meanwhile, the hag called Agnes watched her with a cynical leer. Then, holding the bodkin firmly in her right hand, she thrust the point fiercely into Sara's flesh.

Sara shrieked with the unexpected pain of the pricking. A wall of mocking laughter greeted her agonised cry from the villagers outside. Agnes suddenly found herself in possession of unaccustomed power. With a cruel smirk, she jabbed the bodkin several times more into Sara's flesh, each jab of increasing ferocity, and each cry of pain being greeted by fresh bouts of laughter from outside.

'Confess, Witch!' Sprogg's voice sounded tauntingly from the other side of the wooden wall. 'Confess your love of Satan! Confess that you are *truly* a witch!'

By now, Sara was weeping - weeping with pain, weeping with anger, weeping with humiliation. 'No...' she wailed, 'no... I'm not a witch, you *fools!*'

But to Sara's further humiliation, the gale of laughter only increased. And as the pricking finally stopped, she fell silent. Agnes replaced her bodkin to resume the search.

After a time, one crone spoke mournfully. 'Tis not here!' she wailed.

'It *must* be here!' protested the crone with the bodkin.

'Tisn't! She has the purest, whitest skin I ever saw!'

'If we don't find it, the Parson will free her!' Agnes warned. 'Now get her to the ground, and search again!!'

Taking Sara roughly, the women pulled her so that she slid from the table and onto the straw where the three women resumed thumbing her naked body, prodding her breasts, lifting her arms and turning her over and over, looking for the slightest pimple which could be interpreted as evidence of witchcraft.

Then a yell of delight came from behind her as a figure jabbed at her left buttock.

'Here!!' came a scream. 'I have found it!'

'Found it?' thought Sara, turning to look down.

Then she remembered the insect bite on the beach back at the cottage!

'Aye, there it is!!' screamed another crone. 'In the crack of her arse!'

Running to the door, she burst it open to shout the news to the waiting villagers. 'The mark of Satan is on her!' she screamed. 'We have found the third nipple!!!'

Sara grabbed her dress and speedily slipped it on. Her modesty had just been recovered when Sprogg dashed in through the door. Behind him, the other men. Sprogg's eyes drooped in disappointment that she was no longer naked.

For a few moments the excited sound reminded Sara of the baying of foxhounds. Then as the women left her alone in the barn, Sprogg spoke.

'Satan's kiss is upon you!!' he pronounced with a piety which pleased and impressed his fellows. 'Tomorrow you shall die!' He paused for effect as the crowd of men behind him mumbled assent. Then he added finally, 'And never will a witch more fittingly have met her end!'

Sara shook her head. 'No... no...' she whispered pleadingly. 'You're wrong!'

But it was no good. Sprogg had turned to leave, the others with him. But as they left, he turned once more to regard her for a brief second before reaching out to the door. Unseen by the other men, lust hooded his face for a moment. Then with one mighty crash he hurled the door shut, and Sara heard the wooden bolt being slammed into place. Footsteps receded across the yard.

Left alone, Sara lay still. For a time, she watched the late sunlight filter through cracks. As the sun began to sink, her spirits sank with it until they bottomed in an unbelievably cavernous pit.

Unless a miracle occurred, *in the next twenty-four hours she would die.*

* * * *

Sara rubbed her elbow.

Pained in her head through lack of sleep, and all over her body from the pricking and rough handling, she got up. Slowly, she made her way over to the side of the barn. She sat down on a pile of straw to consider her situation, making herself as comfortable as her aches would permit.

Her coming trial would now be in front of a substitute 'judge'. The Squire was a man Sara had never met. But the weakness of her defence meant that barring a miracle, tomorrow's trial would be no trial at all. In the eyes of the villagers, she was already as guilty as if she had indulged in black magic rituals. They would be difficult to convince otherwise.

Sara hoped that Edward would come to her defence. But now she strongly doubted him. He had recently surprised her by his attitude, for hitherto she had thought that he had believed her. Now she knew better. His reliability was not just questionable, it was non-existent.

Why had he suggested that she be tried at all? Why had he condoned the searching of her body for the 'third nipple' when he himself had claimed not to believe in witches? Why hadn't he spoken in her defence? And why had he suggested this trial tomorrow?

He was an immense disappointment. He had deserted her at the first test of his love. She'd believed in him, wanted to marry him, wanted to forsake all in her own time to be with him for the rest of her life.

Now she could see he was as superstitious as the peasants. And no matter how she looked at it, she could only reach one conclusion. She'd had a narrow escape. She might have been married to him before finding out about him. And at least there was one advantage of knowing she could not rely on him.

She knew she was alone.

And she would have to work out her own salvation.

But what?

She could do one of two things:

Firstly, she could put up such a good defence that she would be cleared of witchcraft.

But as soon as she reached that conclusion, she knew that no local court would clear her without evidence. Why, she could not even prove that she had come from Josephine's - and her claim to be from another century would be regarded as PROOF of witchcraft rather than a defence against it. No, she could think of no way to prove she had come from the cottage... Josephine! Josephine could bear the truth of it! Josephine could be summoned to give evidence on her behalf!

For a few minutes, she felt exhilarated. But then her excitement vaporised as she thought more about it. Why, even if she managed to get a message to Josephine, what then? Would Josephine think her innocent of witchcraft? On the contrary, Josephine might be as convinced of her guilt as the others!

It might be best to try her second plan: To escape from the barn.

But how? The timbers of the barn were stout; there was straw but no tools; in fact, there was little of use.

It was now late afternoon. But outside, the sun still shone brilliantly, although judging by the few shafts entering the barn, it was fairly low in the sky. So how was she to get out?

She tried the door. No chance there. Its timbers would not submit.

She went along the walls, pushing, knocking, shoving, trying not to make a noise, but urgently seeking a plank ready to yield. She pushed each slat in turn, but was disappointed. There were no weak areas.

The barn was a recent construction. The new oak of its walls withstood all her blows, the slats stoutly resistant. No, there was no easy exit.

As time passed and dusk approached, her eyes grew accustomed to the dim light. She continued to examine her prison.

If only something could happen to one of the houses... some distraction in the village... if the inn could go on fire perhaps?... No... there was no prospect of setting the inn on fire. Still, wait a minute? Fire??? That was it! Yes, a plan was suggesting itself. Fire! It was dangerous, but it might work!

Sara carefully pondered the details of her plan. It had to be worked thoroughly and correctly. There would be no second chance.

The barn was strewn with agricultural debris, like the barn back at the cottage. Soon she was diligently looking for what she might find useful, - for the implements she needed for her escape.

* * * *

Today was different.

Normally John Sprogg would have spent the early evening at home with his wife before he quit his cot for the tavern. But today his daughter was dead and buried. His wife lay gravely ill, in the care of his unwed son, Luke. None of the women of Abbots Cross would go near his cot, for fear of catching plague, although the whole village had attended Lizbeth's funeral.

Poor Lizbeth! Only his son now remained. Much older than little Lizbeth; and able to take care of himself. But Sprogg was too overcome both with grief and determination on revenge to think about him.

Lizbeth... Poor, lovely Lizbeth!...

Sprogg's drinking had started early, even before the funeral service, and it had resumed after the witch had been tested. His cows were unmilked, his sheep untended. And they would remain so unless a neighbour remembered about them, for now, already several tankards on, Sprogg was well past rationality. And his anger at the witch in the barn increased with his drunkenness.

'Another tankard, Hal Quincey!' he shouted.

The innkeeper came over to pick up his pewter vessel. 'Don't you think you've had enough--?' he began. But Sprogg snarled him quiet. 'Another tankard!! Now!!!' he yelled, voice raised in drunken anger.

He threw his last farthing onto the table in complete disdain. 'Now get me more ale, Hal Quincey! Before the peace be breached!'

'Certainly John, if you wish it.' Diplomacy replaced the innkeeper's concern as he briefly regarded Sprogg's empty leather tankard before scurrying away. His return was almost instantaneous. He hurried back, his rough, hairy hands clasping another square leather jack of ale. Placing the jack on the rough-hewn table, the innkeeper hastily removed the plug, pouring some of the contents into John Sprogg's tankard as rapidly as he could. Sprogg breached the peace fairly frequently. It was not an event Hal Quincey wanted to see repeated too often.

Time wore on, and the early evening became later and later. John Sprogg became more and more arrogant, talking freely about the witch in the barn.

'We shall swim her!' said Sprogg. 'No matter what the Parson says! Then she shall be hanged!'

'We should prick her first.' said Matthew Smith, the man who had held Sara's other arm on the frog-march to the inn.

'No need.' said the man opposite, palming back his few strands of hair across a dirty bald head. 'We have proof enough. She bears the third nipple!'

'Yes,' Sprogg agreed with a drunken slyness, '...but a confession would be best...' He banged his tankard on the table and leered inebriately. 'Were we to wring a confession from her, that would seal it before the Justice of the Peace!'

He would have spoken further but was interrupted by a loud crash as the inn door was flung open.

The men looked up in surprise. Apart from serving wenches, women did not patronise alehouses.

'Why - Goodwife!' shouted Smith in muddled recognition. 'You should not be here. What brings you?'

'Out the back!' shouted Smith's wife, her voice rising to a shriek. 'Yon barn - where the witch is held!'

'What about it?' Sprogg demanded.

* * * *

At first, Sara found difficulty in raising fire. Rubbing sticks was laborious. She tried scraping wood and metal, flintstone and wood, a stick on the door - before discovering a wooden wheel and spindle lying in a corner.

The small wheel was a toy, fairly loose on its axle. By putting the shaft on the table and standing on it, Sara was able to spin the wheel to create heat on the axle. But although the wheel spun freely, little heat was created, and after few minutes, Sara gave up.

Getting down from the bench, she looked round for some other means of starting fire. As she searched in a corner, her eyes lighted on a grindstone. She regarded it thoughtfully, wondering how she could make it work. Then, using an old knife she discovered in a corner, she worked out how to make it spark.

There was an abundance of straw, and Sara put some of it into the box. Then, praying for success, she began, turning the grindstone, creating sparks with the knife.

Sparks landed on the straw in the box, but at first none seemed to ignite. Like the wooden wheel, she wondered if her attempts with the grindstone would prove fruitless.

Then, suddenly, a spark alighted, the faintest merest glow on the end of a straw stalk. Quickly she blew, gently at first, supplying oxygen to keep the spark alive. The area of glow slowly expanded little by little. An infant flame flickered!

Within minutes, it was a fire. As it began to crackle, Sara carefully carried the box over to a corner. She set it down to build what she wanted - an inferno in the corner of the barn.

The flames licked up the straw, but she had not bargained for the amount of smoke it would produce. The barn soon filled with choking, pungent fumes. They infiltrated her lungs, chasing out the pure air.

Coughing and spluttering as the flames grew bigger, she pushed against the side of the barn away from the inn. Finding a larger than normal crack in the wall of the barn, she pressed her nose against it to absorb the clean pure air. As the flames licked up round the corners of the barn, she got as near as she could, and with the flat of her foot pushed and kicked in an effort to make the burning timbers give way.

But the wooden walls were stouter than Sara had anticipated. In any case, the burning straw made it difficult to get near enough to push. Time after time she was beaten back by heat and smoke. In the end, she could do no more than watch.

For her to succeed, speed was crucially important. If the fire was discovered before the timbers had burned through, recapture was certain.

Sara grabbed a pitchfork, and pushed and jabbed at the timbers with the blunt end amongst the swirling smoke. But it was hopeless. The smoke continued to billow.

Sara started to cough - lightly at first - then more rackingly as breathing became difficult. The smarting in her eyes kept them closed, except for the briefest of glimpses. And because of the dense fog in the barn, it was now impossible to see.

Flames were licking up the side of the barn. But instead of escape, Sara's only concern was to keep breathing. Now the air was filled with dark, grey, choking smoke. It nauseated her, stopped her seeing and interrupted her respiration. Then, just as she was about to suffocate altogether, she heard the sound she dreaded most of all!

Chapter 14

Tankards were cast down. Benches scattered. Tables overturned. Drinkers jolted out of their revelry.

'It's the witch!' shouted Sprogg. 'The witch has set the barn afire!'

'Aye, she has that!' shouted Timkins. He followed closely, staggering from the effects of alcohol.

Bursting open the back door, the drunken crowd staggered noisily over the flagstones to the barn.

'Buckets!' shouted one. 'Bring buckets!'

'Here!' shouted the innkeeper. He reached inside the back door and produced first one, then another half beer barrel, each with handle attached.

But Sprogg and his associates were not too intoxicated to deal with the crisis. The water pump handle was vigorously worked up and down. Buckets were filled. The contents were thrown with remarkable accuracy, considering the drunken condition of the fire-fighters. The oak walls of recent construction were still fairly unseasoned so that the barn did not burn readily. So the well thrown buckets of water dowsed the blaze while still small. It was quickly under control.

Then Si Timkins reminded them of something which, in their semi drunken condition, they had forgotten about.

'The witch!' he called.

'Aye, you're right!' called the innkeeper. 'She'll still be inside!'

With feverish hands, the bolt was thrust aside, the latch lifted, the door flung open.

An enormous pall of smoke issuing from the barn was accompanied by the last hissing of the dying embers of the fire. But of the 'witch', there was no sign.

'Where is she?' asked Timkins.

'The bitch has got away!' yelled Sprogg.

But Quincey grabbed him by the upper arm and pointed. 'No, John' he said. 'She's still here. She remains. And now she has gone either to God or her master Satan. Pray that it be the former.'

In the corner, face down, lay the lifeless body of Sara Goodwin.

Drunk as each person in it was, the crowd sensed that something sombre had happened.

'Poor maid!' said one very young peasant softly, tears welling up in his eyes. But Sprogg instantly whipped round.

'Shut that senseless mouth, Lance Thompson!' he said with a sharp severity.

The young lad recoiled, but the innkeeper interrupted. 'Let him alone, John. She was a pretty wench to be sure. Her passing is to be regretted.'

Sprogg's blazing eyes were turned full on the innkeeper. 'Would you pity a witch?!' he demanded. 'Would you show mercy to a daughter of Satan?'

The innkeeper's eyes fell, and he shook his head. 'No, John.' he confessed quietly.

'But I would.' came an authoritative voice.

A pathway opened up to allow the Parson to make his way forward. 'Witch or not, I would have mercy, for Our Lord will have mercy!' he said openly.

Sprogg's facial expression showed that the rebuke had stung him. 'Was it merciful for The Lord to take my child? and my wife?!' he demanded indignantly.

Edward looked at him with stern surprise. 'Has Rose died?' he asked suddenly with apparent callousness.

Sprogg looked up at him with sudden anger. 'Why... I do not know...' he began.

'Then let me inform you.' replied the Parson. 'Rose has shown improvement during the last hour. I have been to see her. Her face is clearer and she is cooler. Indeed, she may now live!'

'God be praised!' replied John Sprogg. 'He has been merciful after all.'

'Did you not know of this until I told you?' Edward asked.

Sprogg shook his head.

'Why not?' Edward continued cynically. 'Is it because instead of being at your wife's bedside with your son, you're here - at the inn - making merry with ale?!'

The second rebuke clearly hurt Sprogg further. But this time he reacted with anger. 'There's a witch in that barn!' he retorted. 'She must be watched closely. Else she will escape!'

The innkeeper spoke. 'She will not escape now.' he whispered. 'She is dead.'

The effect of the innkeeper's statement on Edward was electric. With one bound he was in the barn, and quickly he knelt beside the prostrate figure. Then he turned, still down on one knee.

'Quickly! Get her out!' he called. 'She may yet live! She's still breathing... but if we don't help her at once, she will surely die!'

* * * *

Sara was desolate. Her fire was creating more smoke than damage to the barn.

She lay on the floor with her nose pressed against a crack between the wallboards. But eventually the stifling smoke overcame her. Just as she began to hear excited voices, she lapsed into unconsciousness. Her last thought before drifting into senselessness was that her escape attempt had failed - dismally.

When Sara began to come round again, it was in response to a gentle rhythmic pushing against her abdomen. Coughing and spluttering with the still-resident fumes choking her lungs, she opened her eyes. She discovered she was lying on a hard surface gazing up at Edward.

Her first reaction was to try to get up. But he restrained her.

'Lie still, Mistress Sara.' he said softly. As he spoke, she realised what the regular pushing was. He was aiding respiration.

She lay back momentarily. Closing her eyes, she made vain attempts to put her mental processes in order. Please God, she hoped, was the incident at the graveside no more than a nightmare?

But her hope was rudely shattered by a voice.

'Give the witch some brandy - that'll wake her up.' John Sprogg growled cynically.

Edward stopped massaging her abdomen. Moments later he reached forward with his left hand to support her head. He raised a small tankard to her lips. The pleasant-tasting brandy had body. And as the warm fluid ran down her throat, she tingled into full consciousness.

'How do you feel?' he asked. His voice sounded concerned. Had Sara been able to forget the events of earlier in the day, she might have been convinced that he DID care for her.

A blinding headache made Sara feel dreadful. But she avoided saying so.

'Very well, Parson Makepeace.' she answered. Her voice sounded tiny, child-like, most unlike her normal tones.

Then, seeing John Sprogg standing behind Edward, she asked, 'How is Rose, Mr. Sprogg? Is there any hope of recovery?'

To Sara's surprise, Sprogg coughed in embarrassment. 'Why... she's no worse... thank 'ee...' he muttered, red-faced.

'Rose has improved, Mistress Sara.' Edward said. 'She breathes more easily, and her temperature is lower.'

Feeling in the lining of her borrowed dress, Sara produced the bottle of pills, and handed them to Edward. 'It's time she had another pill.' she said. 'Please give her one. They seem to be working.'

'I will, Mistress Sara.' Edward replied. He straightened up to look round at the crowd surrounding him.

The faces of the men looked cowed, like naughty children, almost ashamed of being drunk in the presence of the Parson. As Edward began to speak, they stood listening without a murmur.

'It appears as if Rose Sprogg will recover from the distemper which sent poor Lizbeth to Our Lord.' Edward began, his voice ringing against the wooden rafters. 'There is no doubt in my mind - and I hope, in yours, that this wench helped save her life with the remedies she administered to the sick woman.'

A murmur of assent rose from the crowd

as Edward continued. 'This is no witch - but a pure maiden. Her actions hath proved it.'

For a moment after the sound of Edward's voice died away, no sound arose from the assembled peasants. Then Si Timkins spoke.

'I believe you're right, Parson. She saved Rose Sprogg - and for that we should all be grateful.'

'True.' agreed the innkeeper. 'Poor Rose would be with her daughter in Paradise were it not for the wench.'

Sara's head was now throbbing wildly. But greatly heartened to hear the change of attitude of the villagers towards her, she lay back on the bench to close her eyes in soothing relief.

Thanks to Edward's intervention, she had escaped the witchcraft trial! Oh why had she ever doubted him - why? He hadn't forsaken her, he had merely been awaiting the right moment to speak out. Why had she not been able to see that?

She began to raise herself from the table. But she stopped as one more voice was raised in argument, the voice of John Sprogg. At once Sara realised the he was still determined not to allow her to go free.

'She must be tried!' he said in loud protest.

'Why?' demanded Edward, accompanied by an approving chorus. 'She saved the life of your own wife!'

'She brought the pestilence in the first place!'

The floods of relief Sara had been experiencing began to evaporate. Weakly she heard Edward's rejoining plea.

'That's not fair, John. Mistress Sara did not know she was bringing plague when she arrived.'

'How do you know, Parson?' Sprogg was determined. 'Isn't it true that she arrived out of the darkness to thy house without explanation about whence she had come?'

'Well... yes...' Edward began. 'But she was brought by Mistress Josephine from Rose Cottage.'

'How do you know she came from Rose Cottage?' Sprogg demanded.

There was a short silence before Edward replied in a semi-whisper. 'I think it best not to tell you, John.'

His answer was reticent and reserved. From the murmur that arose, Sara could tell that the crowd were changing viewpoint, becoming suspicious of him. But Edward might still have won the day had not Sprogg asked a question which the others found irrefutable.

'Why, Parson,' he asked, 'Are you sure that the witch hasn't placed *YOU* under a spell?'

Sara opened her eyes to see the crowd, wide-eyed to a man. Now it was *HER* turn to speak for *HIM!* Sliding

229

off the table, she stood up. Unsteadily, she faced Sprogg. 'Listen!' she said, her throbbing head helping her anger to boil over, 'If you want to know more, ride out to Rose Cottage. Ask Mistress Josephine for yourself. She will tell you that I came from her cottage.'

Sprogg was taken aback. He was trapped, and knew it. 'Very well,' he said reluctantly, 'I will go.'

Si Timkins spoke from behind him. 'I shall go, John.' he said. 'You're in no fit state to make the journey.' Then he turned to Edward. 'Give me half an hour.'

'We shall await your return here, in this alehouse, Simon!' Edward replied.

By now, Sara's thumping headache had slightly abated. She sat down in a wooden armchair in a corner of the room. Leaning forward, she buried her head in her hands. She longed for this nightmare to be over, but knew it would be once Josephine came.

The thirty minutes or so seemed like hours. Conversation was conducted in low voices. Edward did not sit with her, but stood at one side of the room conversing with two of the villagers. The others stood about, none drinking. All were engaged in conversation. And from the frequent glances thrown at her, Sara was aware that she was their main topic of conversation. She tried not to look, staring at the floor, shifting occasionally to keep as comfortable as possible. Several parts of her body ached agonisingly.

Then from outside, the sound of galloping hooves alerted her. Everyone turned to look at the door as it burst open and Si Timkins strode in.

Edward made forward to speak to him. But Timkins brushed him aside. It was a gesture which Sara found alarming. Especially as he walked straight to John Sprogg.

Timkins was sweating and breathing heavily. And when he began to speak, his words were emitted in breathless gasps.

'I rode to Rose Cottage, John.' he wheezed. 'I tied up my horse, and knocked at the door several times. But I could get no answer. I tried the door handle which opened, and I went in, calling all the time. I looked round, but could see nothing at first.'

He stopped, still gasping for breath. He turned to look directly at Sara with a look of intense hatred. Now thoroughly alarmed, she stood up. Knees trembling, body shaking, she listened as he addressed her in a semi-shout.

'Then I looked over to Mistress Josephine's bed. And I saw her. And at once I knew the reason she had not answered. Mistress Josephine can never bear out your story, WITCH, because, as you already know, she is dead!'

Sara's mouth dried up in a flash. The room swirled. 'Dead?' she croaked.

'Yes!' Timkins yelled, 'Dead! - Dead of plague - plague *you* inflicted upon her!!!'

Mists swirled in Sara's head at the dread news. Not only had she lost her last possible defence! Now she was incriminated even further!

She reached out for support - but the man next to her backed away. 'Get away, *WITCH!*' he almost screamed.

Sara sat down.

Edward spoke. 'There is only one thing for it: We must try her as planned.'

'Hang her now and be done!' yelled Sprogg.

But Edward raised a restraining hand. 'No,' he said, 'we must abide by the law.'

Sara's alarm reawakened at his tone. It was not the voice of a man trying to aid her. And her belief that she would have to get away by her own wits was strengthened while the discussion continued. Still shocked, Sara began speculating wildly on her chances of escape. If she did not get away, hanging was her certain fate.

Suddenly, as her eyes darted round the taproom, nobody appeared to be watching her. For a brief time, she was unguarded. Take your chance!she shouted inwardly, or die!!

Silently, unnoticed, she rose from her seat. Keeping low, she crept round to the back door. It wasn't *much* of a chance. But it might be her last!

Circumventing the crowd of people, she reached the rear door. Stretching up, she gently pressed the latch---

'Hi!' shouted a man. 'She's getting away!'

Yanking open the door, Sara picked up her heavy skirts and started running. She crossed the flagstones towards the field behind the barn. She covered quite a distance. But her dress hampered her movement.

Then panic gripped as rough hands bore down on her. She was restricted. Forward movement was halted. She was pushed down onto the cobblestones.

Now pinned to the ground, her face was blackened by the filth and rocks of the sumpyard. In that position, she heard Sprogg's accusing voice yelling drunkenly at the others.

'We should have swum her!! What we need is a test! A proper test. A test where she will *confess* to witchcraft!'

'She will not confess!' came another scathing voice behind him.

'She will if I have anything to do with it.' Sprogg answered. 'Strip her naked, swim her, make her confess. That's my way of it!'

'Why, John, I do believe you have a fancy for the wench!' the voice taunted.

'Shut that silly mouth, Simon Timkins!' Sprogg snarled angrily. 'My daughter was only buried today. And my wife may yet die tonight. Should I have a fancy for their killer?'

Sara was in pain. Her hand stretched up at an angle behind her. Her arm was held straight while her face was pressed into the mud.

'Let me up!' she said, her voice half smothered by the mud.

'Aye, let her up.' came a voice Sara recognised as the innkeeper's. 'We'll soon find a place to secure her for the night.'

Then came a surprise. Sara heard a voice she had not expected. And what it said made her spirits plummet.

'When we try her, we might wring a confession from her!' said the voice. 'Then we can execute her tomorrow knowing we are doing God's work.'

'Why, Parson,' said Timkins, his voice sounding surprised, 'we've never heard you speak on witchcraft like this before!'

'I never met a witch before.' Edward replied.

'We've suspected people before, but you never agreed.'

'No,' said the Parson, 'but this time it's different. After all, did I not personally shelter the foul beings under my own roof? And even now is not one of her familiars in bed in my house?'

'Why, that's true, Parson Makepeace.'

Edward's words made Sara's spirits sink desperately. Here was Edward, whom she had regarded as a friend, now turning against her for the second time! And why? Why did he want her to be hurt and publicly humiliated?

Then her thoughts were interrupted by a question from Timkins. 'When shall we extract her confession?'

'In the morning at the trial.' said the Parson. 'Too many of her familiars are likely to be around at this time. The hours of darkness are rapidly approaching.'

'The darkness is not only outside, Edward Makepeace' thought Sara. *'It's in your soul, you hypocritical man of God!'*

'So what shall we do with her tonight?' asked Sprogg.

'Put her back in the barn.' said Timkins.

'If you wish,' intervened the Parson, 'she can stay in my house.'

'That would not be secure.' said the innkeeper. 'My barn be a better place. Nor would it be fitting to knowingly have a witch under your roof.'

'She could be secured in the hanging fire.' Edward responded. 'I could make her secure there - with good strong hemp. She'd *never* set that alight!'

'It would be safe from fire,' said Sprogg, 'but not from her leverets. What if the foul being were to summon a familiar? The ropes might very quickly be gnawed through by a rat! And don't forget. We found a RatKing in the shed with her. If that's not the sign of a witch, I do not know what is!"

Edward stood silently for a moment. 'I see.' he said. 'Very well, it shall be as you say.'

'We must secure her.' said Sprogg.

'Bind her wrists ' said a woman. 'Bind them to one of the uprights.'

'Aye...' said Sprogg thoughtfully.

'May I make a suggestion?' asked the Parson. 'Instead of tying her wrists, why not mount a guard? No familiar could possibly free her then, which it might do were she to be trussed up against the pillar!'

Minutes later, Sara's hands were grabbed and the barn door reopened. Daylight had faded into twilight. A guard was being mounted. She would be here for the night - with no chance of escape.

A rope was tied round her. She was attached to a beam in a position preventing her from lying down.

'Will I have to stand all night?' she protested, appalled at the idea of standing for several hours.

'Aye, you will!' laughed Sprogg.

But Edward once more intervened. 'Tie her by all means.' he said. 'But let her lie free. With a guard over her, nothing can happen.'

'It's more than she deserves, Parson.' said Timkins.

'Surely we can show her the benefits of Christianity and of goodness?' asked the Parson. 'We can show her what it means to be one of God's children instead of Satan's?'

For a moment the group murmured one or two remarks then Sprogg said, 'Let it be then, Parson Makepeace. She can have one night of God's peace before an eternity of damnation!' The murmuring chorus grew louder as assent was confirmed.

Once more in the barn, Sara was tossed onto the ground. The straw was still wet from the efforts of putting out the fire. She was chained from her ankle to an upright, tethered like a goat.

But before the door closed for the night, the last voice Sara heard was Edward's.

'Sleep well, witch!' he called with triumphant sarcasm. 'Once tried you shall return to your Master Satan!'

Chapter 15

Lying on the filthy straw, Sara found that the chain tugged at her ankle every time she moved. Quickly, she realised the benefits of keeping still.

She could hear boots on stone outside the door. Even if she freed herself, another escape attempt would be impossible. And, having failed twice, Sara had no doubt that another act of rebellion would result in instant lynching.

Hours went by, and darkness reigned completely. The dirty straw, smelling nauseatingly of stale animal excreta was quite repugnant. But at least it was reasonably soft. And the privations of the last few days, with Connie needing constant attention, made its semi-softness welcome.

Sara dozed off into bouts of troubled sleep. She frequently awoke when aches in her restricted movements became too painful to ignore.

Then another sound alerted her. She opened her eyes to peer across at the barn door. Peering into the gloom, she could see by the light of the moon that it had been opened.

Sara's first reaction was to shout. She felt like creating as much noise as she could to frighten away the intruder. But she stopped when she realised it might be Edward.

She watched breathlessly as a shadowy figure came through the doorway, a small lantern in hands. It lightly closed the door afterwards. Then, silently, it approached.

Knowing that the superstitious peasants were terrified of witches, Sara felt there was only one person it could be. Edward. It *MUST* be Edward. He'd come to free her, come to get her out of her ghastly predicament. And as his figure drew silently close, she breathed a sigh of relief.

'Edward...' she whispered, 'Edward...'

The figure stopped. Then, it spoke in a soft, repulsively soothing tone.

'T'aint the Parson, *witch,* it be me!'

Sara instantly recoiled in horror.

John Sprogg!

Sprogg's rough hairy hand clamped her mouth like a vice as she opened it to scream. Helplessly, she watched as he reached up to hang up the oil lamp with his other hand. The nauseous odour of his body made her want to vomit.

Then he reached from behind his back, and drew from his rough jacket a long needle which glinted, even in the dim light.

Only an angry moan sounded as Sara, restricted by the chain, fought to repulse the nauseating oaf. But the battle was unequal. Even with all her faculties, Sara would have found him difficult to beat off. Restricted, it was impossible.

Then a sharp pain in her left buttock made her yelp like a dog. She realised what he was doing. He was 'pricking' her, trying to wring from her the 'confession' she might have to make the next morning.

'Confess!, Witch, Confess!' he whispered gruffly as he withdrew the needle. Then again she felt a sharp stab of agony. It was a little higher this time. Then once more he thrust the needle into her skin through the heavy dress.

Sara had to stop him. She had to get him away, to stop his maniacal pricking. Frantic to put an end to it, she did the only thing she could think of.

She bit hard into the hairy hand.

Like a pig in agony, Sprogg let out a short scream. Roughly, he pulled away his injured hand. 'Bitch!!' he screamed.

But Sara wasn't listening to his ravings. 'Help!' she yelled with all her power.

Instantly Sprogg's filthy hand clamped back where it had been. This time it was positioned to make biting impossible.

Shivering with detestation, Sara closed her eyes in revulsion. Once again Sprogg produced the long needle. Her eyes closed as she waited for the pain she knew she would have to endure.

'Mmmmm!!!!' she screamed as first her thigh, then her back and finally her neck were subjected to the agonising needle.

'Confess!' he shrieked again, beginning to lose his drunken reason as he desperately tried to torture her into an admission. 'Confess!... Confess!!!... Confess!!!!!' With each word, he thrust the needle into some part of her anatomy.

239

Fortunately, the thick wool of her dress cushioned the depth to which the needle sank into her body, so that although the pricking was agonising, it did not harm her as it might have. Shaking her head from side to side under his huge hand, she fought cattishly to free herself from the agonies.

But his strength completely overpowered her. Quickly she realised that struggling against this vile, ignorant drunk was in vain.

Dreading further prickings, Sara stopped struggling. She knew that the battle was lost. To continue would simply result in bruising and rough handling. In a frenzy, for the first time she wished that her hanging would come - that her life could end now. Being dead must certainly be better than the pain and indignities she'd endured that day.

Then, suddenly, Sprogg stopped. He moved away from her and got up. 'What...?' she heard him say. Then he gave another yelp as a second shadowy figure dragged him away from her and threw him to the floor.

'Leave her - *DRUNKEN ANIMAL!!*'

Sara's body flooded with delight at the sound of the voice she had come to know so intimately.

Edward!

Chapter 16

It had been a peaceful, if uncomfortable, night's sleep. Edward had pulled the foul Sprogg from her and had dragged him away across the inn yard. She had half-expected that perhaps Edward would return, but he did not, and in the end she had fallen asleep on the dirty straw.

Sara spent the last few hours of her life watching the sun rise through cracks in the panels of the barn wall. She had watched it for more than an hour when she heard footsteps coming over the yard. This was quickly followed by the loud raucous scrape of the bolt. The latch was lifted, the door opened, and in the opening stood a now-sober John Sprogg, leading a number of village men and women. Foremost amongst them stood Beth Quincey, an extremely sorrowful look of regret clouding her features as she regarded Sara soulfully.

Sprogg stood arrogantly in the doorway for a moment, then strode with exaggerated purpose into the barn. As he walked, his heavy boots slushed through the piles of filthy straw on which Sara had spent the night. Sara recognised the bundle in his hand.

'Here, witch!' he yelled. 'Take off that dress, and put back on this witch's finery! We have cleaned it for you. Now you'll look like a new pin on the end of the hangman's rope!'

'No need for you to talk like that, John Sprogg!' Beth Quincey said. 'The wench has not been tried yet, let alone convicted!'

'She'll be convicted soon enough!' Sprogg retorted.

'Until then, treat her properly--'

'Get back to your house, woman. And be quick about it!' the voice of Hal Quincey interrupted.

With a surly look, Beth Quincey obeyed her husband, but from her gait as she left, it was clear that her movements were both grudging and resentful. Meanwhile, Sprogg grabbed Sara by the elbow, unhooked the ankle chain and thrust her purple suit into her hands.

Sara looked down at it in surprise. An attempt had been made to wash it. And obviously a lot of effort had gone into its laundering. But the attempt had been less than successful. Regarding her suit with disdain, she thought, *Clean? That's not clean!!* Taking hold of the collar between finger and thumb, she lightly rubbed her fingers together to feel the material . But the limp greyness of the collar simply underlined the differences between Seventeenth and 20th Century concepts of cleanliness.

'We'll be back at once - ready to try you!' Sprogg shouted, adding, 'And to find you guilty!'. He turned away and heaved shut the door, leaving her once more alone as the footsteps of the crowd receded back across the inn yard...

Quickly, Sara changed. She tossed Edward's mother's dress, now filthy and smelly from the rancid straw, into a corner of the barn. Then dressed in her comfortable suit, she waited.

She did not wait long. The door clanged open again within a minute. Once more she submitted to rough handling. She was pulled out of the barn, hauled over the cobbles and as soon as she was through the rear door, a buzz of excitement greeted her ears.

She traversed the kitchen and entered the taproom. There her eyes opened in surprise. The room was greatly altered from last night.

Almost all the tables had been removed. Only one remained, and had been placed across the front window. Benches stood against the rough plaster of the white walls. The dogspit had been carried away. No ale was in evidence.

Every inch of benchspace was occupied by someone. It seemed that the entire population of Abbots Cross had taken a day off to see her convicted.

At the table sat three men. One rotund figure in his mid-fifties wore a barrister's wig. Well and expensively dressed, he sat smoking a long pipe with the arrogant air of a figure of importance. Sara thought his facial features reminiscent of somebody else. Then she remembered: He was Edward's father. And despite his obvious pomposity, she sensed that he was likeable.

The man on his left, dressed rather like James, held a goosefeather quill. He was already writing in a noisy, scratchy manner.

The third man was Edward.

Sara was handled more gently in the presence of the Squire. She was brought forward and made to stand in front of the table.

The scribe stood up to face her. Indicating the pipe smoker, who eyed Sara up and down with studied indifference, the clerk said, 'This is the Squire of Christ Church. He is Acting Magistrate for this District. He will conduct the proceedings today. I am Simon Williams, Perukemaker in Norton, and tithingman in that town. I have been appointed to that office by the Courts Leet, and was sworn in by the Justices, under whose direction I act. Therefore I am today under the direction of Squire Makepeace.'

He looked round, raising his nose pompously, clearly aware of his high – if temporary – position, before continuing. 'It is because of my ability to write that I have been appointed Clerk to this Court for today. Therefore, the records of today's proceedings will be made by me and lodged in the Parish Chest.'

Sara turned to face the Squire. 'Good Day, Your Worship!' said Sara with dutiful politeness.

The rotund Squire, removed his pipe, pushed against the table with both hands, leaned casually on two legs of his chair and regarded her with a stare which ran parallel to his nose.

'Be quiet, wench!' he spat out with complete disdain. 'Speak when you're spoken to - and at no other time!' He replaced his pipe.

The words cut Sara deeply. As she glanced over to Edward, he pointedly ignored her. And considering the attitude of the magistrate, the venom of the villagers and the indifference of Edward, she realised that chance was greatly stacked against her. She hung her head in despair.

The Squire turned to his clerk and nodded.

'Call the first witness!' the Squire's Clerk said.

From the front doorway emerged the old woman who had been next to Sara at Lizbeth's graveside. She halted at the opposite side of the table to Sara.

'State your name!' said the Squire's Clerk.

'Goody Thompson.'

'State your evidence, Goodwife.'

Goody Thompson turned to look at Sara, pausing before speaking. For a moment, Sara could have sworn that she made her eyes narrow with dislike. Then, suddenly and quickly, she poured out a torrent of story.

'Last night I heard my hens start clucking and clacking in the middle of the night. When I got up to see if it were a fox, I saw something in the air. When I looked closer, I saw it was the witch - here - flying by on a broomstick.'

'Was that all, Goodwife?'

Goody Thompson nodded. Then she bent forward to the magistrate. 'This mornin', several of my chickens be dead!' she added.

'Thank you, Goody Thompson.' said the Squire's Clerk. Then he went on, 'Call the next witness.'

'May I question the witness, Your Worship?' asked Sara.

'Certainly *not!*' spat out the Magistrate.

Sara lapsed into silence as Goody Thompson, momentarily the centre of attention for the first time in her life, smiled toothlessly to all around. The Clerk motioned her away.

'Call the next witness.' the clerk repeated.

A shuffling from the rear indicated the arrival of a plump woman dressed in an all-brown dress and holding a little girl with each hand. The woman bowed to the Squire, then took her place at the stand.

'Tell the court your evidence.' said the clerk

''Twas my twin daughters here, Daisy and Dorothy.' the woman began. 'They were down by the river one mornin' not two days sin'. And they arrived home in a *terrible* state.' She paused to draw breath. 'Daisy said to me that they had seen the... the...'

'Accused?' supplied the clerk.

'Aye, th' accused. Standin' at the side o' the river. Dressed all queer like, all yellow, like a buttercup.'

A gasp rose from the gathering and the woman went on. 'Then across the river came Satan himsel'. Leadin' a horse. He made his way across the river without steppin' in the water at all! And when he arrived at the other bank, th'accused spoke to him and nodded to him. And it seems they was well known to each other!'

'That was the reddleman--' Sara interrupted. But again she was stopped.

'Quiet!!!' the clerk called. Then he asked the woman, 'Be that all?'

'Aye, Sir, Aye. But it be true. She be in league with the Devil!'

A huge moan of horror escaped the assembly. Then the clerk said. ', 'Call the next witness.'

The woman and her twin daughters shuffled off. Meanwhile, the next witness, a simple-looking young man of about sixteen, arrived at the table.

'State your name.'

'Lancelot Thompson, Sir.'

'And what is your evidence?'

The lad looked at Sara, then back at the bench. 'Two days ago,' he began, 'I was up the hill looking for a rabbit for dinner. I often try to catch a rabbit. It's good meat, you see, sir, and---'

'Get on with it!' sighed the Squire.

Lancelot Thompson nodded with servility. 'I was coming past one o' the ponds up in the hills when I saw a prancin' and a playin' in the water, like.'

'What kind of prancing and playing?"

'Well - splashin' the water round, like.'

'Was it the defendant?'

'Eh?'

'Was it the witch?'

'Oh - yessir, it were.' He inhaled deeply, then spoke his next sentence deliberately, as if making each word count. 'She were *NAKED!!!*' His announcement over, he glanced round the whole room with huge eyes. He stood drinking in this temporary admiration as a buzz from the spectators arose. This was instantly silenced by the clerk.

'Go on.' he said, once quietness had settled on the assembly again.

'She were divin' down in the water.' the simpleton continued. 'Three times she dived in. And she were under water for more'n ten minutes at a time.'

'How long were you there?'

'Oh... Only two or three minutes, sir, no more'n that... I weren't spyin', ye see...'

'Then how did you know she was under water for three times ten minutes? That's thirty minutes altogether!' The Squire's voice was impregnated with irritation and disdain.

'Oh…aye… I were there only two or three minutes *more*'n the thirty, Sir.'

The Magistrate's opinion of the simpleton remained evident.

'That'll be all. Next witness.' said the clerk.

As he left the front to resume his seat, Sara eyed the last witness, Lancelot Thompson, with contempt. Had he truly believed her to be a witch, he would have been afraid of her at the glebe pool, and would not have taken hold of her the way he did. His "evidence" contained a germ of truth - no more. Under water for ten minutes at a time, indeed! Ridiculous!!

But clearly the simpleton's version of events had been accepted by the court. She had to try to refute it.

'I was taking a bath!' protested Sara.

'Quiet!' snarled the Magistrate.

A number of 'witnesses' followed in procession, each making an accusation more fanciful and absurd than the previous one. Numbed by the whole proceedings, Sara listened as she was accused by simple peasant people of flying on a broomstick, which she thought ridiculous; of setting fire to a barn, which was true; and of having familiars. This was a particularly bizarre piece of evidence from the nineteen-year-old from Lizbeth's funeral.

'Three leverets she had, Sir. I saw them go into the barn last night while she were in there. One were a three-legged cat with a mouse's head she called Jopling. Another were a fat dog with no legs that squirmed under the door when she called it. And a rat with a calf's head called Sugar Bill.'

'Can you swear to seeing all these familiars?'

'I can Sir, every one, with my own eyes.'

Sara shook her head. Not only was the evidence so obviously trumped up - it was childishly contrived. Yet the 'audience' reacted with 'oohh's and aahh's' to every statement, each of which became increasingly bizarre as the trial continued.

Finally, the 'evidence' appeared to be done. Then one more witness arrived. As Sara watched, she recoiled in distaste. John Sprogg.

Yet Sara had to concede a grudging admiration for the way in which he told the truth as he saw it: How his wife had been tempted with finery such as she had never seen before. How she had dressed Lizbeth in it. How Lizbeth had caught plague. How she had died. How Sara had come to gloat at the funeral. How Rose now lay sick, and had only begun to recover once Sara had been placed in captivity.

This evidence was not derisory. Sprogg was not fabricating anything. He truly believed every word he said.

And once he was finished, the squire turned to look at her. It was an unremittingly pompous, superior look, and when Sara was asked to put her side of it, she knew it was pointless.

'There is little I can say, My Lord--'

'Ha! Ha!' shouted Sprogg. 'She admits--'

'*Quiet!!!*' yelled the magistrate. Then he turned to Sara. 'Have you nothing to say in your defence?'

'There is no answer to these risible allegations, My Lord.'

'So you have nothing to say?'

'No. '

'Very well.'

249

Sara had hoped that perhaps Edward might rise and speak on her behalf. But during the entire trial, from beginning to end, Edward said not a word. Then a figure stood up at the back. It was James, Edward's servant.

'My Lord, may I ask a question?'

The Squire nodded, and the Squire's Clerk asked, 'Yes, what is it?'

'What happened to the familiar in the form of the girl the witch brought with her?' he asked.

For the first time Edward spoke - in a low, detached voice.

'My lord, I can answer that. Last night, while the witch was in custody, she died - died of the plague Satan so hellishly sent to kill all of us. I have locked the room in which her earthly remains lie, and will bury her in unconsecrated ground along with the witch following the execution.'

Sara felt faint. Then fainter. Then consciousness fled as she disappeared into an all-embracing, claustrophobing suffocating blanket of black nausea.

* * * *

The black night of her unconsciousness started to turn grey as Edward's voice began to penetrate her understanding.

'Wake up!... Wake up, Mistress Sara!... Wake up!...' His insistence started softly, then rose in a vocal crescendo until her eyelids started to flutter and she prised them open with some effort.

'What...? Where...?' she stammered incoherently as the blurred figures standing over her prostrate figure began to focus.

'Wake up, Mistress Sara!' Edward said again. 'You fainted!'

As he bent forward to cradle her head in the crook of his arm, he heard a warning from the Squire sitting at the table. 'Touch her not, Edward! He who touches a witch risks being tainted with the blood of Satan!'

'Worry not!' Edward affirmed. 'I am a man of the true faith. Witchcraft cannot harm me. I am immune from its influence!'

Without further delay, Edward took Sara's head in his arms and gently assisted her to sit upright.

'What happened?' she asked.

'You fainted, Mistress Sara.' Edward said. Turning his head sideways, he called, '*A CHAIR FOR THE DEFENDANT!*'

A chair was quickly placed at the front and Sara assisted into it. Then, satisfied that she was fully alert once again, Edward withdrew.

As if from afar, Sara heard the Squire's next words, curiously matter-of-fact and unfeeling.

'Will you need help to remove the leveret's body from the Parsonage, Edward?'

Edward turned a deadpan face to him. 'No, thank you Sir. I am a man of God, and the Devil cannot touch me.' Then solemnly he addressed the crowd. 'But any person *NOT* of my calling may find the spirit of Satan transferred from the corpse to his own living frame.'

'Be that true, Parson?' came the clearly surprised voice of John Sprogg from the back. 'Anyone who touches a witch risks becoming one?'

'Exactly!'

'Then many of us are tainted!' Sprogg proclaimed. 'For we handled her when we brought her here!'

"Twas not proven then!' Edward assured him. 'So you are all free of the evil touch! But molest not either of these women from now on, lest the mark of Cain be upon ye!'

The reaction of the peasants spoke pages about their level of superstition. To see them recoil in horror from the idea of touching either Sara or Connie's body was ludicrous.

'Where shall the witch be hanged?' asked Squire.

Sprogg leapt to his feet. 'There's a fine English oak tree on the green.' he said. 'That be where we were going to let her dangle for a couple of days! So why not dangle her there now? As a warning to other handmaidens of the Devil?"

'Aye!' agreed a crone. 'That'll be a lesson to other witches!!'

A chorus of 'Ayes' approved these suggestions. Sara shook her head in frightened disbelief that the superstitions of these simple people were spelling her death-knell.

Then Edward spoke. 'The oak will not do.' he said quietly. 'By rights she should not be hanged there.'

'Where, then?' Sprogg demanded.

Edward turned his gaze to face him. 'The Hanging Fire.' he said softly.

A subdued reaction greeted this remark.

'Why?' asked the Squire.

"Tis the obvious place.' said Edward.

'But isn't one place as good as any other?' asked the Squire.

'True, My Lord. But in anticipation, I have already arranged it. The gallows in the Hanging Fire is already prepared!'

As the Squire nodded, Sprogg said, 'My Lord, it matter little where the gallows be.'

Again, the Squire nodded. 'Very Well,' he agreed, 'let it be the Hanging Fire.'

Again a chorus broke out. 'the Hanging Fire... the Hanging Fire... aye, the Hanging Fire...'

'Oh, Edward...' thought Sara, 'can you not wait to see me die? And I thought you were going to rescue me!' Her eyes felt moist with overpowering disappointment and grief, both for herself and for Connie as she gazed with crushing misery at the cobbles of the stone floor.

Raising his plump, well-fed form from his seat, the Squire turned to Edward. 'I shall leave you now to carry out the execution.' he said. 'My work is finished. The witch is guilty!'

The benches clattered as all rose in respect. In stately manner, the Squire strutted out of the inn. Through the window Sara caught a glimpse of him getting onto his horse, held by a stable boy, clearly giving no further thought to the innocent he had just condemned.

As the carriage pulled away, Sara found herself being taken once again by strong arms. Powerless, she was pulled along to the inn door. Once outside, she perceived what she could not see from inside the inn. A horse and cart stood waiting, quite unlike that in which she had arrived at Abbots Cross.

The cart reminded Sara of a French tumbrel. A small cart, it had one pair of solid wheels. And Sara recognised it at once. This was the cart which had been used at Lizbeth Sprogg's funeral.

As Sara was thrust up onto it, she felt just like the French Aristocracy were about to feel just over a century later as she stood on the back of the cart, jeered at and humiliated by a howling mob of ignorant nonentities. Sara suspected that their gaiety and taunting laughter came from their feeling of gladness not to be in Sara's position themselves. The louder they shouted, the more secure they felt.

Then, just before they set off, to Sara's surprise, Edward stepped up onto the tumbrel. He started mumbling interminably from his open prayer book. Incensed by what she saw as insincerity, Sara shouted abusively at him.

'Forget the prayers, false man of God!' Her voice rang above the noise of the crowd. Sara knew if they heard it, the peasants would take her remarks as further proof of her guilt. But to her own surprise, she had no fear. Now that she had learned about Edward's true character, she no longer cared.

The tumbrel staggered and jolted its way along as it rumbled and shook its way to the Parsonage. As they entered the gate, Sara fleetingly thought of Josephine. Poor Josephine, now dead of plague. Josephine who might have saved her from this fate.

And Connie, too, was now dead. That was the biggest tragedy. That young Connie, in her care, should succumb to the plague. And now she, Sara, was also about to die...

What would Harriet think? Doubtless a search would be instituted around Abbots Cross. The conclusion would possibly be reached that they had been swept out to sea from the cottage beach. Harriet would be upset, a little for Sara, a lot for Connie. But once over the initial shock, Harriet would also milk as much publicity from the event as she could!

Allowing her mind thus to wander freely was the best thing Sara could have done. When, suddenly, the tumbrel stopped, Sara realised they had already arrived.

She looked down. Was there a chance to get away even at this late stage? No. The crowd milled round, determined that she should not escape at this late hour.

Then Edward stepped lightly down from the tumbrel, and held up a hand for Sara. Disdainfully, Sara ignored it. She stepped down unaided, ready to face her execution with as much pride as she could muster.

Sara was swept along by the flood of people into the ruin. Once there, just as she remembered it, she saw the Hanging Fire.

But now there was something slightly different about the Hanging Fire. The ladder leading up the side was of recent date. Yet it was the central feature, missing when she'd last been there, which turned blood to ice. For down the centre, hanging from what had been the cooking fulcrum, dangled a hangman's noose. And she realised what had frightened her so abjectly during her first visit - when she had read the 20th Century sign.

The executed witch was - *herself.*

Chapter 17

A ll during Sara's trial, John Sprogg sat on a bench near the back listening intently, still smarting from his failure to extract a confession from her. He was almost convinced of her guilt, but he had to admit, if only to himself, that he was not quite certain whether or not she really *WAS* a witch!

But that mattered not. Even if not a daughter of Satan, there was still the fact that she had been responsible for the death of his daughter. And for that, he was determined to get revenge!

The idea that she might be a witch had first come to him at the graveside of his daughter. The more he thought about it, the more he had wondered about her involvement in sorcery.

He was well aware that accusations of familiars or of riding about on a broomstick were just so much flummery - tattle put about by the wagging tongues of jack-puddings. And such accusations did not always bring a conviction. There had been cases, more frequently recently, particularly in the big towns, where nonsensical fairy tales had been laughed out of court, and a witch suspect freed.

But even if she were innocent, nobody would be able to blame him, for he would make sure that his testimony would relate only to the facts. He would speak only the truth without any embroidery when his turn came to give evidence.

During the trial, he would make sure that his evidence would be given last. It did not matter so much what kind of evidence tosspots like Goody Thompson and her idiot son gave so long as *HIS* was strictly factual.

But on the way to the hanging, he felt sorry for the witch. She bore her ordeal well. And admiration added to infatuation as he watched her taking her last journey on earth.

He wanted her to confess. Had she given him the confession he desired before the Parson had interrupted, then he might have testified for mercy on her behalf. Being the aggrieved party, he had an important voice during the trial.

But as she would not confess in the barn last night, he was determined to try to persuade the Parson that *HE* should carry out the hanging. Then he would be certain that she had gone, never again to carry out her foul practices.

Parson Makepeace stood with the witch at the Hanging Fire. The Parson, dressed in his white surplice, read from his prayer book. His eyes never flinched, never looked at the witch.

Yet even now, with death staring at her, the witch was not afraid. Sprogg glowered from beneath large eyebrows as he grudgingly admired the bravest wench he had ever seen in his life.

Sprogg pushed forward to the front of the crowd, to stand next to Parson Makepeace. 'We're wasting time, Parson.' he said.

The Parson raised his eyes and looked steadily at him. 'Thirsty for blood, John?' he asked.

Sprogg felt himself flush. 'No, but I fear I may become bewitched unless she goes to Our Lord shortly.' He knew he spoke the truth.

Parson Makepeace looked at him steadily for a moment, and saw that what Sprogg said was true. 'Very well. I will go up with her.' he said, to Sprogg's immense disappointment.

'But, Parson---' began Sprogg.

The Parson shook his head. 'She will need someone up there to comfort her. That is my job. You can pull the rope to drop the trap. You shall be executioner.'

Sprogg's disappointment turned to satisfaction. He smiled broadly.

'It shall be as you say, Parson.'

Turning, Sprogg went out to the end of the rope controlling the trapdoor. Sprogg could not quite see the end of the walkway. It was partly obscured by the arch. But he could see the central platform.

Parson Makepeace moved towards the wooden staircase, and motioned to the witch to mount the stairs. By now the crowd were making much noise in anticipation.

The noise of the crowd freshened in anticipation as they saw the witch move, followed by the Parson. Then as both figures reached the platform, the noise began to abate. The Parson continued chanting monotone psalms, and although the words were unfamiliar, the crowd assumed it to be a new psalm of Parson Makepeace's especially designed to thwart Satan's interest.

At the stairhead, the witch stopped. Parson Makepeace indicated a sack. As the crowd stood agape, the witch climbed in. So this was how a witch was executed! Nobody in the crowd had ever seen it done before.

Then suddenly, the sacked witch appeared to collapse. 'She's fainted!' the Parson yelled at the top of his voice while catching the witch in the sack as she fell against him.

He pushed her against the wall in the corner to steady her. But for a moment, despite his efforts, he was unable to revive her.

'Let me help!' shouted Sprogg. 'We cannot hang her if she's lifeless!'

He moved towards the wooden staircase, but Parson Makepeace held up his hand. 'Stay, John Sprogg!' he called. 'She'll hang now according to the law. She'll go to her maker whether she's aware of it or not! Now go back to your rope, John. I will tell you when to pull!'

The force of his tone was such that even John Sprogg stopped. He nodded meekly, surprised at the Parson's determination. He stepped back off the bottom step to return to the rope end.

Watched by the crowd, the Parson pulled the witch in the sack back off the wall, and heaved her over to the noose. Not a sound issued from any person as the Parson struggled to get the noose round her neck. At first he could not manage it. But eventually it was done, and he held the witch on the platform, ready for execution.

Then the Parson shouted, 'Now, John Sprogg, send her to God!'

Excitedly, Sprogg yanked at the rope. In turn it pulled away the centre of the platform. A great shout of cheering burst instantly from the crowd as the bag fell through with a heavy jerk. Now dangling on the end of the rope was the sack containing the freshly dead body of Miss Sara Goodwin.

Edward Makepeace stood despondently on the platform. With remorse, he watched the sack dangling at the end of the hangman's rope. He felt no emotion about the sack's contents. But he regretted the necessity of what he had done that day.

Transferring his gaze, he looked down the baying crowd. He felt sickness as they cheered the death of the witch, and particular disgust at John Sprogg's unhealthy satisfaction.

Edward moved across the elevated area, past the still-slowly-swaying rope holding the sack, then began dismounting the stairs. As he reached the foot, the crowd began to move forward.

'Cut her down!' shouted Timkins.

'Aye, Cut her down!' shouted Quincey, the innkeeper.

'I shall do it!' came the commanding voice of John Sprogg. 'I shall do it, and I shall carry her away for burial.'

Edward looked across at Sprogg. The cotter put his hand to his belt, pull out his long knife, and began walking towards the dangling body.

Edward moved forward with hands raised, pushing a way through the crowd. 'No, John, No!' he shouted.

Sprogg stopped, looking curiously at the Parson. He glanced at the crowd all around him, then back at the Parson again. 'In Heaven's name, Parson, why not?' he asked.

'Don't you know that to touch a witch may put the mark of Satan on you?'

Sprogg stopped and thought awhile. That was true! The Parson had explained it during the trial!

The noise of the crowd had by now died away to complete silence. For a few seconds, the only sound that could be heard was the creaking of the rope at its fulcrum as the body still swayed gently from side to side.

'You're right, Parson.' Sprogg finally conceded softly, breaking the silence. 'The body shall be left.'

'A wise decision, John.' Edward answered. Then he addressed the crowd in commanding tones.

'She shall remain here for the rest of today. And thus act as a warning to all witches! This be what will happen to them if they practice their foul habits in Abbots Cross!' He pointed melodramatically at the sack. 'I shall cut her down tonight after darkness. Then shall I take her for burial. Along with her familiar who still lies in my Parsonage.' He turned back, casting a solemn look round them all. 'Now let us pray!' he added quietly.

The crowd, now subdued, bowed heads. The Parson spoke a short prayer. Then he looked up. 'Now disperse.' he said. 'Go back to your homes. I shall remain here for a time to pray to God. I shall ask for the soul of our recently departed sister who fell into the ways of Satan to become one of his daughters. We trust that the merciful God, at the Day of Judgement, will accept her into his fold.'

Talking with a hushed gravity, the crowd began to disperse. Edward turned to face the dangling corpse, bowed his head, made the sign of the cross, then remained in an attitude of prayer.

For a long time, he stood thus. And even when the last sounds of the departing villagers had died away, he remained standing in sorrowful attitude, silent and motionless.

Chapter 18

After stepping from the tumbrel and entering the hall of the hanging fire, Sara could not help but hear the conversation between Edward and Sprogg. She'd seen Sprogg leering at her. But strangely, his goading look made her all the more determined not to show fear.

When she heard Edward say, 'Very Well.' she knew her time had come. Now she would be taken up the ladder, her neck noosed, the trap jerked away. Her neck would break instantly, her breath would be choked out of her, and her soul would depart. Neither rescue nor escape were possible

But to her own surprise, her major feeling was not fear, but disappointment. She had trusted Edward. He knew she was innocent. But now he was following the direction of the ignorant and superstitious. He was no better than they were.

And Sara was more shocked about that than afraid of her impending death.

As she slowly mounted the stairs to die, she only half-listened to his monotonous voice as he chanted his psalms.

Hypocrite! she yelled inwardly.

Reaching the top of the stairs, she looked round. The rope which was to take her life dangled in front of her. Down below, the animal pack called and bayed, dry tongues languishing in mouths thirsty for death.

At the side of the platform, out of sight of the crowd, she could see two identical brown hessian sacks. One lay empty. The other was filled and held lightly with a piece of hemp round the opening. Next to the filled sack was a space. It was hardly large enough for a human being. But it set Sara wondering.

'I wonder if that was a priest hole?' she thought. 'If so, I hope the priests had better luck than I'm having!'

Then she smiled to herself. She had just made her last-ever joke!

Edward continued the monotony of the Gregorian chant. Yet there was something about the words she found unfamiliar. Something about the way he chanted them. The words were being repeated over and over, in an unusual way. Suddenly curious, she listened intently. A flash of mental lightning struck as she comprehended what they said:

> *'Climb into the sack and pretend to faint...*
> *'Climb into the sack and pretend to faint...*
> *'Climb into the sack and pretend to faint...*

She looked round carefully at the empty sack. As she looked, he bent down picked up the sack and held it out. Suddenly bewildered, she stepped into it.

He continued to chant as the sack was pulled up over her head and loosely tied with hemp just like the other sack beside her. Then the words changed.

...Faint into my arms...

...Faint into my arms...

...Faint into my arms...

...Faint now... faint now...

'Mine is not to reason why' thought Sara, dumbfounded. Without questioning anything, she faked a collapse, falling in his direction. She hoped that her sense of direction had not been misjudged.

With relief, she felt his arms grab her from outside the sack. 'She's fainted!' she heard him shout.

Although continuing her pretence, she made it easy for him to move her. Holding her with both arms, he pushed her against the side of the priest-hole. She felt herself being thrust into the opening, the stone cold and rough through the hessian.

'I can't revive her!!' she heard Edward shout.

From below she heard a response. Then Edward took one hand away and shouted. 'Stay where you are, John Sprogg!'

Sara trembled at the name. But fear was replaced by wonder as Edward told Sprogg that she would hang whether conscious or not.

Then she heard him move, and whisper in a barely audible tone. 'Stay still. If you put value on your life, in God's name, move not an eyelid!'

Her body shaking, she stayed leaning motionless in the damp corner. She could clearly hear him shuffling about, moving away two or three paces. There was a short silence, then she heard Edward shout again.

'Now, John Sprogg!' he called. 'Send her to God!'

Through the floorboards she felt the sickening jerk. A great shout rose from below as the entire village cheered. She stood statuesque, not only because Edward had told her to, but because now there was an unexpected chance of escape. Silently, not moving, and paralysed with fright, she felt the hot trickle of tears start to run down her cheeks.

As the noise of the crowd began to subside, Sara remained hidden, silently listening. Still in the sack, she heard Edward telling the crowd to disperse, and that he would return later to bury the witch and her familiar in unconsecrated ground after dark. Sara knew at once that he was referring to herself and Connie.

Cramped in the uncomfortable priest-hole, and still in the sack, she wondered how long she would have to stay there. She heard the crowd begin to disperse, and she began to relax slightly. But she took great care not to move. Then finally, all was silent, apart from a constant, muttering sound. Somebody was still there!

After an age, the muttering subsided. A minute later came the sound of feet on the staircase. She remained immobile, but now she closed her eyes in prayer.

'Sara!... Sara!'

As Edward's voice broke her fragile alertness, she relaxed instantly. Without thinking further, she flung off the sack. Now, for the first time since she'd pretended to faint, she could see all around.

It was a shock to see the identical sack to her own dangling at the end of the rope. But when she turned to see Edward, she knew at once how greatly she had misjudged him, and how cleverly he had saved her life.

'What's going on?' she asked suspiciously. 'What's happening? Why are you here? You wanted me hung!'

'But... Mistress Sara... I had to--'

'You made them search me for a third nipple!' she went on angrily and in great confusion. 'So what convinced you of my guilt--?'

'I was convinced of your *innocence*!' he replied, speaking with uncharacteristic anger in his tone. 'That's why I was determined to save you.'

'By having them nearly hang me--?'

'There was no other way!' he said firmly. 'The only way I could save you was by pretending that I wanted to go through with a trial and conviction. That's why I went along with their stupid superstitions!' His chest heaved as he paused for breath. 'I'm glad you're still well.' he added, in a much softer voice.

Suddenly, she realised what a fool she had been to ever doubt him. His plan had been excellent - well thought out and executed - and he had saved her from certain death. And now all she could do was shout at him! What an idiot she had been!!!

'Oh, Edward...' she said, 'Thank you - Thank you!' She meant it sincerely. Yet it seemed poor recompense for the risk he had taken. She regarded him silently for a few seconds. Then she asked, 'I thought you were convinced of my guilt?'

'Never!' he replied.

For a moment, nothing was said by either of them. But, now safe at last, she wanted explanations for actions which had led her to disbelieve in him.

'If you wanted to save me, why did you suggest a witch-trial?' she asked. 'And why did you condone a search for a third nipple?'

He smiled. 'Because the alternatives were worse. Had they not found a third pap - and witchfinders always do! - then you would have been swum, or pricked into a confession - as Sprogg tried to do!!'

Sara nodded as he spoke, understanding the logic. Then she argued, 'But I could have escaped before then!'

'It was difficult for me to contact you while you were under guard. I didn't want to betray my desire to free you! In any case, Mistress Sara, speaking in your strange tongue, and without someone to go with you, you'd have been spotted like a two-headed horse within the day. Then you would have hanged instantly, without trial! No, what was done was best, and it threw off suspicion that I might be trying to help you. Only so long as they believed that I was convinced of your guilt was your escape possible.'

'I doubt if you will hold credence in the eyes of your father, the Squire, after this!' she said.

He laughed. ''Tis of little consequence. My father and I hold opposing views. Had I been of age to fight during the war, we would have fought on different sides.'

'You mean - you are not on good terms with one another?'

Edward chuckled. 'I do not think I would so express it.' he said. 'My father is a bluff man who has not had the benefit of so advanced an education as I have. He tells me that his parents - my grandparents - considered education a drain on their purse, so spent as little on him as they could. I am indeed glad that my father did not take that view with me!' He smiled genially. 'Ours is an amicable relationship. And he will understand should he ever discover the trick I have played in assisting your escape from execution.'

Like an almost-completed jigsaw, the picture started to materialise. 'So you looked for the priest-hole?' she asked.

He shook his head. 'Not I! That was James! His finding the priest-hole gave me the idea.'

'So I owe part of my freedom to James?'

'A large part - yes!' he said. 'And it was James who made the dummy for the sack while I diverted the attentions of all the villagers at the inn by telling John Sprogg of his Goodwife Rose.'

'I see...' Sara pondered a moment. 'Sprogg seems to be an evil man.' she went on.

'He is beyond himself since Lizbeth died!' the Parson agreed. Then he sighed. 'Far from promoting Christian virtues of Love and Charity, plague does the reverse. And country people eye refugees from London with suspicion. In truth, I fancy they would rather fall into the hands of the Spaniards!' He chortled, then his smile died. 'But I must confess Sprogg has pursued me diligently on the subject of witches. This witch finding was all his idea. Without him, there would have been no witch hunt, trial or execution!'

Looking back at the dangling sack, Sara asked, 'Can I come out of the priest-hole now?'

She had expected him to agree. But she was surprised by his answer.

'No. You will not be able to come out until tonight. When I 'bury' you.'

'So what shall I do all day?'

'You must remain here in the priest-hole alone. All the long hours until dark. Nobody must know you are here and alive. Make yourself comfortable. Rest easily until I come back for you.'

'When will you return?'

'After the sun has gone down.'

'And what will happen then?'

'Then you must leave Abbots Cross - forever.' Sadness edged his voice. 'If ever you come back, we will both hang. You for witchcraft, I for sorcery.'

'Thank you, Edward. ' she said softly. Then, as an afterthought she added, 'Oh - and thank you for trying with Connie. Please don't blame yourself for her death. It was no fault of yours.'

As he looked deeply at her for a moment, she frowned. A curious half-smile played on his face, and she could not understand why. Then, to her surprise, his smile broadened.

'I have something to tell you.' he said.

'What? What have you to tell me?'

'About Constance---'

'What about her?'

'She is not dead.'

Sara's chest swelled with uncontainable delight. 'She's not???' she almost shrieked. 'Then why did you say she was?'

'To stop them from hanging her too. In fact, she is much improved. I think another day will see her cured.'

'And when James asked about Connie at the trial---?'

'He and I arranged that to deceive the witch-hunters, particularly Sprogg.'

Lightly, she raised her hand to rest it on his upper arm. 'I have much to thank you for.'

His genial smile broadened. 'And I have much to learn from *YOU,* Mistress Sara.'

'Well, now, isn't this a pretty picture?'

Coming from below, the coarse voice startled Sara and Edward who both shot sudden looks down to the flagstones below.

Looking haughtily up at them was the arrogant, deeply-scratched face of John Sprogg.

Chapter 19

As he watched the body fall through the trapdoor, John Sprogg felt gratified and satisfied. He had destroyed the witch! And when the cheer went up from the crowd, he cheered even more loudly than the others.

For a few moments, he felt exhilarated that the witch had met her end.

After the Parson's prayer, the crowd began to disperse. They talked rapidly in wonder, amazed at having seen the witch's execution. For although the tales told at the trial had been more than just tall, all were convinced that she *HAD* been a witch. So a witch had been executed, and they, the villagers of Abbots Cross, had dealt a mortal blow for God against Satan.

Wandering off in twos and threes, the villagers gradually dispersed. But although Rose was recovering, she was still at home. So Sprogg was on his own.

He stood regarding the dangling sack. In it hung the body of the witch he had just executed. But now his exhilaration was evaporating. He found it difficult to tear his eyes away.

But the Parson was already urging them towards the exit. And gradually Sprogg wandered through the door with the last stragglers. As he went, he constantly looked back, beyond the now-praying Parson, at the swinging bundle on the rope's end.

He followed the others up the corridor. But instead of going through the exit and away, he remained, creeping back to have one last glimpse of the sack.

The witch was dead. But her body still inhabited that sack. And Sprogg, having been annoyed at the Parson for stopping his pricking just when he felt that a confession was imminent, was now further aggravated that the Parson had prevented him from mounting the platform to tie the rope round her neck. At probably the only time in his life when he might have the chance to do so!

He remembered Sara at the trial just one short hour ago. He had admired her standing at the side of the table, a creature of stunning beauty. He'd repeatedly had to remind himself that this had been the foul being whose undoubted fiendishness had been responsible for the death of Lizbeth.

Sprogg had expected to experience pleasure at having had his revenge. But he was filled with an empty feeling. He'd expected his hunger for revenge to be sated. But it was not.

As Sprogg watched Makepeace, he began to discover how much he disliked the Parson. As he cast blazing eyes at the kneeling figure, Sprogg saw him begin to rise, and wondered where the Parson was going.

As the Parson turned, Sprogg leapt back out of sight. Then, hesitating momentarily, he gingerly peered round the corner again. The Parson was climbing the stairs.

Before reaching the top, the Parson stopped. His feet were still visible on the upper step. Sprogg strained both ears and eyes. What was happening?

Then, strangely, he heard a faint noise - the noise of the Parson calling. It was followed by a faint cry of pleasure and delight, not of pain.

Further conversation followed. But infuriatingly, it was too quiet to be intelligible. So, still keeping his eye on the figure up the ladder, Sprogg stealthily crept forward.

When half way to the hanging fire, Sprogg suddenly heard a noise from behind. He whipped round, darting glances everywhere. It would be difficult to explain his presence had someone come back for some reason.

But the passageway through which he had just come was empty. The outer door was open, swinging in the breeze, and Sprogg realised that this must have made the noise.

Turning slowly back again, he continued his watch. The Parson's feet had now ascended the rest of the stairs. He was out of sight.

Now Sprogg could see nothing and hear little. Inquisitively, he stealthily crept forward. He peered up underneath the arch of the hanging fire. What was the Parson doing on the platform?

Then Sprogg's jaw dropped open. The Parson was talking to a girl! And it was not just any girl, but the girl he had so recently executed for witchcraft!

Knowing he was eavesdropping, but no longer caring, Sprogg gazed up. The two people were oblivious to his presence. As he listened, he was amazed to hear the Parson's story of the younger wench.

Furious at the way he and the others had been tricked, Sprogg was just about to speak when he heard the Parson and the witch talking. And as frustrated anger surged into him, his hatred of the witch resurfaced.

But Sprogg's evil mind worked at high speed. Realising the vulnerable position he had found them in, he wondered how it could be turned to his advantage.

He quickly decided what to do.

'Well now, isn't this a pretty picture!' he called, a supercilious grin on his face.

To his satisfaction, the Parson and the witch looked down at him, their eyes suddenly wide in amazement.

'Why... John...' stammered the Parson. He clearly did not know what to say.

'Aye... John Sprogg...' answered Sprogg. Suddenly he was in the unaccustomed position of command.

Sprogg walked forward to the staircase and put his hand on the rail. 'Do not forbid me to come up this time, Parson.' he said mockingly. 'This time I'm comin' - an' *you* won't stop me!'

He continued to grin as he started to mount the stairs, slowly, each step creaking under his weight. He reached the top, and balanced precariously beside Sara and Edward.

'Now look, John...' began the Parson. But Sprogg turned a look which made the Parson think protest unwise.

Sprogg eyed Sara up and down for a moment. Then he said, 'Well, thou art a comely wench. But how did you escape the gallows, eh, witch?' Then he brushed Sara aside as he looked round, examining the area closely.

For a few moments, Sara and Edward stood watching in silence as Sprogg continued to think it out. Then suddenly, he saw the priest hole. His face broadened into a wide grin. 'So *THAT*'s how you managed it, Parson!' he exclaimed.

'Look, John, she's no witch...' began the Parson.

'She was tried and found guilty!' Sprogg retorted. 'In front of the Squire - your father - all according to your wishes. And now you want to go against the findings o' the court and cheat the hangman's rope?!'

The Parson looked at him with a withering look. 'Yes, but you *know* she is no witch! Why, you could have explained to the court how Rose clad Lizbeth in plague-ridden clothes against Miss Sara's instructions! *And*you could have told how Miss Sara gave you pills which saved Rose from the clutches of the pestilence!'

Sprogg stood silent for a moment. And when he spoke his tone was no longer sarcastic, but contained a menacing evil which chilled Sara.

'I could *still* tell them...' he said with a cold dampness to his tone. 'But the witch must confess!'

'I would rather die...' she whispered.

'And would you rather the Parson die too?'

It was unanswerable, and he knew it. Then the Parson spoke.

'God will never forgive you for this, John Sprogg.' he said. 'But I would rather both Miss Sara and I die at the hands of the village people than have her confess!'

Sprogg snorted. 'Brave words, Parson!' he mocked. Then he became earnest. 'Stand aside and let me go on my errand of witch arraignment!'

Sprogg half-expected the Parson to argue. But to his surprise, the Parson simply moved over, leaving a space through which to pass on the way down the stairs. 'I will let you pass.' the Parson said quietly.

'But I will not!' called a strong voice.

Suddenly alarmed, Sprogg looked down. The strong, muscular figure of James was climbing the stairs.

'Now... James...' Sprogg stammered. 'My argument is not with you!'

'No matter.' James answered, continuing to climb.

Sprogg realised what he would have to do. Resigned to a struggle, he stood ready.

By now James had reached the platform.

'No, James...' the Parson began, but James held up his hand.

'I am sorry, Parson Makepeace.' he said. 'But what must be must be!'

No sooner had he spoken than Sprogg, taking advantage of a moment's relaxation of vigilance, ran at James. Hands held out, ready to grab him by the throat.

'Look out, James!' Sara called.

Warned at the last instant, James moved with a speed belying his large weight. Sprogg tripped. He missed his target, and fell off the platform.

For a moment he seemed to be suspended the ten feet or so above the cobbled floor below. Then he fell, and as he hit the hard stone, blackness engulfed him.

The three figures on the platform looked down in horror at Sprogg lying on the stone.

Then the Parson moved. His feet rattled down the wooden stairs. He was followed first by James, then Sara.

'Is he badly hurt?' Sara asked as the Parson leaned over his chest, placing an ear to Sprogg's heart.

Then the Parson looked up with a face which told them what they needed to know without speech.

'He's dead.'

'Now he cannot spread our secret round the village.' said James confidently. Then, clearly reflecting that he might be thought callous, he went on, 'But I'm sorry he's dead.'

James, Edward and Sara circled round the lifeless figure. James went on, 'I hope our Good Lord will understand. It was done accidentally.'

'Don't blame yourself, James,' Edward said. 'He was guilty of his own death.'

Horrified at the crooked figure lying in front of her, Sara found it difficult to speak. 'I feel sorry for Rose.' she croaked. After his fiendish activities of the last few days, she could feel nothing for John Sprogg. Only revulsion at his death. And sadness for his family.

Edward agreed. 'So do I.'

'But she has a son.' said James, 'John Sprogg will be small loss to her.'

Edward nodded, turned and spent a minute or so once more looking down at the body. Meanwhile James began to fidget, plainly disturbed.

'What is it, James?' Edward asked.

'Parson... I'm worried in case they return and find Miss Sara here with Sprogg's dead body! She must hide at once while we conceal the carcass. In fact, best she remain concealed until nightfall.'

Edward turned to Sara. 'James is right.' he warned her. 'Return to the priest-hole. Remain there until sunset. I shall come back for you then.'

Sara nodded. Taking one last look at the horror sprawled in front of her, she turned, and made her way over to the foot of the stairs.

'What shall we do with Sprogg, Parson?' asked James.

'I don't know.'

As Sara started to climb, she turned to face the two men.

'The corpse...' she said thoughtfully.

Edward looked up. 'Yes, Mistress Sara?'

'Why not put it in the hanging sack? Nobody will search there. And even if they do... well... the sack *IS* supposed to contain a dead body, isn't it!'

'Aye!' laughed James grimly. 'Yours!'

Sara shrugged her shoulders. 'If they discover that the sack contains the body of John Sprogg instead of me, they'd think it an act of witchcraft!

Edward looked at James. To his surprise, the servant's face bore a strange expression. 'You have a doubt, James, have you not?' he asked.

James nodded. 'I have, Parson.' As Edward and Sara waited, he went on, 'What shall we do with the corpse come nightfall? We cannot leave it to dangle in the sack forever.'

Edward looked back at Sara. 'James is right, Mistress Sara.'

Momentarily, all three were silent, then James spoke again.

'You recall last year when old Giles Turnbull drowned? His body was fished out of the river. Nobody could tell what had happened.'

Edward gave a sage nod. 'That's right.' For the first time that day, he smiled. 'It's a knavish trick! But it might work.' He slapped his servant's shoulder. 'Come, James, we'll do it. We'll put Sprogg into the sack now. Then tonight, while I go back to Rose Cottage with Mistress Sara, take my horse, go a furlong upstream and dump him into the river. No doubt he will be 'discovered' some time tomorrow!' He turned to Sara. 'Now, Mistress Sara. Into the priest-hole with you at once. Before someone sees you!'

Once ensconced in the hole in the wall, all Sara could see was the dangling rope. She listened as the two men removed the dummy Edward had put there. By the noise, she knew they were replacing it with the corpse of John Sprogg. Then Edward climbed the stairs.

'Not a sound for the rest of the day!' he commented. And although his tone was light, she knew he was in earnest. 'I'll be back at dusk.'

The day ground on.

Wedged in the priest-hole, Sara sat for long, cold hours watching a shaft of light flooding down from the roofless top of the ruin. The sun lethargically approached its zenith. Then with agonising slowness, it moved across the sky.

From time to time, the rope holding Sprogg's corpse creaked as light breezes caught it. As it swung back and forward, chills of unbelievable cold ran wildly through her body. These movements made her think of Sprogg, of the effect he'd had on her and how, in front of her eyes, he had been dashed against the cobbles below. And now it was made worse by new feelings of reservation over her macabre idea of swinging him at the end of the rope in the place originally intended for her.

Finally, the late summer evening began to arrive. By now, Sara was in an agony of discomfort, cramped into the priest-hole. All parts of her body aching, she wondered how much longer it would be until Edward finally arrived.

But when the sound of horses hooves finally stole into earshot, she almost didn't believe it. She listened with apprehension as they slowly made their way round from the parsonage, accompanied by the grating of cartwheels on the track. Relief, not excitement, possessed her when she realised that Edward had arrived at last.

But, remembering the earlier unexpected arrival of Sprogg, Sara didn't move. She remained motionless in the priest-hole as the sound of footsteps echoed across the cobbles below.

Then she felt her heartbeat accelerate as the feet mounted the staircase. And although certain it was Edward, she took care not to move prematurely.

When the figure came into view, she sighed with relief.

'Very well, Mistress Sara, you may come now.' Edward said.

Gripped by a creaking, crushing stiffness, but thankful to be able to move at last, Sara began to raise her agonised body out of the priest-hole. *Thank God the long hours of motionless waiting are finally over!* she thought as agonies of stiffness sought out every muscle.

The evening shades of daylight still sent illumination down through the absent roof. It lit up the wooden ladder and the hanging fire. As she descended, she cast a glance at the swaying sack. Again she shivered as it swung in silent eeriness.

Quickly, with Edward by her side, Sara pattered stiffly over the cobbles towards the exit. Reaching the door, she paused and cautiously looked out. A horse and high-sided cart very like Josephine's stood in the area just opposite where she stood.

Apprehensively, she walked over and looked over the cart sides and into the floor. A bundle of blankets covered an inert figure. In addition, the Seventeenth Century dress Sara had borrowed was also covering the sleeping form. Connie was lying in the back, dressed once more in her original clothes. Her apparel was now clean. She was sleeping peacefully, no longer delirious.

'Why, Edward!' said Sara. 'She's wearing her own clothes!'

'Yes.' said Edward, 'The plague has not spread further. And when I last gave a pill to Rose, I collected Connie's clothes. I think the plague flea has by now gone, but in order to be certain, I washed the clothes in hot water. I did it myself as I did not want to risk the life of Daisy, the servant girl. Although once the clothes were dry, I asked Daisy to dress Mistress Connie. Now the clothes are clean and pure without any of the plague-bearing fleas you spoke of. With luck, your pills, and God's good grace, the plague has been stopped.'

He looked furtively round to make sure they were not seen. 'Please climb aboard.' he said, pulling himself up onto the driver's seat.

Sara reached up, grasped the rail and, helped by James, swung herself on to sit beside Edward. She twisted in her seat and looked down at James, standing beside Josephine's cart. His enormous figure was silhouetted in the moonlight. 'Goodbye, James.' she said. 'I owe you my life. I'll never forget you.'

'Nor will I forget you, Mistress Sara.' he said. 'Goodbye!'

Edward and Sara set off.

'Where are we going, Edward?' Sara asked.

He looked thoughtfully at her. 'Fear you the plague?'

'Why do you ask?'

'Because the safest place for you is Josephine's cottage.' he said. 'And nobody will think of searching for you there. They all fear the plague too much.'

'True.'

'There is an outhouse there.' Edward went on. 'I have packed some food and drink for you. Stay in the outhouse. There is straw and hay, so you will both be comfortable.'

'Connie will not catch it again.' said Sara, glancing back at the sleeping form. 'And I am healthy and young. Plague is very unlikely to molest me!' She did not mention that she did not expect to be long in Death Cottage. Once she had passed through to the 20th Century, and delivered Connie back to Harriet, she planned to return to him.

'Then Josephine's cottage it is.' he said. 'But I am worried about plague, nonetheless.' He turned to her. 'Did you not say that the sicknesse was carried by a flea?'

'It is.' she said. 'A flea which hosts on black rats--'

'Hosts?'

She nodded. 'Lives by drinking its blood.'

'So if there are any rats in the cottage, the plague will continue?'

'I think it will. But tell me - *ARE* there any rats at Death Cottage?'

He nodded wistfully. 'There will certainly be rats there.' he said. 'They will live in the thatch of the roof.' He pondered for a moment. 'My father, Squire Makepeace, has been thinking of rebuilding that cottage, adding an upper storey.' he said. He pondered further before adding, 'I think 'twill be a good plan to burn the thatch of the roof, then rebuild the cottage. That will prepare the cottage for its improvement and rid us of the rats at the same time.'

She shot him a look of alarm. *If he burned the cottage, then she would have no means of returning to him!* 'When do you plan to do this?' she asked.

He thought for a moment. 'I do not wish to draw attention to the cottage.' he said. 'So I will leave it for two or three days before coming out here again. I shall speak to my father in the meantime, and elicit his permission. So it will be at least three days hence.'

She nodded. *That would give her time to get Connie away and return!* 'That's good.' she said. 'And in the meantime I shall remain in the outhouse for tonight, then set off tomorrow.'

'Where will you go?'

'I will journey to Newcastle. Connie's mother has a relative there. I hope to leave Connie in her care. If that is possible, then I shall return.'

'How will you get there?'

Sara hadn't really thought about it - because she had no need to! But she could not tell him that. 'With luck, some farmer will be taking a load of hay south, and will allow us to travel on the top of the load.'

Edward nodded. 'I'm sure there will be.' he said. 'Especially at this time of year. And there are always supplies being taken into the city for the population there has to be fed! So there will be numerous carts going to Newcastle, carrying all manner of produce to feed that vast city.'

'How big is it?' she asked curiously.

He rolled his eyes. 'Enormous.' He responded. 'There must be at least ten thousand souls live there... probably more!'

She nodded. 'Enormous...' she said, trying to hide her tongue-in-cheek from him.

He regarded her obliquely. 'Are you worried some farmer might know of your witchcraft conviction?' he asked. 'Because if so, you need not fear about news of witchcraft traveling.' He went on. 'The gossip and tittle tattle about that will largely be confined to Abbots Cross and Christ Church.'

Will I return by haycart too?' she asked.

He pursed his lower lip. 'There may be a coach going from Newcastle to Edinburgh.' he said. He fished in his pocket and produced two coins. 'Here are two sovereigns.' he continued. 'They will pay for your return journey from Newcastle, should that be possible.' He turned to look at her. 'How will you get to

Abbots Cross from Fenwick?' he asked. 'Shall I ask James to meet the coach?'

She shook her head vigorously. *If only she could tell him!* 'No, Edward.' she said. 'I am young. And fit. I can walk that short distance.' She smiled. 'And I will do it with great pleasure!'

'The coaches are very fast.' He told her. 'So make sure you get an inside seat.'

'How fast?'

'The slowest only make some four miles an hour. But on good roads the fastest travel at eight or ten miles per hour – sometimes more!' he said. 'With a good road and a following wind, you might even return from Newcastle in six or seven hours!' His tone was confident and a little boastful. 'Although there will be at least one stop for a meal. The standard rate for a meal is half a crown. Expensive, but the money I have given you will cover such an expense.'

She nodded and looked away, trying to hide the tears which lurked, ready to appear at any second. As they continued the moonlit journey, Edward fell silent. 'Why so quiet?' Sara finally asked.

He turned to look at her, his doleful face reflected in the white lunar light. ''Tis just that... well... I wish you could stay...' he said, almost pleading, '...if only you could stay...'

An edge at the top of her throat almost prevented speech. 'I have to get Connie home...' she whispered. 'Were it not for that...' She left the rest unsaid.

As Sara looked back at him, she knew that life with Edward, albeit in a different Century, was all she wanted. *But was return to him possible?* Once she had traversed Josephine's room into the 20th Century, would it revert to a junk room? And would her return route then be cut off? She had no way of knowing.

Please God, let me return to him! she prayed silently. *Let me deposit Connie with Harriet, then come back to this Century, and this man.*

The journey progressed. But as they covered the well-known track to Death Cottage, Sara's desperation mounted. She said nothing. She was increasingly tempted to risk all and return with Edward to the Parsonage. Immediately. No doubt it would be possible for her to hide in that huge house for a few days. Once the hue and cry died down, things might be different. With Sprogg gone, Edward would be able to convince the villagers of Sara's innocence.

Then Sara turned to look down at Connie. Her cousin was sleeping peacefully in the rear of the cart. And Sara's delight drained as she realised the truth. What she dreamed was impossible.

To stay by herself in the Seventeenth Century would be a major step. But at least if it were a mistake, she would face it alone. Nobody else would be effected - least of all her aunt!

But for Sara to remain, Connie would also have to stay. And to trap Connie in an alien century would be a selfish liberty with the adolescent's future. Instantly she felt her happiness drain. She could not do it.

She turned to look once more at Edward. Speech was unnecessary. He recognised her train of thought and nodded.

'I understand, Mistress Sara. You must go back home because of Constance.' He inhaled hugely. 'Go then, with my blessing... And may it bring the happiness I yearn for you.'

'Oh, Edward' she lamented. 'I wish I could stay. With you. But I can't. I must take Connie back.'

'Is your return here impossible? After Constance has been returned?'

'I don't know...' she said. 'I *MAY* make it back. but there are other considerations... things I have not troubled you with... I just don't know...'

She wished she could tell him the truth - that she was from a future time That she had to revisit that time to take Connie back.

But it was such a bizarre notion - so apparently ridiculous - that it was impossible to tell him. She hated being devious, but there was no alternative.

She had been thinking furiously. There was a chance that Connie could be left with a cousin of Harriet's. And if Sara phoned the next day, she would be able to arrange it immediately. Sara needed desperately for Harriet's cousin to take Connie.

Her future happiness depended on it...

'Let us leave things like that.' she said. 'I fervently hope to return. But if I cannot...'

He nodded understanding. 'But if you're not back shortly,' he went on, 'I'll know you've decided to remain in your own Country.'

Then almost at once, the moonlit cottage loomed up. Edward approached it, then pulled the cart to a stop at the side of Death Cottage. While Sara dismounted, he tied up the horse and went round the rear of the cart. Lifting the sleeping Connie, he carried her round to the rear of Death Cottage and made his slow way down the garden path to the outhouse.

Sara followed him, and when they reached the wooden building, she leaned forward and opened the door. A strong smell of fresh hay greeted their noses. Clearly Josephine had been busy on the day before her death!

'There is not much light in here.' he said as he carried Connie forward. 'But 'tis risky to light a candle because of the risk of fire in a wooden outhouse.'

Straw and hay piled against the sides of the outhouse. Sara looked for and found a comfortable area, indicated it, and with a gentle movement, Edward laid the sleeping Connie down.

Once Connie had been made comfortable, Edward stood up. "Tis time for me to go.' he said. "Twould be best were I not away from Abbots Cross too long.'

Sara nodded. 'I'll see you off.' Her voice croaked agonisingly.

Together they walked slowly to the front of Death Cottage where the horse and cart stood. Then as Edward stopped by the cart, he turned to take one last look at her. It was a look which both knew would have to last forever.

Then - almost without realising it - she was in his arms. And a lingering embrace from across the centuries filled her with such longing and such despair that tears which she had hitherto kept at bay breached the wall of her resistance.

'Goodbye, Edward' she wept.

She saw him force a smile. 'I'm not going to say 'Goodbye', for I hope and believe we shall meet again.'

On the instant his face changed. Athletically, he turned and leapt onto the cart. 'Giddup!!' he yelled. He slapped the horse's rump smartly. It jerked into life. The speed at which it set off demanded Edward's total concentration. He was too involved in controlling the animal to look back.

Chapter 20

Sara watched the cart through shimmering vision until it disappeared over the rise. Then, drying her eyes, she turned back. She went to the gable door of Death Cottage, reached forward and turned the handle with one hand.

The door creaked open. Without looking at anything, Sara went into Josephine's room. The moonlight streaming through the window gave enough light to see an oil lamp. Quickly she applied a flame to the wick. Josephine's lamp created a primitive glow. Then she started back in fright.

In the bed still lay the plague-ravaged, dead body of Josephine.

'Oh... poor Josephine...' she whispered.

She went out of the door again and round to the outhouse. Connie lay on the straw, half sleeping, half awake. 'Where am I, Sara?' she asked dreamily.

'We're at the cottage, Connie. You fell asleep in the outhouse here. Let's go to bed.'

In her dreamy state, Connie readily accepted the banal explanation. Sara helped her to her feet, and together they made their slow, unsteady way round to Death Cottage. Going in through the gable door, Sara took care to shield Connie's gaze from Josephine's dead body but the young girl was too half asleep to notice the carcass.

By the lamp glow, Sara could see a wooden chair on the landing down the spiral steps. She helped the semi-sleeping adolescent across the room, out of the door and down the three spiral steps. Lightly she sat Connie on the chair.

She walked across the room and closed and barred the outer door, taking care not to look at Josephine's lifeless form. Then she returned and went out of the door above the spiral steps, closing it behind her.

Connie had roused a little and was sitting up in the chair. 'Sara!' she complained in irritable sleepiness. 'I want to go to bed!'

Helping Connie up from the wooden chair, Sara supported her into her bedroom. And it was not until back in the bedrooms that Sara realised she had never doubted her ability to re-enter the 20th Century.

The bed in Connie's bedroom was just as it had been when Connie had left it. Gently, Sara removed Connie's outdoor clothes, put on her the same night-dress she had been wearing when she fell ill. Connie scrambled immediately into bed, fell onto her pillow, and was asleep at once.

Sara stood up, to be startled by a noise. It was the sound of a car engine approaching from outside. As it squealed to a stop, Sara recognised George's old Ford. Then footsteps approached the cottage, to be followed by a loud pounding on the downstairs door.

Startled, Sara dashed away from Connie's bedside, completely forgetting the low beam over the door. Instantly, she paid the penalty a second time. Her head collided with the beam.

She staggered back, stars flying, and fought to retain her consciousness. Momentarily, the passageway took on a life of its own, spinning and dancing round her like children in the playground. Stunned and briefly insensible, she dropped onto the soft carpet, desperately striving to stay alert.

But the battle was not there to be won. And eventually Sara stopped fighting as a cloud of insensibility completely engulfed her.

Sara gradually became conscious of some pain in her cheeks as her face was gently slapped from one side to the other, and a voice she recognised called, 'Sara... Sara... Wake up...Come on, wake up!'

'Mmmm? mumbled Sara, and her eyes opened, then gradually focussed. Then they jerked into full vision. She was looking straight into a well-known face.

Harriet!

* * * *

'What are you doing here?' Sara asked.

'We'll discuss that shortly, My Girl!' Harriet responded tersely, but it was a terseness with which Sara was extremely familiar, and she took little notice of it. She looked quickly from one side to another to see that she was lying on her bed, still completely clothed. Then she faced her aunt again.

'What are you doing here, Harriet?' she repeated, levering herself up on the bed.

'I came to see how you were getting on. It's as well I did - isn't it?' Harriet spoke hotly. 'Connie in bed asleep. And you lying unconscious on the floor for God-knows-how-long!'

Sara looked out of the window. The sun was high. Another fine day was in prospect. She tried to get to her feet. But a feeling of dizziness prevented her. She lapsed back onto the bed.

'Don't go back to sleep!' warned Harriet. 'You could end up in a coma!'

Sara shook her head. 'I don't think so, Harriet.' she said. 'I'm fully awake now. This dizziness will pass. Anyway, how did I come to be here? I heard you knocking on the door last night. Just before I lost consciousness.'

'George had a key to the front door. He let us in when we realised there was going to be no response. We looked around downstairs, then came up here to find you lying on the floor.'

'I banged my head on that low beam.'

Harriet nodded. 'I thought you must have done that. George said he warned you about that beam.'

'I forgot. But how did I get here? On he bed?'

'George and I carried you through - George mainly. We laid you on the bed. We thought it best to leave you as you are rather than try to get you undressed.'

'I see.' Sara sat up again, and this time her dizziness had evaporated. She got to her feet. now she was feeling quite steady. moving towards the door she went into the corridor and looked into Connie's room. Connie was fully awake. But clearly a little drowsy.

'Hello, Sara.' she said, sitting up.

By now, Sara had begun to control her nausea. 'Hello, Connie, how are you this morning?' she asked.

The adolescent face creased into a thin smile as Connie responded in a thin voice. 'I feel a bit strange. Very weak. As if I've been in bed for a few days.'

'Well - you had a headache. And you were sneezing all the time.'

'Well - my headache's gone, and I've stopped sneezing.'

'So... you've recovered...?'

Connie's forehead furrowed. 'Recovered?' she asked. 'Recovered from what?'

Harriet looked askance at Sara. 'Has Connie been ill?'

'Well...er... yes, she has. We took her to Abbots Cross to see the Pars--- er, Doctor... didn't we, Connie?'

The puzzled frown deepened. 'Doctor? I've seen no doctor! I've been in this bed all the time.'

Sara laughed. 'Have a look at the inside of your thighs - and under your armpits!'

Connie rolled onto one shoulder, and lifted an arm. The buboes had disappeared. No evidence of disfigurement remained. 'I can't see anything! Have I had spots or something?...'

Suddenly and irrationally angry that Connie should remember nothing of her illness, Sara snapped at the young girl. 'You've had Bubonic plague!' she shouted.

A shriek of cynical laughter from Harriet made Sara whip round.

'Bubonic plague!' scoffed Harriet. 'Don't be ridiculous! Where would she catch Bubonic plague?'

'From a rat we found in the barn.'

Harriet snorted his disbelief. 'You don't catch plague in Britain *NOW!*' she said. 'It only exists in Third World countries! In remote areas of the world! Not in Britain!' Her mocking tones crescendoed. 'Where do you think you are? In the Seventeenth Century? That bump in the head must have been worse than we imagined!'

For a few moments, Sara was consumed with anger. Harriet didn't believe her. She turned a resentful look to Connie. But when Connie stared blandly back, Sara's irritation evaporated. Clearly Connie remembered nothing of her 'sicknesse'.

Sara turned back to face her guardian. 'Why are you here?' she asked. 'Why aren't you in America?'

'The gig in America is off.' Harriet said, suddenly abashed. 'But guess what? Great news! I have a part in a play in Edinburgh!'

'Edinburgh?'

'Yes,' said Harriet. 'I'm on my way there. I want you both to come with me. It'll be a great experience for Connie. Think of it! Seeing a *REAL* play acted by *REAL* actors and actresses! And you can look after her while I'm onstage!'

Sara's spirits slumped. *Harriet was going to use her as a childminder again!*

'I don't think so.' Sara said.

'But Sara... think of it... I'm going to take part in the Edinburgh Festival.'

'The Edinburgh Festival?' Sara was, for once, genuinely impressed.

But Harriet was reticent. 'Well... not exactly.'

'Not exactly?'

295

'No,' said Harriet. 'Actually, it's part of the Fringe Theatre.'

'The Fringe Theatre?'

'Well... perhaps not the *Fringe*, exactly, more the fringe of the Fringe, if you see what I mean - the *Forward-Looking* theatre. I don't get paid for it, of course, but it's a real play. You can come too. That will be great for Connie.'

'I don't think so, Harriet.'

Harriet's manner changed at once 'In that case you can stay here by yourself, Sara Goodwin.' she suddenly snapped sternly. 'I might have expected that kind of selfish reaction from you!' She hesitated, overcome with fury. 'And I think it will be a good idea for you to move out of my house and find somewhere else to live.' she said, as if playing a trump card. 'Then we'll see how well you get on, my girl!'

'I've only stayed in your house because I don't think you're fit to look after Connie!' Sara retorted , knowing she was being cuttingly brusque, but also knowing that it was the truth.

'Hmm!' Harriet retorted. She turned to Connie. 'Get dressed, my girl. You're coming with me!'

'Aw... can't I stay with Sara?--'

'Get dressed *NOW!*'

Connie looked despairingly at Sara. But Sara spoke quietly. 'Go on, Connie. Go with your mother.'

Sara bestowed a wan smile on Connie. Despite her adolescent moods, Sara felt sorry that Connie would be leaving. Then with a sudden burst of ineffable joy, she realised that it also had its reward.

Now she would be able to return to Edward within the two-day timespan!

Later, when Harriet spoke to Connie about going with her to Edinburgh with her. Connie's reaction was unexpected.

'Well I'm not going there on my own!' she said. 'I'm only going if Sara goes too.'

Harriet turned to Sara. 'See?' she demanded. 'See what you've done with your selfishness?'

But Sara had had quite enough of Harriet's moral blackmail. 'It's not my scene, Harriet.' she said. 'What's the point of me going to the Fringe theatre in Edinburgh? It's of no interest to me! So whoever goes - I'm not!'

'Do you know what's wrong with you, Sara? You're jealous! Just because **you** haven't the presence to be an actress! You have no adventure in your soul - none at all! You'll end up living a boring, uneventful life! I despair of you!'

Sara smiled sadly. *'I could tell you a story...'* she thought, but said nothing. It was pointless to argue.

That night, Sara went to bed feeling much better. She slept well, and next morning, she was completely recovered.

Then she thought about the two knocks on her head. Suddenly alarmed, she wondered about her adventure.

'Has it been a hallucination?' she asked herself. 'Did it only take place in my mind?'

She looked round for something tangible - something that would *prove* where she had really been.

Had she brought anything back with her?... clothes, for example?

No, her clothes were still the same - and so were Connie's. The dress she had borrowed still lay discarded in Quincey's barn. The nightdresses Connie had worn had been left in the Parsonage.

Did she still have the bar of Bristol soap? No, that had been returned to Edward.

Then she knew there was only one way to confirm the truth. 'The door...' she said in a half-whisper as she went past a bemused Harriet. '...the door...'

Arriving at the small spiral of steps, she reached hesitantly up for the handle. The lamp would now be out, of course. But the room should be as she left it.

The door was solid and stubborn. Even with both hands on the ring, Sara found it difficult to move the catch. She began to fear the worst.

'Edward...' she pleaded with a soft, frantic sadness, '...Edward...'

Then, watched by an amazed Harriet, and using strength she did not realise she possessed, she forced the key. The mortise moved, the door swung aside.

In the darkness it was possible to see little. She fumbled for the light switch, found it and flicked it down. Accompanied by the electrical fizzing George had first noticed, the lamp went on. The room was illuminated with a flickering light.

The lamp lit up properly to reveal nothing more than the junk George had promised to clear away.

Sara stood peering into room, thinking a number of things, regretting and wishing. She extinguished the light, then silently turned to swing shut the door up the spiral steps. Meanwhile, unheard, the lampholder continued to make the slight buzz of its electrical fault.

George's car stood outside the front of the cottage, its engine 'put-putting' quietly while George waited patiently behind the wheel. Connie had finally been persuaded to go to Edinburgh with her mother and sat sulkily in the back of the car.

'Remember what I said, Young Lady! I think it's time you moved out of my house and went to live by yourself.' said Harriet, repeating her earlier threat with one foot poised melodramatically on the running board. 'Your selfishness will soon come home to you then My Girl! Your attitude isn't good for Connie, and it *certainly* isn't good for me!'

Making an outrageous attempt at dramatic exit, Harriet stumbled into the rear seat, sat back beside Connie, closed the door and opened the window. 'If you're not able to fit into my family, then you're better on your own.' she continued in a voice high with petulance. 'I shall arrange for you to have your mother's legacy any time you like. Let me know your arrangements after I return from Edinburgh.'

Harriet's words held no terrors for Sara. In fact, she welcomed them. For some time, Sara had considered living alone. She'd only stayed with Harriet for Connie's sake. Now that Harriet had told her to leave, she felt relieved.

Now, more than ever, it would suit Sara to live alone. If she couldn't be with Edward, she didn't want to be with anybody. Least of all Harriet.

She could have matched her guardian's venom in her response. But Sara was more tactful than that.

Quietly, and with measured civility, she said, 'Very well, Harriet. I shall arrange to live elsewhere as soon as I can.'

Further piqued by Sara's calm, Harriet sat back and closed the window. Sara saw Connie lean forward and begin to wave. Sara's hand was half-raised to respond when Harriet pulled the girl away from the window forcing her to sit back in the seat where Sara's couldn't see her.

The old car proceeded off along the cart track in a cloud of blue smoke. Sara watched it go, standing at the front gate, thinking. It disappeared over the rise just as Edward had disappeared over the same rise last night.

Or had it been three centuries ago?

Or had it been that the bang on her head had created hallucinations?

Now completely alone, Sara went back into the house. She plumped into an armchair. Listlessly, she gathered together her books and started to thumb through them.

But she was unable to concentrate. Within a few minutes she knew that before anything else, she would have to do some investigating.

Chapter 21

Had it all really happened? Or was it one long hallucination? Could she prove to herself that she had been to the Seventeenth Century and back again?

Laying down her books, Sara stood up and began to wander round the house. 'There must be something here!' she told herself. 'Something which can remind me, something which will prove that it *did* actually happen!'

Had anything changed? Had anything tangible figured in her adventure? And if she could find proof that she *had* been to another time, could she also find the means to get back there?

She wandered upstairs. Carefully, she examined her clothes. But nothing in them bore evidence of Edward or his time.

Several times she opened the door up the spiral steps. Light from the skylight illuminated the junkroom. No Josephine.

She looked in the barn. Nothing. Nothing at all. Nothing anywhere.

The day was wasted in futile searches and pointless activities. Repeatedly she went over and over the same things, revisiting the same areas of the house, examining its contents, searching its environs. Not a clue.

Day was followed by troubled, restless night. Sara woke several times, now feeling very alone in Death Cottage. Next morning, Sara was no closer to solving her dilemma.

Her first thought was to return to London. Today. She could make the effort to resume something approaching a normal life there. In time she might get over it.

But her emotional reaction was different. If she was to get back to Edward, she was convinced it would happen *here.* In Death Cottage. Or at Abbots Cross. So to leave Northumberland would be to lose forever the man she loved.

There was no longer any possibility of return through Josephine's room. And she knew of no other way back to Edward. Yet a lingering reluctance to quit Death Cottage, which would finally cut her off from Edward, prevented her from going.

Next morning she went down to the beach and tried lying in the hot sun. She tried a book. But concentration was impossible. Wherever she went and whatever she did, Edward was there. As if his spirit had come with her. Haunting her from over the centuries.

In the end she decided. There was one thing to do. One place to go. One journey to make.

She would visit the Parsonage for the last time. Say Goodbye to Edward's portrait. Then she would cut her stay short and leave for London the following morning.

She climbed back up the path from the seashore, re-entered the house and took a bath. Fresh and changed, she ate a lunchtime snack, then set out to Abbots Cross, just as she had with Connie on that fateful afternoon.

She pondered for a moment, desperately trying to disguise her hurt at being parted from Edward, now knowing that the parting was permanent, and that she and Edward would never be together again.

During her week at Death Cottage, she'd found out exactly what love was. Love was what she had felt for Edward. But the concrete block now residing in her stomach was a constant reminder that Edward was no longer attainable.

But she needed time... Time to reflect... Time to come to terms.

With her own feelings.

* * * *

As she turned up the drive to the Parsonage, her mind raced. The last time... This is the last time I'll come here. Then I'll never see him again...

As she approached the house, a great thrill possessed her. Was it too late for something magic to happen when she was inside the house? Could she return to Edward's time after all? Had he another plan to pull her back over the centuries like the one he had used to free her from execution?

As she mounted the flight of wide, stone steps, she felt her bones tremble. Her lungs took great gasps of expectancy. Yet a football stuck in her throat. Tears hovered just below the surface of her eyes. *Please, God, I implore you, let me get back to him!* she mumbled repeatedly.

Once inside, she made straight for the gallery and the portrait. Again, Edward's eyes spoke to her. But this time she knew what he was saying. And her response. *'I'll come, My Darling. I'll come. If I can.'*

Sara lingered so long at the portrait that visitors behind began to accumulate. Finally, with a mountain of reluctance, she moved off. 'Goodbye, Edward!' she whispered out of public earshot.

She cared not whether or not they heard her. The words were spoken to the man in the portrait. The man she would never see again. The man without whom life was worthless.

She quit the portrait gallery. Yet her purpose for coming to the house was not yet complete. She had one more part to visit.

This time, she knew better than to hurtle away in fear from the Hanging Fire. Nor did its inscription hold any terrors for her.

IN AUGUST, 1662, A YOUNG WOMAN OF THE VILLAGE WAS FOUND GUILTY OF WITCHCRAFT.

SHE WAS ALSO HANGED IN THIS PLACE.

'Oh no she wasn't!' whispered Sara, smiling with inner knowledge of the truth. 'She escaped! She's here to prove it!'

She continued to stand and look. Just as John Sprogg had done a few minutes before he died. No longer afraid, she mentally reworked the rescue which Edward had pulled off at no little risk to himself. He'd put his life in jeopardy to save her. Had she been discovered, he too would have been charged with witchcraft and executed.

When, finally and dejectedly she left the Parsonage altogether, gloom was beginning to gather. And as she breasted the rise on her way back to Death Cottage, she turned to look at the panorama of Abbots Cross.

For the last time.

As the minutes passed, one after another, she stood looking, thinking, wondering, remembering, longing...

Then finally she turned and steadfastly strode out through the deepening murk back to the cottage.

Remaining in this place without the possibility of ever seeing Edward again would be an unbearable torture. Better to be back in London with friends - and see what the future held. Yes, she *HAD* to go tomorrow.

Life in Seventeenth Century England was short. But with Edward, it would be Heaven. If only the choice were hers!

A blanket of dusk had settled when she arrived. And she was tired. The last few days - whether real or imaginary - had been fatiguing.

But although dejected at not finding the proof she sought, she was still convinced that it had all happened. And despite the problems she would face if ever she got back to Edward's time, Sara longed to find the way. Desperately, she thought what she would do should it come about.

She would return to the Parsonage under cover of darkness. She would hide in the huge house for a time, until her conviction for witchcraft was forgotten or quashed.

Alternatively, she and Edward could leave Abbots Cross to start a new life elsewhere - London, perhaps.

Caring little, Sara wandered amongst the junk George had intended to move. Listlessly, unable to summon much enthusiasm, she pulled at pieces of carpet and metal. But the exercise was pointless. And finally realising that what she was doing was no more than self-torture, she turned back to the doorway.

She swung shut the door, descended the three spiral steps, and went sadly downstairs.

Meanwhile in the junk room, the forgotten light bulb continued the slight buzzing of its electrical fault...

The evening waxed long. Darkness fell completely. Sara tried everything to raise her spirits. She ironed her suit. Again she tried reading, but without success. There was no television set - not that she could have concentrated anyway. And when she tuned on her radio, none of the programmes poured solace on her deep wounds of yearning.

She wandered upstairs yet again. She aimlessly looked into the room where Connie had slept. The bundle of blankets covering her on her way back from Abbots Cross lay at the foot of the bed. Idly, she eyed them. Then, suddenly startled, she saw what she had sought.

The dress!

Edward's mother's dress lay at the bottom of the pile!

Knowing it was pointless, but wanting something to remember Edward by, she slipped out of her own clothes and pulled on the Seventeenth Century dress. Now - everywhere - Edward's voice was with her. She wandered along the landing and again turned the key in Josephine's room door, but when it opened the landing light only fell dimly on George's junk.

Once more downstairs, over yet another cup of coffee, and still wearing the woollen dress, Sara decided that tonight she would keep vigil. In the forlorn hope that at some point Josephine's room might revert to its Seventeenth Century condition.

She knew it was hopeless. The door could not be opened by Josephine. Josephine - poor innocent, trusting Josephine - was dead, dead of the plague she could only have caught through her act of kindness to Connie.

The final push over the cliff edge of complete heartbreak came when once more Sara turned the tuning dial on her radio. She found herself hearing an introduction to music of the Restoration period.

It was during the first piece, when the lute began to play that Sara could resist her grief no more. Eyes watery, she climbed the stairs and looked hopefully at the bottom of the junkroom door. Darkness. No glow of an oil lamp.

Now she knew it. All was lost. Edward would remain nothing but a beautiful and serene memory against the brash, empty life she would lead in London from now on.

Sara descended the stairs, sat again at the table, leaned forward and laid her head sideways on her arms as they rested on the table. The tears were irresistible. The lute continued to play its beautiful melody. Sara started to sob quietly.

She must have sobbed herself to sleep. A deep, deep sleep.

When she lifted her head, the lute was no longer playing. There was no longer any sound from the radio. And the sun was up in the sky. And at once she realised that she must have been in that position all night.

But Sara had not been awakened by the sunlight. There was something else. Something was different in the cottage.

But what?

Then she noticed. A strange odour. A smell had begun to assail her nostrils.

At first it was only the lightest of whiffs. Then it strengthened.

Suddenly alert, she looked round. *Black smoke!*

Sara leapt to her feet. Hurriedly, she looked round. It came from above.

She bounded upstairs and looked into the two bedrooms. As she hunted, George's words on the day she and Connie had arrived sprang to mind.

'The cottage was burned down and a young girl killed.'

Both rooms were all right. Then her glance flew up to Josephine's door and she realised she had found the source of the fire. Smoke was pouring through the gap between the bottom of the door and the three spiral steps!

Grabbing the key and praying that she would succeed, Sara turned it in the door lock, then pulled at the door, swinging it open. The room - poor, dead Josephine's room - was ablaze. And instantly, the cause of the fire was evident: The roof was already alight, as if it had been set ablaze from outside. In addition, the lamp Edward had lit for her had been blown over and was now lying on the floor, oil spilling from it.

Every second was vital! Sara *had* to prevent the oil from catching light. If it did, the fire would rapidly get out of control.

Grabbing a blanket, Sara rushed into the room. With enormous vigour, she set about the job of bringing it under control. With great swings, she beat the fire right then left in an attempt to smother it.

At first her efforts were such that it looked as if she might succeed. But suddenly the rivers of oil flowing from the lamp caught light. Abruptly, the blaze flared up. Sara was instantly surrounded with leaping flames.

For a moment - the briefest of moments - she hesitated. Then, realising that the fight was lost, she sought to escape.

But now the door itself was alight. Her eyes turned to terrified saucers. There was no way out. Back. Or forward. She was trapped. And doomed.

Sara made one last despairing attempt at escape. She flapped the blanket to beat the inferno. First one way. Then another. Fighting her way towards the door. But the heat beat her back.

And now another hazard. Just as it had in the barn, smoke began choking her. The swirling pungency cut off her air supply - just when she needed it most urgently.

The thatched roof was now ablaze from end to end. And Sara realised the inevitable. She stopped fighting, knowing she was about to die. Sense slipping from her, she remembered George's story, and knew, too late, that *she* was the girl burned to death in the cottage.

Then an inexplicable calm fell on Sara. She felt no fear in the final moments before death. And as her knees began to weaken, she realised how rapidly death was approaching. The heat intensified, the smoke thickened and the volume of the crackling, roaring fire increased. As the heat became unbearable, and as she felt herself beginning to take her leave of life, Sara began to hear all kinds of sounds and see things.

Shouting. Yelling. A huge white light. Her end had come...

She knew her soul was leaving her mortal body, for suddenly through the white light there appeared two apparitions. Edward and James - huge, sturdy James, - both with wet caps on heads and damp cloths over noses. Gripped by sheer amazement, she watched as they both emerged from the flames.

And, distantly, she imagined herself powerless as she was grabbed by two pairs of muscular arms which lifted her up and carried her away, out of the burning cottage and into the coolness and freshness of a fine summer's evening. And although she continued to cough, she no longer felt hot, and no longer were pungent smoke fumes choking the life out of her. When she breathed in, her lungs no longer filled with pungent, gaseous toxins, but with God's clean, pure air.

Now that she was able to breathe easily again, she knew she was in Paradise. She could feel the gentle turf, and, half-smiling, closed her eyes in the blissful peace of death, waiting...

Then she became conscious of being shaken with gentle care. She opened her eyes, knowing she had arrived in Heaven. Edward was there, towering over her, gazing down with loving care.

'Wake up, Sara, wake up!' she heard him say in encouragement.

'Edward...' she whispered, opening her eyes.

Then the faint dreamy smile gradually died. The burning cottage was still there, now completely engulfed in flames. But she was outside, no longer in danger as she lay, recumbent and relaxed, on luscious green turf

But she had no eyes for anything other than Edward. His apparel was dirty and dishevelled. Concern masked his soot-blackened face.

'Edward?' *Was* she dreaming?

'Yes, Sara?'

'Is it really you?'

'Yes, Sara, it is.'

'What happened?'

'I waited for you, as I said I would. Then, thinking you would not be coming, James and I set the cot roof ablaze to destroy the plague.'

With an explosion of joy, Sara realised she'd made it back. 'I tried to return sooner, Edward, but I couldn't.'

'Do not worry.' he smiled. 'For you are here now.'

'Yes,' she agreed, 'thanks to James - and you!'

Even in his soot-covered clothing, James managed a dignified bow. 'I thank you, Mistress Sara.' he said. Then he added, 'I would not have set the house ablaze had I known you were in it!'

'How *did* you know I was there?'

'I saw you at the window.' said Edward. 'Flapping at the blaze like a great bird after we had set the roof alight. So we entered the furnace to try to save you.'

For a time, Edward, Sara and James sat on the cart, watching the blazing cottage, saying nothing. Illumination from the enormous fire lit up three grime-covered, happy faces. Roof supports began to yield to the flames until, like standing dominoes, joist after joist succumbed, falling with a crash and a myriad of sparks into the interior of the cottage walls.

Edward was first to break silence. 'Are you staying this time?' he asked.

Sara shrugged her shoulders. 'I have to, I suppose.' she joked. 'There's no way back now.' She indicated the now-ruined cottage with a wave of the hand.

'Are you glad?'

She nodded. 'I'm glad to be with you. But sorry you'll have to give up your Parsonage for me.'

His face broadened into the widest of smiles. 'Mistress Sara,' he said happily, 'I can tell you: We no longer have to leave.'

'But... what about the witchcraft charge?' she protested. 'We'll both be hanged!'

He shook his head. 'In the two days since your departure, events have moved with a winged swiftness.' he said.

Her brow lined as he continued. 'Recognising that Lizbeth Sprogg's death was Rose's fault for giving the girl the dress which you had ordered burned, one or two of the more enlightened villagers - along with James and Daisy - spoke for you to my father, the Squire of Church Cross - the Magistrate at the trial. This deputation told the Squire that John Sprogg had made the charges against you when demented by the death of his daughter.'

'But - what about the other witnesses at the trial?'

'Under James's urging,' Edward continued, 'Goody Thompson and her foolish son, Lancelot, have confessed to perjury. Consequently, and on my advice, the Squire has set aside your conviction. That means it is still on record, but will not be enacted upon as long as we live in the parsonage as man and wife.'

'So - you still want me to marry you?'

'I do.'

'Is this to retain your position as parson? Or because you want me?'

'You need not ask such a question, Mistress Sara. And if you do not want to wed me, you are free to go.'

'And free to remain?'

'Yes.'

Delight flooded through Sara. Then she sobered. 'But the villagers were so *hostile* to me.' she argued. 'They will *never* accept me as their Parson's wife!'

Edward shook his head. 'Their hatred was under the direction of John Sprogg. Now he is gone, a pall of shame hangs over this village.'

'Shame?'

'Yes. Guilt at your near-execution. But relief at your escape, of which I informed them after the Squire's action over your conviction. I know you'll be welcomed back by the people of Abbots Cross.'

Gleefully, she turned to look back at Rose Cottage. 'Poor Josephine...' she said. 'Now she is completely gone - consumed by the fire!'

'Yes.' he said. 'And when next we pray, we shall remember Mistress Josephine, for she will not now have a proper burial. It will be as if she perished in the flames.' He turned a meaningful look at her. 'And that is what shall be entered in the Parish Register. The less my Parishioners hear of plague, the sooner it will be forgotten - especially for *your* sake!' Then he added, '*Now* are you glad?'

'Are *you?*' she asked.

'I shall be more glad when we are wed.' he told her.

'So shall I!' she exclaimed ecstatically, 'Oh - so shall I!'

Epilogue

EXTRACT FROM 'The Norton Courante', August 26th 1962:

GIRL DIES IN COTTAGE BLAZE

From our own correspondent

A twenty-four-year-old nurse died last night in a blaze which completely gutted the Seventeenth Century thatched cottage in which she was staying.

Miss Sara Goodwin of 17, Finchley Place, Kensington, was alone at 'Rose Cottage', one mile south of Abbots Cross, Northumberland, when the fire started. Preliminary examination tends to indicate that it was caused by an electrical fault in the roof.

Miss Goodwin's body was almost entirely destroyed by the intense heat. But although the remains are virtually unidentifiable, local sources think they can only be Miss Goodwin's.

The position in which she was discovered suggests that she was in the loft when the fire started.

Miss Goodwin's step-mother, Miss Sandy Smith (real name Mrs. Harriet Hopkins), an actress currently working at the Edinburgh Festival, was today overcome by emotion at the news.

The house was known locally as 'Death' Cottage because it had been the scene of a previous conflagration in August, 1662. Parish records show that another young woman, also alone in the house, met her death in *THAT* blaze. The cottage was later rebuilt.

The present owners have yet to make a decision on whether or not to rebuild the cottage a third time.